Little Bird Unbroken

-

A. F. Ryser

Little Bird
UNBROKEN

Behind every strong woman is a
story that gave her no choice.

A. F. Ryser

Imprint

Copyright © 2024 by Anette Faye Ryser
All rights reserved.

No part of this publication may be reproduced, distributed, or transmitted in any form or by any means, including photocopying, recording, or other electronic or mechanical methods, without the prior written permission of the publisher, except as permitted by U.S. copyright law.

The story, all names, characters, and incidents portrayed in this production are fictitious. No identification with actual persons (living or deceased), places, buildings, and products is intended or should be inferred. The views expressed in this book belong to the characters speaking and do not represent the author's opinion.

Cover design: Adam Hay Studio, UK
Copy editing by Heloise Murdoch
Formatting by Daniela Rohr / www.skriptur-design.de
Proof reading, guidance, friendship and unlimited kindness by Craig Buchanan

ISBN: 9798328504072

1st paperback edition 2024

Published by Anette Faye Ryser
anettefayeryser@hotmail.com

Germany 1992

1

I had agreed to meet Yvonne in the library. Of all places, she had to be in the "bunker"—the name students used to refer to the concrete, windowless library of Cologne University—now that I was bursting to scream my news from the rooftops.

My insides reverberated like thunder from my drumming heart as I lurked between the rows of bookshelves. *Had they always been this long?*

The carpet's rough and ribbed structure prevented any rapid movement. I rolled my foot from my toes to the heel, ensuring not to make a noise. The fabric released my shoes with a delay, as if covered with Velcro.

Argh, where the hell is she?

Industrial silver lampshades dangled low above the dark reading tables, spilling a grey shimmer over shadowy figures below, engrossed in silent study.

I recognised my friend by her bright yellow pencil case. Hidden behind a pile of hardcovers, she bent over an opened book. Like everything else in the room, her blonde curly hair appeared dusted with an indiscernible grey. Only the shiny little stationery pouch resisted conforming.

Had she not made me promise, I would have reconsidered disturbing her. "Swear you will find me as soon as you know, no matter what."

Watching her engrossed in reading, I wondered if my news could wait.

She gazed in my direction and narrowed her eyes.

I grinned and made a "thumbs-up" sign.

Yvonne slammed her book shut with a thump. Someone released a deep exhalation from their throat.

I placed my index finger before my mouth, but it was too late. She reached out and embraced me. I inhaled her sweet and heavy perfume, patchouli.

She whispered into my ear, "How was it?".

"I passed!"

"Quiet please … Shhh … silence …" Subdued voices hushed from behind the dimly lit bookshelves.

"Let's talk outside. I want to hear everything," she hissed. "Let me just grab my stuff."

"I'll wait in the cafeteria," I whispered, glad to escape the depressing building.

A line had formed at the counter. A young woman holding a toddler was standing in front of me, unaware that I was queueing behind her. It was Susanne. We had started university together and met in lectures during our first term before she became pregnant. Her son and I made eye contact. I blew out my cheeks and crossed my eyes, then released the air with a "Boh", opening my mouth wide in surprise.

His pink lips parted in surprise. I blew him a kiss. He giggled.

His mum spun around. "Is he flirting with you?" She transferred the infant from her right to her left arm.

"Oh yes, he's a right little heartbreaker." I tapped his nose with my finger, and he shrieked with joy. The line shuffled forward.

"It's been a while since I last saw you here. A lot has changed, I can see," I said.

Months before, I was impressed by her candour when she told a group of students that she was "up the duff" after a one-night stand. Her lack of shame impressed me.

"What about your parents?" I asked at the time.

"They weren't pleased when I told them. However, they assured me that they'd support me, no matter how dire the circumstances. So, they came round really quickly, thank God."

I recalled her folding her hands as she spoke about her family. I experienced a twinge of envy.

"The father doesn't want to know and prefers I end the pregnancy." She caressed the swell of her tummy. "I've considered it, to be honest, more than once. In fact, if it's a boy, I'll name him Vincent—the survivor."

Her son extended his arm towards me. His tiny fingers shone wet from having sucked them. I offered my hand.

"Wow, he's got a good grip," I said.

"Yes, Vincent's thriving." She tilted her head back. "You are, aren't you, little man? Thriving, you are." The boy squealed. "Unlike your mummy, who is knackered every moment of every day. But we don't mind, do we?" She muttered the last words as she brushed her nose against his. Vincent seized her hair, drawing her towards him.

"Ouch, careful, Vinnie!" she exclaimed, laughing. She shifted her head and squinted at me from underneath her messy hair.

"Oh dear ..." I was out of my depth.

"Mind you, he is an exceptional kid. I could not continue my studies if he had not been this charming. He's easy to love," his mother said.

The lady behind the counter waited for us to finish talking and asked, "What can I get you?"

Susanne ordered a slice of plain cake and a carton of juice, while holding Vincent, who leaned forward, admiring the food display.

"I'd better have this outdoors; he's getting restless." She paid and nodded a "bye" as she made for the exit, balancing what seemed like her entire life in her arms: toddler, shoulder bag and a pile of books, while carrying her tray on top.

I ordered and heard hurried footsteps as I settled at a table with two cups of coffee. Yvonne hugged me under the bright strip light. I got to my feet, the chair scraping across the floor. She grasped me by the shoulders, extended her arms, and beamed at me.

"Well done, you. How did the meeting with 'Grumpy Tash' go?" Her voice echoed around the room. The surrounding murmur subsided; heads turned our way.

She took a seat across from me. "Well?"

With my head tilted backwards, I closed my eyes.

"I got a 2:1. I can't believe it. Pinch me, will you?" I let out a breath.

The sound of Yvonne's laughter forced a smile onto my face. Then, a grimace.

"Ouch." I winced, rubbing the mark that appeared on the top of my arm.

"You asked for it. Come on, tell me. Was it awful?" She rolled her eyeballs and mimed smoking a pipe. I laughed.

"Yes, we had the pipe. Very 'Dupin', as usual."

"And the tweed waistcoat?" Yvonne propped herself up on her elbows.

I pushed my thumbs into the fabric of my jumper and under my bra straps. With my bottom lip curled out, I leaned back, forcing my chest towards the ceiling.

"Tell me, Miss Olbig," I replicated the professor's austere voice, "what are your intentions now that you have passed your degree?"

Yvonne slapped my arm. "You imitate her so well. What did you say?"

"I told her I wanted to live in England. And guess what the pretentious cow said? 'That is not a job'. Can you believe it?"

"No way. For a lecturer of English literature, I'd have thought it was the biggest compliment you could have paid her."

"Exactly. I told her I didn't care if I couldn't find a job teaching. As far as I'm concerned, I can work in a supermarket. You should have seen her face. You'd think she'd swallowed sour milk."

"Oh dear, another waste of academic potential."

I cringed. "You sound like my father." I continued, "I need to check the announcements upstairs. Who knows, there's still hope for a research position here. Are you coming?"

Yvonne checked her watch. "My lecture starts in twenty minutes." She nodded. "Sure. There might be something for me. I wouldn't mind staying at uni a few years longer. Cologne has grown on me since meeting you."

I stood up to return the tray, leaning over to collect her empty mug, when a gangly young man in a denim jacket approached our table.

He gave me a weak wave and smiled at my friend.

"Oh, hi ... how are you?" Yvonne said, the colour of her face intensifying to a soft pink. She fluffed up her hair.

"It's been a while since ..." he said, but Yvonne did not give him a chance to finish his sentence.

"I've been quite busy lately. I had to help Pippa here type her thesis. She finished today and got a 2:1. Isn't that great?"

There could only be one reason Yvonne was keen to deflect and redirect the topic: He didn't 'float her boat,' as she called it.

I left the table, suppressing a smile. Yvonne stood up and let the man hug her. He held her before she picked up her bag and joined me.

"Sorry to keep you waiting, Pippa. I know you're in a hurry," she exclaimed with urgency and caught up with me. "Phew, thank God for that." She let a breath escape as we reached the stairs. "Keep moving. Is he following us?"

I laughed. "How do you do it? Honestly, you're such a hussy." Glancing over my shoulder, I saw her admirer standing in the queue, pointing at the display.

As we entered the corridor to the English department, one of the staff was pinning a sheet onto the notice board. He stepped back to check the alignment.

Yvonne held my arm.

"Wait," she whispered. "I recognise him."

I turned to her. "Are there any cute guys you don't know?"

She rolled her eyes and pulled a corner of her mouth into a tired smile.

Unaware of us, he tucked in the seam of his polo shirt and disappeared behind a door.

"Let's have a look," I said and moved to the board.

A padded fabric covered a wide stretch of the wall outside the administrator's office. In order of title, I stopped in front of a poster with photos of lecturers. Prof. Natasha Werther stared straight at me. Her hair, parted in the middle, drew my thoughts to the back of her head, where the thick, grey strands met in a bun. *Who's afraid of Tasha W.?* A tiny line in the corner by her eyes gave a clue she'd attempted a smile for the photographer. In our fresher year, Yvonne had pointed out the imperceptible hint of a moustache above her top lip. "Did you notice Tashe's stache?" she asked after a passionate lecture on Wollstonecraft. Now it was impossible to unsee.

"I could become a post-lady. I am an early riser," I said. Yvonne lingered by the job section.

"No, you won't. Oh no, you won't. You will be a teacher, Pippa!" She spoke the words in slow motion. Without turning her gaze from an A4 print, she stretched her arm out, summoning me with her hand. I followed her silent gesture and stared at the sheet the young man had pinned up.

> *Why not study at York University and learn how to teach German? The Department of Modern Foreign Languages is looking for native speakers for the academic year 1993.*

A rush of adrenaline shot through my veins. My head spun. Raising my eyebrows, I blinked. As I reread the text, my vision focussed on a photo of a red-brick building set in a landscaped garden in front of a lake. I held on to Yvonne's arm.

"When does the academic year begin?" I asked.

"In three months. September. You'd better start writing your application."

"I can't." The rush subsided and gave way to a sobering heaviness in my stomach. "All hell will break loose at home."

"Pippa, it won't. This is a brilliant opportunity. They'll be proud of you. Surely, they realised what they signed up for when they sent you to university to study English?"

Yvonne had no clue about the actual extent of my family's dynamics. The few times my parents visited, she'd pass me in the hallway of our shared flat, rolling her eyes. As much as my dad tried to speak in "Olbig code", consisting of unflattering nicknames and sarcastic jokes only to be understood by our immediate family members, anyone who overheard him would prick up their ears.

"Yvonne, they didn't finance me to bugger off abroad."

"Which year do they live in? It's the nineties, not the fifties." Without waiting for a reply, she tore the paper off the noticeboard.

"Wait, you can't do that. He only just put it there. Others …"

"… need not apply. This chance is yours, Pippa." She folded the sheet in her hand and pushed it against my chest. "Does this make your heart leap 'like a rainbow in the sky'?"

Heat rose in my neck as the inside of my ribcage was thumping. I suppressed a smile and nodded.

"Well," she said, grinning in triumph. "I'll see you at the flat later. Don't lose this ticket to freedom."

"I won't," I said, burying the folded paper deep in my jacket pocket as I left.

A few minutes later, I sat on the subway platform opposite the university, the metal of the bench pressing into my legs. With a wheezing sound, a tram picked up speed and left the station. The stale air came to life, and the draught of the leaving train sucked up my hair. Passengers aimed straight for the escalator, leading them to daylight. It was the third line I let pass. A determined, tiny bird picked at a fry glued to a paper bag with a blob of mayonnaise. *How did you get here?* I peered into the dark tunnel to the right and turned my head to follow the overhead wires connecting the complete subway network. If one broke loose, would the entire network collapse?

I glanced at the advertising board opposite me, on the other side of the tracks. Oversized smiling faces with perfect skin exposed sets of bleached teeth. A man and woman with a girl and boy in front, overlooked by a detached house with symmetrical dark windows above the front door. The white-rendered walls stood out from the treelined backdrop. Letters in the cloudless sky read: *We build your dream home — Luxhousing.* Maybe that was how Mum and Dad got the idea at the beginning of the seventies. A similar billboard may have planted the seed twenty years ago. The first Olbigs to become "proper homeowners". A house that the rest of the village dubbed "the mansion". My insides tightened as I recalled my mother's anger when she spotted track marks on the high-pile living-room carpet. "Lift your feet, for heaven's sake."

My stomach churned. I clenched my fist around the paper Yvonne had shoved into my hand. With closed eyes, I drew in a deep breath through my nose. A cool breeze and the squeaking of brakes announced the next train. I sighed and looked up at the departure board. Ehrenfeld. My friend Ursula lived there. *I wonder if she's at home.* When the carriages came to a halt, I walked up to its sliding doors.

Her house was only a few stops. *This can't be a coincidence*, I thought, when I recognised her dog in the crowd of people outside the metro station. His coarse brown coat had a glow of silver in the sunlight, and his pointed ears bounced to the rhythm of each step. The dog's hips jiggled as the stiff hind limbs came off the ground, letting this Alsatian crossbreed appear older than it was. Ursula declared he had the gait of a donkey when she announced his adoption from a local charity. The vet had guessed that the animal was two years old and that someone had tied him to a chain from an early age. It took half a year for the fur to grow back around his neck and for his body to fill out.

As much as I had admired Ursula for the confidence for rescuing Jackson, jealousy gnawed at me. I had begged my parents for years to have a dog but was constantly told I was too young to be handed this responsibility.

I had echoed my father. "You're on your own with a full-time job. How can you take on a dog? You won't have time for it."

Ursula had reacted with a dismissive wave, using both hands. She was not impressed by my opinion. When she turned up at the flat with shaggy Jackson for the first time, I swallowed hard, hoping nobody discovered how I envied her determination.

My friend navigated through the busy high street. Jackson followed her on a slack leash, nose pointing in various directions. His upright, bushy tail performed its job flawlessly, wagging with metronomic precision. I focused on the couple, in no hurry to draw level with them. Ursula wore a baggy linen dress with a translucent scarf matching the ribbon holding her ponytail. Even the Birkenstock sandals looked elegant on her. A shiny, square cardboard bag swung from her hand. The pair went into a side street, off the main shops. Her house was nearby—time to catch up.

"Pst, pst …" I hissed. Jackson stopped in his tracks and turned his head. I crouched and spread my arms. "Jackson, my boy," I shouted as he charged up to me, leash dragging on the ground. I heard Ursula's voice come closer as I pressed my face into Jackson's neck, juddering. "Grrrr … did you miss me? Who's a good dog?" I squeezed my eyes shut as his warm, moist tongue licked my cheeks.

"Ok, that's it. Come on, Jackson," Ursula interrupted our greeting. Jackson hung on to me as I stood up, inviting me to continue our game.

"Sorry, Urs." I placed my hand on Jackson's shoulder. "There you are. That's enough." I winked at him.

"I saw that." Ursula laughed. "You are incorrigible. Why on earth go to university, I wonder? You should run an animal sanctuary."

"Who says I won't? After all, I'm free to do whatever I fancy," I replied and spun with my arms outstretched, ignoring the nagging thought of my parents.

Ursula shrieked before covering her mouth with her hands. Jackson tilted his head and pricked up his ears.

"Oh my God, I forgot. Your final exam … it was today. How did it go?"

I stopped pirouetting and made an awkward bow. "Tadaaah! I passed. 2:1. Isn't that great?"

Ursula stepped forward and put her arms around me. "An honours? Abso-fucking-wonderful, Pippa." Jackson jumped up and rested his front paws against us. "Group hug," we both shouted, including him in our embrace.

2

"Hello?" My fingers clutched the spiralling cord connecting the receiver to the telephone.

"It's your mum. Whom were you expecting?" My mother's voice sounded tense.

"Nobody. Erm, you. I mean … I was about to call you," I stuttered.

"I see. We appreciate you eventually granting us your attention." Her voice dripped with sarcasm. "Shouldn't we be the ones to learn your news ahead of everyone else? We funded your education, remember?"

"Listen, I'm sorry, Mum. I just came back from uni. I was held up in town."

"Oh, I don't want to know who kept you. I'm not interested in hearing any excuses. Have you had too much to drink?"

"No, Mum. Why would you say that?"

"Why didn't you phone us? Instead of partying with your friends. Who are they, anyway?"

The nails of my left hand grazed across the rough surface of the kitchen table, dragging a muesli grain and burying it in a knothole.

"I passed. 2:1."

There was a muffled silence at her end of the line.

"Mum, are you listening?"

She murmured something I was not allowed to catch. My stomach tightened upon hearing her whisper, "Yes ... she did ... I don't know ... you ask..."

There appeared to be a scuffle, and I pictured my dad snatching the receiver out of my mum's hand.

"Dad?" I called into the phone as if hollering at the end of a tunnel.

"Yes, so you made it. Congratulations, I guess."

"Thank you," I said, a tang of bitterness rasping in my throat. I coughed to clear it.

The tension of the moment was palpable. My face tingled, and my knees faltered. I secured a chair from under the table and sank, paralysed by the memory of the day I received my A-level results. My parents would undoubtedly also recollect the evening I'd been out celebrating the end of my secondary education.

My dad put a stop to my overthinking. "Right, it's time to become focused on your future. I'll have a word with …"

"Are you planning to return home this weekend? To celebrate with the family?" There was a tremor in my mum's voice.

I recoiled. "I … erm … can't promise. There's a chance that I will have to work. They're … erm… expecting a large shipment of cars at the dealership."

There was no delivery, but the lie lessened my guilty conscience. I could not face my parents yet. Instead, like most Saturdays, I stationed myself behind the reception desk of the Ford car dealership. On my first day, the manager had led me to "the heart of his business" through the shiny, perfumed showroom. A board obscured the coffee-making area and a complex telephone switchboard from the eyes of any customers whilst positioning me in the centre.

"Cologne Cars -- Drive Your Dreams". He told me to smile while I answered the phone with his pet slogan. The sales team took turns to ring reception from their offices. "Who am I speaking to?

Can I talk to Dixie Normus, please?" It did not take long to link the laughter behind closed doors to my anonymous callers. Afterwards, they'd pour themselves a coffee, wiping tears of amusement from their eyes. We'd clink the plastic cups and giggle at their "new girl" japes.

The swirling rays of sunlight in the revolving glass door captured my attention. With a flawless posture, a familiar figure entered the showroom. My sister walked up to the reception with her shoulders back and her neck exposed. I jolted and turned, collecting my thoughts, tinkering with the coffee machine. *I should have asked for the day off after all.*

"Hello." She dragged a stool over to sit by the corner of my station. I looked up. Sandra tossed her thick, dark hair back, squinting at me with a stiff smile.

"Hi," I answered and pivoted towards the worktop, wiping the lid of the water compartment of the Melitta machine.

When I had composed myself, I poured a coffee and placed it beside her.

"Are you on your way to town?" I asked.

"I hear you passed?"

Why the need for confirmation?

I gazed across the showroom. A senior salesman leaned across the wide-open door of a glistening Mitsubishi and explained its technical specifications to a customer. He held the sheet displayed on every windshield in his hand, detailing the price, year, and model. As he caught my eye, he lifted the document to a wave. I pushed up one corner of my mouth and shifted my gaze to my sister.

"Yes, I got a 2:1. I'm so chuffed." *Don't let your guard down.*

"Whatever," Sandra said, gesturing with her hand. "As long as it gets you a job. Presumably, you don't want to deplete our parents' savings for longer than required?"

I examined the rotating door, wishing it would move. Nobody came to my rescue.

"Of course. I can finally focus on my future." My heartbeat pounded in my ears.

"I hope you consider Mum and Dad part of that focus." A smirk spread across her face. I rubbed my neck and studied the switchboard.

A green light flashed. I released a breath. "Sandra, I have to take this. Cologne Cars – Drive Your Dreams. How can I help you?"

Sandra stood and corrected her posture. "Bye," she snarled before the spinning entrance swallowed her.

The dealership grew busier towards the afternoon. It was a sign that sales had gone well, time went by without notice, and there was an upbeat vibe. I opened the dishwasher, collecting milk tubs and sugar sachets.

A sales assistant put down his Filofax and helped me pile up the saucers.

"What a day that was. I had three sales, and the couple looking at the red Colt are showing genuine interest. With luck, they'll sign on Monday."

"You really don't have to help me," I said, wiping a milk ring off the surface with a yellow dishcloth.

"No, let me. You've had a tough day as well. Who was that woman you spoke to before?"

I came to a sudden halt.

"My sister. Why?"

"When you were talking, I thought she was sucking on a lemon!" He chuckled, squinting his eyes to gauge my reaction.

"Yes, she can appear somewhat uptight." The hairs on my neck tingled.

"A bit? I wouldn't like to cross her when she's pissed off." He handed me a few cups.

"Thanks," I muttered, relieved I could turn my back on him to fill the machine.

"Don't take it the wrong way. I can't imagine you being siblings. Ah well, families, eh?!"

"Yes, families," I repeated and busied myself.

Ursula had arranged to meet me outside the cable car ticket office on Sunday. "Hello, there." She fluttered a leaflet in the air.

"What's this for? I rode on here many years before you joined the organisation," I said, taking the folder from her hand. "Take off for sky-high fun with the Rhine cable car." I arched an eyebrow. "And they pay you for conjuring up slogans like this?" I laughed.

"No, that was communications. It's your lucky day, a complimentary ride, Pippa." She winked and tugged on my sleeve. I followed her to the platform by the terminal, where the grimy hauling cable above our heads moved nonstop, a steady hum droning like a beehive.

"Ready?" she asked and nodded at the ticket officer, who held open the gate for us to enter a cabin. We sat opposite in the rickety enclosure before the brake loosened. With a jolt, it swung up and stabilised. The stuffy air transported me into a reminiscing mood.

"The scent of my childhood," I said. The terminal shrank as we passed the treetops at the edge of the Rhine.

"Yes, and the stillness. A vacuum, like being underwater." Ursula took a meaningful breath.

The cabin bumped as it swayed underneath a supporting pillar before it swung higher, leaving the riverbank. My organs felt disconnected and tumbled weightlessly. I gasped, enjoying the rush of fear, followed by relief as we glided high above the grey surface of the river.

Ursula gave me a knowing smile. "I'm forever indebted to you for alerting me to this job."

Despite being a couple of years older than me, we had been friends for over a decade and had never lost touch, even when our paths parted after secondary school. At sixteen, she started working as a junior officer for a local construction firm. I envied her for her financial independence. She had moved to a compact apartment above the bakery opposite the church. After Sunday service, I'd often pop in and pour my heart out after another fight at home.

Despite her reluctance to see me go, Urs encouraged me to enrol at Cologne University. In my opening year, I spotted a job advertisement in the paper for a human resources manager for a cable car company. I sent her the clipping, never expecting her to apply for the opportunity or get it. But she did.

"My dad met yours, by the way. He sounded boastful, he said." I hated Ursula's overkill of pronouns.

"Who was boasting?"

"Yours, he said."

I jerked my head, my eyes bulging in astonishment. "I don't get them. You should have heard him on the phone," I said.

We reached the mid-section of the cable car tour. I looked at the cars crossing the bridge below us.

"Damn it, still can't do anything right by them, can you? I wonder why your parents are forever on your case. They never fussed with Sandra, did they?"

"Oh, just leave it," I muttered, regretting mentioning the phone call. But it was too late. Ursula had long abandoned any degree of politeness when we spoke about my parents.

"Your dad is dreadful, and your mum should stand up for you. When he called you a whore for wearing nail varnish …? How old were you? Sixteen, for goodness' sake."

I cringed. "Please, shut up. I regret confiding in you."

"No, you don't. You wouldn't have survived the madness that is your parents had it not been for me."

She was spot-on. During my teenage years, I'd spent hours huddled on the floor by the telephone, whispering into the receiver, which was covered by my palm.

I looked through the window to estimate the duration of our journey.

"He wants me to work at his company. Can you imagine me selling insurance?" I shrugged.

"Have you not mentioned York? You *must* apply, Pippa. It's your *destiny.*"

"No way. Thinking about it turns my stomach."

Ursula's expression hardened. "Look behind you," she ordered. "Right over there, that's your beloved England, your dream destination. You are about to set foot on the opposite side."

I huffed at her comparison. "It's not that easy, Urs."

"Getting there is the easy part. You hop onto a ferry. The journey in your mind is the challenging part. It's time to drive your dream." She sang the final three words. "You left home to study in Cologne. If you're not prepared to take that subsequent logical step, you might as well never have moved out of your parents' house."

The cable car hovered for a moment, then we passed another supporting pillar, and my organs plunged into free fall once more.

3

On Monday morning, my flatmate had set the breakfast table for three.

"Who is our mystery guest?" I asked, examining the fridge's contents. "Blast, it was my turn to buy orange juice. Sorry."

"Not to worry, Tom just popped to the corner shop," she said with a blustery undertone.

"*Tom?*" I pushed the refrigerator door shut and turned. "What did I miss?" I asked.

Yvonne arranged a jam pot on the cheese platter. "I thought I'd brought him up. He's …"

"Let me guess. Sweet? Super cute? *The one?*"

Yvonne snatched a boiled egg and pretended to hurl it at me. "Watch out, you hussy." She laughed.

I tossed a tea towel at her. It landed on her shoulder. The entrance door lock clicked.

"You gave him a *key?*" I mouthed.

"Shush." Yvonne locked me with a stare and pressed her index finger to her lips.

I mimed "joking".

"I'm back," a stranger's voice called. The door to our kitchen swung wide, and a tall figure froze mid-movement.

"Hi, I'm Tom." He widened his dazzling blueish-green eyes and beamed, exposing impeccable teeth.

"Nice to meet you, Tom." I took a step forward and reached out to him. "I'm Pippa. You must have heard *loads* about me." The three of us giggled as he clasped my hand.

"I hope you're ready to eat, ladies," our visitor announced, lifting a paper bag before setting it on the table. "White, brown, wholewheat, sesame, or poppy seeds. I got three of everything."

Yvonne grabbed the breadbasket and emptied the rolls into it, spilling a couple on the table.

This wasn't the first occasion a stranger had become part of our morning routine. I had noticed the bathroom locked many times while Yvonne rushed around the kitchen, preparing a breakfast tray for two to return to her room.

It would have been easy to judge my flatmate for her uninhibited love life. It contrasted with the norms and values my parents raised me by. But I never did. The men she introduced me to were pleasant, well-mannered, and good-looking. I envied her, hoping her carefree behaviour might rub off on me.

In the following thirty minutes, I discovered Tom was studying business and economics and had recently returned from a scholarship at Durham University.

"Tell Pippa about your year in England, will you? She's applied to York. Isn't that a coincidence?"

I raised both my hands in protest. "Wow, Yvonne, hang on. Nobody mentioned *application*," I said.

"Well, you should." She placed her fists on the table and leaned forward, glaring at me. Then, she pivoted towards Tom. "Pippa has this one ambition: to live in the UK. So, guess what? There's a course at York for her to become a teacher." To emphasise her concluding words, she nodded with every syllable. "Tell her she has to do it, Tom."

"I think we should leave our guest to eat his breakfast," I said, seeking her shin under the table, and nudging it with my toes.

"Why not apply? It sounds like an excellent opportunity," Tom said.

"That's out of the question," I replied, adding, "financially," hoping he would not pursue the matter.

He didn't. Instead, he suggested a list of solutions for what he referred to as "insignificant obstacles." Various grants and an exchange programme for teacher training courses were accessible. He knew this from a friend of his flatmate. Yvonne looked on in awe.

She caressed his arm, tossing her hair, and then looked at me. "Isn't he a-ma-zing?" She gestured in my direction whilst Tom scribbled keywords on a notepad. His speech did not leave me unimpressed, either. The pair of them outnumbered me in my scepticism and, at least for the duration of this breakfast, I believed it was possible to fulfil my dream.

"Thanks for the pep talk, both of you." It was time to give the couple space. "I must return a few books to the library. See you this evening."

The short walk gave me plenty of time to reflect on the conversation at breakfast. *Insignificant obstacles*—Tom could not imagine the consequences of a move to England, and neither could I. However, I knew that my parents had different expectations regarding my future.

The English Department had not replaced the flyer Yvonne had torn from the notice board. As I vacantly scanned the leaflets, the door opened, and a lady from the admin team passed. She flashed a smile. "Hello," I said without shifting my focus.

She came back carrying two paper cups, spreading an aroma of freshly brewed coffee.

"Can I help you?" she asked.

"I, erm, I have a question about grants." What had Tom outlined about a range of options?

With the drinks in her hands, she motioned towards the door. "Come in. I need to put these cups down." She winced. "The university only buys budget-friendly ones, and I'm forever scalding my fingers."

Another lady sat in the back of the room, head lowered, typing.

"Watch out. It's hot." She placed one cup before her colleague and rubbed her fingers on her tweed skirt. The rhythmic clicking of the typewriter drowned out a muttered "thank you."

The lady opened a filing cabinet. "Did you want to apply for a bursary?"

"Erm, yes, to study in the UK." I struggled to recall the terms Tom had mentioned at breakfast.

The lady looked at me. "You're one of Professor Werther's students, aren't you? You passed your B.A."

"Yes, Phillippa Olbig. I want to apply for a teacher training course in England." *Phew, at least that went smoothly.*

"Congratulations," she said as her hands moved from file to file, fingers pulling folders out and parting pages. "Are you in a grant scheme?"

"No, my parents … I mean, no, I'm not."

"I see." The clerk removed a folder from a shelf and unclipped the bracket. "Here is an application form. You need to complete this so we can determine if you meet the requirements."

I gulped down the lump in my throat and nodded.

"And here,"— she slid a booklet on top of the filing cabinet and nudged it in my direction with her finger— "you specify the details of the course you're applying for, and the duration, etc."

"And you'll have to write your motivational letter," she said. "Don't worry. The documentation is incredibly concise. There's even an example letter somewhere in there." She presented me with a bundle of leaflets. Thanking her, and with the paperwork in my bag, I left. Walking in the shadow of the grey blocks of university buildings, I pulled my collar close around my neck. A chill crept through the fabric and my shoulders tightened. Students hurried by, anxious to make it to lectures in time.

I did not want to intrude on Yvonne and Tom, who certainly would have crept back under her duvet.

Perhaps I should toss all of this in the next bin I stumble upon. I could see the doors shut on my future. My stomach felt like a key had turned, as it often did when thoughts drifted to my parents. *If*

I apply, they must never know. The key pushed further into my gut as memories of sitting at their kitchen table unfolded.

"Mindless drivel." My father had dismissed my motivation for studying. Mum hunched in a chair in the corner of the room, her head lowered, looking at the fine lines on her hands.

"Hush, Karl, the neighbours."

"How can you be so ungrateful? Instead, here I am, presenting you with a position in sales, and you want to go to u-ni-ver-si-ty." He articulated the word with a heightened lisp. Tiny molecules of spit escaped his mouth.

"I can put in for a grant," I had said.

"Don't be so bloody stupid! Handouts are for the kids from a council estate, not for an Olbig. I worked hard for this family to move on from that."

"What will people think, Pippa? Use common sense," my mum said without lifting her head.

"Please, Dad. I assure you I will consider your office. But let me finish my study. With a degree in English, I could …"

"… join a queue of jobless idealists."

It was impossible to defeat the "Olbig plan." In disdain, my dad belittled my life's plan and reiterated how indebted I was. "After everything we've done for you."

My mum's sagging mouth spoke volumes: I was an ungrateful disappointment, and she asked herself what she had done to deserve a daughter like me. It was an unspoken rule that I beg forgiveness, and after days of stifling silence, my mum delivered the verdict.

"We've been talking, Pippa. You may go to university. But after that, there will be no more silly manoeuvres. And Dad has yet to agree."

Deep in thought, I had reached the park connecting the campus with the ring road that circled the city centre. The sun had driven the shade off a wooden bench, the surface still cool. I took a seat, clutching the bag of forms to my chest.

The key in my insides turned full circle and pressed my stomach up, creating a sour taste at the back of my throat.

I recalled Yvonne's words, "This is ridiculous." There was vexation in her eyes. She'd clenched her jaw as she tapped her fingers on the table, listening to my reasons not to apply.

A shiver ran up my spine, culminating in my scalp prickling. By this point, Yvonne would have filled Tom in with family anecdotes I had disclosed. My mum always warned me not to reveal what happened behind closed doors. "Washing your dirty linen in public", she called it, putting her hand to her throat, choking down her discomfort as if she had sampled something foul. She never pointed a finger at Sandra for "soiling the nest."

With a heavy exhalation, I opened the bag and removed the paperwork. Mindful that the breeze didn't scatter them, I turned the pages, searching for the sections I had to complete. There was no need for a parent's signature. How naïve of me to assume there was. Heat spread across my cheeks. I could submit an application without informing anyone, not even Yvonne. I'd most likely face a rejection, anyway. That'd be the end of it. Considering my family's economic background, they would not consider me for a grant, thus taking the decision out of my hands. I'd never have to tell my parents. I could agree to an apprenticeship in my dad's company.

My thoughts became sharper, and my heart rate slowed. *I will ring them, Mum and Dad, and visit. There is no need to mention the application or England. Of course, the University of York will decline my application, but at least I will have tried.*

4

I found my parents on their patio. Mum was perched upright on her sunbed, peeking out under the palm clutching her forehead. With the other arm, she waved her fingers at the side of the building as if conducting a jazz ensemble.

"For heaven's sake, Waltraud, I said *mine in the shade*." My dad bent over a collapsed garden chair. A faded floral cushion lay at his feet.

I paused in the kitchen, having let myself in, watching from the safety of the shadows.

"Draw up the armrests from behind, Karl."

"What do you think I just did?" He wet a finger with his tongue and swung his hand in front of his chest, flinching. "Bloody hell. I *never* sit in the sun until the afternoon," he growled.

I tiptoed over the threshold of the back door and into the dazzling sunlight.

"Hello." My voice held a phoney cheer. "Surprise!"

My mum lowered her hand and sank her skinny legs to either side of the sunbed, toes angling for her plastic sandals.

"Pippa, why didn't you call? Your father could have collected you from the station."

She rose, smoothing her summer dress, and hugged me. Her bare arms shimmered. I drew in the unmistakable odour of sunscreen.

She angled her head. "Two hours on the train and the bus, in this heat." My mother tutted.

"The wanderer returns." The plastic legs scraped across the aggregated concrete tiles. My father leant the collapsed chair against the wall.

"Hi, Dad." I untangled myself from my mum's embrace. She snatched my wrists and scowled. An anxious flame engulfed my gut, soaring up into my rib cage. I yanked my arms loose and crossed them in front of my chest.

"They gave you a pass, did they? How many terms did it take?" my dad said.

The heat in my body intensified. My cheeks burned. I felt the fabric of my blouse stick to my back.

"Dad, that *extra year* was part of the course." My voice lost strength. "They expected us to spend time abroad."

"Yes, yes." He flicked his hand across his ear to swat away a fly. The insect encircled his head and landed on the side of his chin. He whacked it. "Gotcha, you little bastard."

During a gap year, I had worked as an assistant teacher in Surrey. An opportunity set up by the university, the position was full-time, well-paid and included accommodation. It was a straightforward application, and whilst my fellow undergraduates swapped news of their suggested schools and made travel arrangements, I waited in vain. I never doubted their honest intentions, so I gave my parents' address for formal correspondence.

By the end of July, I had accepted that my application had been unsuccessful. That was until a visit home in the middle of August.

It was a sweltering summer. People yearned for a fresh breeze and were desperate for rain. When thunder rumbled in the far distance one afternoon, everyone in the street opened their windows, expressing anticipation on the faces of the houses. Black clouds blocked the sun, turning the daylight into sober darkness. I checked upstairs to ensure nothing could slam shut in the impending storm. The tiles warmed my naked feet as I walked across the landing, ready to step down the stairs. I paused mid-flow as I caught my mum chatting to a neighbour by the front door.

"No, we haven't mentioned it. She's wasted enough time." I pulled my foot back. The certainty that I was the subject of this conversation constricted my breathing. I bit my lower lip, slanting my head. The neighbour's voice sounded muffled.

"I cannot understand how gallivanting across England would benefit her education. She needs to complete her degree and prepare for a proper life," my mother said.

The roots of my hair felt like they were burning and scorching my skull. I swallowed the hurt at the back of my throat. My chin trembling, I turned back, mindful not to alert them to my presence.

When the heavy layer of lead-coloured clouds eventually burst, torrential rain hammered down on our house. I sat on my bed, my arms around my legs, sinking my teeth into my knees. A gush of pellets bounced off the window's glass pane, cancelling out my mother's raised voice.

"… care that the…" she said mid-sentence as she flung open my door. "There you are. Did you not hear me shouting…?" She checked the wall, confirming that no water had leaked onto the parquet. As her gaze settled on me, her posture stiffened, and her eyes widened.

"What's the matter with you? Don't tell me you're afraid of thunder?" she asked.

I turned my face towards the window. Bruise-coloured clouds boiled across the sky. The branches of our lime tree reached sideways, the gale tugging on the leaves.

"Mum." I cleared my throat. "Mum." My vocal cords were stronger this time. "Has there been a letter about a teaching post in England?"

Her lips thinned. "You should be ashamed of yourself." She stopped me, her hand raised. "Listening in on my conversation."

"I wasn't doing it on purpose. I couldn't help …" The rainfall intensified as my voice cracked.

"Yes, that's right. Tears. Play the victim, as usual," she said before she hurled the door shut, leaving me to the thunder.

When the storm had cleared into a drizzle, I opened the window to take in the ozone-saturated air. From below, I heard the whisking of a broom darting across a surface. My dad was pushing the rainwater that had formed pools on the terrace into the flowerbed. My mum was picking up torn-off petals from the lawn.

I rinsed my face and went downstairs. An envelope from the university lay on the counter. They expected me to start at a Guildford school within three weeks.

I snapped back to the present when my mum asked: "Are you hungry? There's cake left over from yesterday. Sandra made it."

The sun pricked my skin. "What was the occasion? Me finishing uni?" I realised the absurdity of my question.

My mum looked at my dad quizzically. He turned to his deckchair, jiggling it so the parts unfolded.

"Well, your success, yes. But erm, Sandra, well, she had *fantastic* news." The whites of my mother's eyes glinted.

"Karl, will you wipe the table and lay the wax tablecloth?" she called across my shoulder.

With a disgruntled moan, my dad shuffled towards the summerhouse.

"Right," my mother grabbed hold of my wrists. "I can't wait to tell you. Sandra is pregnant. We're going to be grandparents."

My head felt light like a helium balloon. The corner of my mouth twitched, and I choked.

"Isn't that marvellous? Our first grandchild," my mum said.

I battled to grasp the thoughts that spun through my mind. My brain hummed. When did I last see my sister? It was a week ago.

"How long has she known?" I asked, attempting to sound upbeat.

"Does it matter? It's wonderful news. That's what counts. At last, a grandchild." My mum studied me. "Are you not happy?"

"Of course, I am. It's just … I saw her the other day. After I got my final grade."

"I guess your sister opted not to inform you in case it might distract you from your studies. I mean, she only disclosed it to us yesterday. Isn't that thoughtful of her?"

I put my hand against the fence to steady myself—a thick fog built up in my mind.

"There's no need to pout," my mum scolded. "Everything doesn't have to revolve around you."

"I'm not; it's the sun." I creased my face. "I'd better take my stuff upstairs and freshen up," I said while my dad moved past me into the kitchen. The rattling of china and the cutlery drawer being jerked open sounded from inside.

"You do that. I'll get on with the coffee. A hot drink is the best in this weather. It kills the thirst."

My bedroom faced northeast, and the cooler temperature refreshed my senses. Barry, the stuffed St. Bernard, lay on a tartan cushion in a wicker armchair. He had eased my anxiety as a child. A doily I had embroidered for my mum one Christmas decorated a chest of drawers, my only attempt at needlecraft. "You couldn't balance a wine glass on this without it falling," she'd said, holding my present in the air, studying the back. "You worked at the stitches so carelessly, Phillippa. There are far too many knots. Leave the fine craft to your sister. You will find something you're good at one day."

I pressed the dog against my face. Its coat felt chalky. I brushed my finger across his cold brown eyes.

A metal shelf stood where my desk used to be. It contained several houseplants, none of them thriving. My glass bird still dangled from a nylon thread in the window. My face softened into a smile. A thin layer of dust dulled its fragile body. I cupped my hand underneath it as I untangled the string from the hook in the ceiling. I folded it up in the doily and inserted it into an inside compartment of my bag. Then I rejoined my parents in the garden.

They had placed the table in the half shade, with my mum catching the full glare of the sunlight while my dad sat with his back against the brick wall of the house, making the most of the shadow.

My sister's cake tasted delicious. I did not ask if her visit had been spontaneous or arranged, in which case it would have been easy for me to get a lift. She worked as a civil servant in a state pensions department. Within a few months of starting, she'd bought a car and moved into an apartment overlooking the river. My father suggested that Sandra could arrange something for me, but I never got excited about it, as much as her ambition impressed me. I could not see myself working nine to five behind a desk, carrying a leather briefcase and matching shoes.

"What's your plan now?" My dad rolled up a newspaper and aimed at a wasp that hovered over the chocolate-covered cake.

"Karl, don't. It angers them, and I'll get bitten," my mum said, waving her hand across the table.

"Some research posts are coming up at the English Department," I lied, testing the water.

"Wait a minute, young lady." My dad confirmed my suspicion. "You're not telling us you're going on with this *eternal student act*, are you?"

The coffee mug left a round imprint on the plastic tablecloth as I lifted it to my mouth.

My mum squashed crumbs with her fork. "The baby is due in late January. Who knows, it might be February. You were later than expected, too," she said, pushing her fork across the plate, leaving streaks of melted chocolate.

"Let's hope it doesn't inherit its aunt's traits. One underachiever in the family is more than enough." My dad slapped my thigh. "What, can you not take a joke now that you are one of these academics?" he added as he caught my eyes.

"All the more reason to get on with life, Phillippa." My mum aimed to make light of his comment.

My father had no intention of copying her bright-hearted tone. "I guess it's our fault you're drifting through life without purpose."

"Karl, please." My mum placed her hand on his arm.

"Why, Waltraud? It's true, isn't it?" He turned to me with a look of disdain. "If we'd bought you a dog, you'd never have gone off to *study*, would you?"

He settled back in his seat and placed his hands on either side of his plate. "Have you given my offer any thought? The deadline has passed, but I can get you an interview. They owe me something after my years of service." There was a tone of superiority in his voice.

35

"If you'd waited longer, you would have been born on New Year's Eve." My mum tapped my arm and forced a smile. "Imagine that, in between the years."

I gave a faint smile and dissected the layered cake, lifting the cocoa icing with my fingers. "I don't know, Dad," I said. "There's also …"

"For crying out loud, child. Let me tell you what: you finish everything over there, pack up your stuff and move back in here." He pointed his teaspoon towards the sky. "Sandra agreed to vacate her old room, and you'll have the run of the place upstairs."

"You discussed my future with her?" I shouted, and my mum hushed me.

"The neighbours," she whispered.

"Your mum and I decided this is the best choice for you—no more education. You have freewheeled for long enough. It's time to earn a living. I didn't work myself to the bone to support you until I retired. It took me years of night school to get where I am. Years of coming home covered in dirt, washing off the coal dust and off to evening classes. Years of sacrifice to create a better future for your mum and our children. My patience is running out, young lady."

My skin burned. I averted my eyes and watched a bee humming above the flowerbed before disappearing between the lush petals of a yellow rose.

"Let's face it," my dad continued, "you'll never afford a place of your own in the city, not with a degree in–" He drew speech marks in the air with his tablespoon and fingers. "Languages."

I gasped.

"And don't turn on the waterworks," he added. "That won't work this time."

The telephone rang from inside the house. "That'll be Sandra," my mum said and jumped up. "You get it, Pippa. It will give you a chance to congratulate her; go on." She nudged her head toward the kitchen door, and I obliged, glad to escape the heat and my father's demands.

5

After my dad had driven away from the train station, I searched for a public telephone and dialled Ursula's number—one of the two close friends I could trust without fearing judgment.

"That bad, huh?" she said when I described where I was and why I'd called. "Pippa, come home. When's your next train?"

"In half an hour," I murmured.

"Take that train, and I'll see you at the central station. What time will you get there, nine-ish?"

I stared at the yellow sheet of departure times on the wall. "Nine-thirty-two. Are you sure?"

"Of course, my dear. I'll meet you at the main exit."

Two hours later, we hugged underneath the illuminated 4711 sign that welcomed travellers to the city of Cologne. We scampered down the stairs to the underground and took Line 17 to the college quarter. The "Scholars' Retreat" was a popular pub with students, non-students, lecturers, and locals.

Urs held the door open for me and curtsied, her arm gesturing for me to enter. I filled my lungs with the sweet scent of hops and fresh nicotine.

"Ah, that's better." I sighed with relief and looked for a space to sit. The place was packed, and people's chatter drowned out any discernible music in the background.

"May we join you?" Urs took the lead and wiggled past the tables to a narrow corner with one free chair. A group of girls glanced up, all smiling. One of them nodded at a single, empty seat. "Of course," she said.

"Excuse me," a waiter shouted from behind my shoulder, nudging me to one side. He wielded an empty beer crate and a thick telephone directory in one hand. With a skilled movement, he rotated the crate in the air and stood it on the floor before placing the phone book on top. He smacked the makeshift stool. "Sorry, no backrest. Perfect for your core." He patted his belly and laughed.

I sat, clutching my travel bag on my lap.

"Give that here. It looks uncomfortable," Ursula said, snatching my luggage from me, cramming it on the floor and shoving it under the table.

"Careful with that." My abrupt shout startled the girls from talking, and heads swivelled towards me like a mob of meerkats.

"What's in there? One of your mum's famous cakes? Bottle of red from Daddy's wine cellar?"

"No," I explained, crouching to retrieve my luggage. "Far more precious. My little glass bird."

"Whohoo… ahaa…whohoo…ahaa…" Urs sang, clapping her hands along with the rhythm.

"What? Stop it," I urged.

"You know the Annie Lennox song, right?"

I shrugged my shoulders.

Urs shrieked and leaned her head against me, singing, "Piiiiippaaaa, she is real low. Piiiiippaaaa, when will she go?"

I opened the zip of my bag and fished around, looking for the hidden treasure, grabbing the doily with it rolled up inside. The contents appeared intact. The clustered threads of my botched needlework had preserved it throughout its journey.

"So, tell me how it went with your parents."

"As foreseen, to be honest." I groaned and took the glass of lager the waiter placed on our table. He marked our beer mat with two pencil strokes and left.

"Ouch." Urs flinched. "They were not pleased, huh?"

"Oh yes, they were *pleased*, all right," I jeered.

Urs fumbled with one of the cardboard coasters, which was steeped in liquid. She blew out her cheeks and released her breath. "I take it that's sarcasm?"

"You could say that. My sister is pregnant. It trumped anything I had to say."

"What?" Urs jerked back her head whilst her mouth fell open. "Holy Sandra. Talk about timing."

"Indeed. Knowing her, I wouldn't put it past her to time her conception to coincide with the week of my results."

"Argh, do you think so? I guess she'd do anything to spite you."

I balled my hands into a fist. "I'm serious, Urs. A few days after I passed, she appeared at my parents' place and performed the whole happy dance. My mum's over the moon." The intensity of my voice heightened. "With her, of course."

Urs swung her head in disbelief. She studied me, her lips pursed. "You need to see it from the sunny side. A baby from the *prodigal daughter* will be a splendid diversion from anything you get up to."

I gave her a stern glance.

"Sorry, Pippa, it's a joke. Remember, I know your parents." She turned her hand, opening her palm.

"It's cool. I know." I laid my hand in hers and squeezed.

"So, what did they say when you brought up ..." She sank her head and watched from under her fringe. "Hang on, Pippa. You told your parents about York, right?"

I cringed. "There was no point. Everyone was on edge. I couldn't bear to drop that bombshell on them."

"So, what will you do? Accept a job at your dad's office?"

I remained silent.

"Pippa, no. I won't have that. You stick to your dream. It's time to spread your wings and fly, little bird."

When I arrived at the flat, Yvonne was working on her coursework at the kitchen table.

She shoved her books and paperwork aside and grabbed a bottle of wine from the fridge.

"Look what Tom left us." She chuckled. "He had counted on an evening of rumpy-pumpy, but I have to get this damn paper written before the end of the week."

Without pause, she placed two glasses on the table and searched the drawer for a corkscrew.

I knew that the white wine would blur my mind, having enjoyed a few beers with Ursula earlier, and welcomed that prospect.

When I filled Yvonne in on the visit to my parents, she urged me to make decisions independent of my parents' negative judgment.

"It would be a shame to let this opportunity pass. You could at least call York and get an idea of the place, the course, and the people. You're an exceptional judge of character, and you'll know if it's an opportunity worth pursuing."

I downed my glass in one go and enjoyed the soothing effect of the alcohol.

"You're spot-on. I'll review them before I start submitting for the bursary. The thought of the paperwork puts me off, and I don't want to waste my time," I said, feeling confident.

Yvonne poured me a refill and held hers in the air. "Cheers," she called out to an invisible audience. "Here's to Pippa's future."

When I stirred the following day, my head felt as if it was stuffed with cotton wool. I ran my tongue around my teeth and realised how dehydrated I was. Soft light twinkled through my curtains.

The kitchen clock displayed 11.45. My throat burned, and my heart raced. At weekends, Mum used to roar into my room without warning, yanking back my sheet and jerking open the window.

"Late nights, early mornings" was one of her favourite greetings, followed by a list of household chores waiting for me.

Yvonne had cleared away the bottle and left me a note: *Good luck with the call to York.*

Ouch. I remembered.

After a toilet break and coffee, I settled on a chair with the phone, pen, and paper. I looked at my checklist with keywords that Yvonne and I had scribbled the night before: *start date, funding, accommodation, and job guarantee.* Yvonne had added *the knight in shining armour* and drawn several hearts around it.

I dialled and listened to the dual ring, each followed by a momentary pause. Brrringbrrring … brrringbrring … the receiver clicked.

"University of York, Language Department. How can I help you?" a woman answered.

"Yes, erm, hello…" I cleared my throat. "My name is Phillippa Olbig. I'm calling from Germany."

"Hello, Phillippa. What can I do for you on this fine morning?"

"Erm, do you have any vacancies for the …" I bent over the paper to read the advert. "PGCE?"

"What subject are you applying for?"

"Languages," I said. There was a brief period of silence. "German, I mean."

"Can you hold the line for a moment, please? I will be back with you shortly." Listening to the silence, my father's voice became clear in my mind. *They're having a good laugh at you.*

Clicking sounded from the receiver.

"Thank you for waiting, Phillippa." *She had memorised my name.* "Do you plan to apply for the upcoming semester? And have you obtained a degree in German?"

"Yes, and English," I added. "I just got a 2:1."

"That's fantastic, congratulations."

A pang shot through my body.

"Yes, thank you. When does the course commence, and what is the fee? I'll need to seek funding."

"Do you want the good or not-so-good news to begin with?" The smile in her voice was inspiring.

"Both, in whatever order," I said, wiggling my feet underneath the table.

"The good news is that you qualify for course funding. It's on condition that you provide the necessary reports and diplomas. The not-so-good news is that it's late in the year, and classes start the first week of September. You will need to act fast if you intend to apply."

My blood charged through my veins. The hangover vanished, and fireworks went off in my stomach. *June, July, August...* Oh my God, less than three months to go.

"Right, yes, that's no problem. It's not a problem at all. What do I need to do?"

I heard my dad's voice resonate in my head. *What a foolish thing to ask.* I brushed it to one side with the sheet of keywords on the table.

"Well, we would be delighted to have you on board if you join us." *Join you? You must be joking. I can't wait.*

The lady told me she'd send the application form in the first-class post- that day. *First class? How great was that?*

"In the meantime, you should prepare your CV and arrange certified copies of your qualifications, including school exams."

"I will, I will," I said with urgency.

She laughed. "Oh, and you will need to have two independent references. Not family or friends, but someone who knows you in an academic or work environment. There's plenty to keep you busy while the paperwork gets to you. Where do I send it?"

My heart jolted. *Was I soiling the nest?*

"I'm in Cologne," I said, giving her my address.

6

At the beginning of July, we celebrated my dad's birthday with a small gathering. The family had diminished since my parents had become homeowners.

"Envy is a fatal affliction," was my dad's phrase to dismiss our relatives' infrequent visits. Mum had more trouble not seeing her siblings. I watched her shield the receiver with her hand when talking on the phone with one of my aunties.

This year, they hosted a small gathering at Sandra's place and I prepared myself for an afternoon of cooing over my pregnant sister.

I had not foreseen the presence of my brother-in-law's parents. My dad made no secret of how much he disliked Harald's mother, a "stuck-up cow", nor masked his loathing of her husband, who owned two small hotels on the banks of the Mosel. After meeting the Lindenthals for the first time, my father had worked himself into a temper. He called Harald's father a "pompous twat" for mentioning that he was about to be "published in a travel journal". My dad air-quoted the words with a disgusted smirk.

When I arrived, hushed voices came through the living room door. Harald held his hands out, ready to take my coat.

"Let me." He picked up a hanger from the wardrobe.

"It's only a cardigan," I replied whilst he tugged at my collar behind me. "Have they been here long?"

"Yes, we had brunch together."

A shiver ran down my spine. I took a deep breath and entered the room with a vague wave. "Hello, everyone," I said, smiling. My dad stood on the balcony, in conversation with Harald's dad. As I passed my mum, I stroked her arm before stepping out through the open glass door.

The men had their backs to me and turned, startled, when I tapped my dad on his shoulder.

"Happy Birthday." I hugged him, breathing in the sharp scent of fresh soap, and handed him my present. A biography of Bismarck, my mum's tip, gift-wrapped in black and silver striped paper. I rubbed my nose discreetly.

"Thank you, you shouldn't have," he said in a sarcastic tone that was meant for me only to pick up on. "You're still a penniless student, after all."

"Good afternoon." I shook hands with Herr Lindenthal, who scanned me from head to toe. I wore a cotton skirt down to my ankles, and the blue clashed with my brown sandals, giving my outfit a frumpy appearance. They were the only pair I owned.

Harald stuck his head through the door and offered me a glass of summer punch.

"Food is ready," my sister shouted from inside. We took seats at the round table, admiring her delicate blue and white porcelain and matching linen napkins.

"Sandra told us you passed. Well done." Frau Lindenthal leaned across the table.

I glanced at my sister, who was pointing a polished cake slicer at three homemade cakes on the table.

"Black Forest? Chocolate? Cheesecake? Mum made the gateau."

I nodded at a slice covered in whipped cream with a cherry in the middle.

Sandra flopped a piece onto my plate. It landed on its side.

I turned on a fixed smile, aware that nobody suspected my discomfort throughout the dreary conversation.

"An aunty with a degree," Harald's dad said, placing his hot drink down with a wince. "Will you have time to be godmother? I guess you will want to start climbing the career ladder?"

I dabbed my lips with a napkin, peeping over to my sister. She lifted the corner of her mouth.

"We've not asked Pippa yet." Sandra nudged her husband with her elbow.

Harald choked. "Oh, yes, of course. Well, Phillippa, erm, Pippa. Will you do us the honour of being our firstborn's godmother?"

My dad clapped his hands like two cymbals. "Well, what a title, Pippa, and quite a responsibility." He threw me a knowing look.

Harald's mum took her husband's hand, the precious stones in her golden rings glinting.

"You're so fortunate to have two lovely daughters." She turned to my mum. "I so much longed to have a second child, a girl, but ..." She turned towards the window with moist eyes.

"So, Pippa, what do you say?" Harald had composed himself. Blood shot to my face, and my cheeks blazed. My heart was pumping in my chest as I thought of the letter I had sent to York University two weeks earlier. *Godmother,* what did that involve?

"Wow, that is... an... honour indeed," I stuttered, "and a surprise."

"Well, you were our obvious choice. Harald and I believe in *keeping it in the family.*" Sandra smirked.

The family. I cringed: did they know of my plan, and was this a scheme, a ploy they had orchestrated to make me stick around?

No way could I pop their bubble in the presence of Harald's parents. His mum, with the designer jewellery, begrudging her husband for not giving her a daughter. Here he was, a hotel owner with a Michelin star and an article published in a magazine. I could not bear to wreck my dad's birthday and disappoint my mum. This round table of seven was my *entire* family.

"Of course, I'd be ... thrilled." My mum's face lit up, my sister exhaling with relief.

"I'll fetch the champagne." Harald walked to the kitchen.

The conversation flowed as we toasted my sister, who sipped pressed orange juice from her champagne flute. The grandmothers-to-be reminisced, recalling christening gowns and agreeing to swap photos at the following visit. My official duties started with the christening in spring.

"Unlike our generation, baptisms do not happen within days of birth," Harald's mum explained.

"Eroding traditions," my dad muttered.

The following week, I received confirmation that I had been accepted at York. My grade entitled me to full funding without applying for a bursary. Yvonne performed a vigorous victory dance in our kitchen whilst I stared at the letter with an incredulous grin.

"I can't believe it!" I whooped at Yvonne as she hobbled along our corridor. She paused before me, gripped my arms in a tango pose, and pulled me along with vast strides. "Taram, taram, taramtamtam …" she sang.

Laughing, we bumped into the coat stand on one side of the corridor.

"Stop it, please. I am going to wet myself," I shrieked, squeezing my hand between my legs. She let go of me, snorting, and I rushed to the bathroom, just in time.

"Pippa, I'm so delighted for you." Paper crinkled on the other side of the door. "It's the 12th of September. Perfect timing. Tom wants to move in," she shouted through the crack.

"Hold your horses," I said as I appeared from the bathroom, buttoning up my jeans. "I must let this sink in. Flipping heck, I was bracing myself for a rejection."

"For a rejection? Boohoo." Yvonne simulated a sob, circling her fists in front of her eyes. "Well, Miss Olbig, you are evidently more than just a pretty face. They want your brains."

I bit the inside of my cheek.

"Go on, be happy. This is what you wanted. Since I've known you, you've had this obsession with England. I mean, God knows why you want to live in a wet country, drinking milky tea and warm beer. But hey, if it's what you fancy …"

Holding back my news from my parents was torment. Unable to focus on my plans until I overcame this last obstacle, I grappled with how to tell them. Every day, the need to confess grew.

What a coward I was. My thoughts shifted from self-loathing to wishing I could turn back the clock and erase what I had done. If only I had not applied. If only Yvonne hadn't spotted the notice. If I hadn't gone upstairs to the English department that day… In my mind, I retreated, wishing I had never developed a passion for England, never wanted to set foot in *this green and pleasant land*.

When Yvonne found me one afternoon with a shot glass and an unsealed bottle of Tequila left over from a recent party, she took the phone and planted the receiver in my hand.

"Tell them, or I will."

I picked up the glass. Yvonne jerked it out of my hand, and the clear liquid sloshed on the table.

"No, Pippa. Enough of this prevarication. It's time to reveal the truth. The earlier you do it, the quicker they'll learn to accept your decision. You deserve to be over the moon. Not getting hammered before the sun sets."

"I'm not drunk."

"Even better. Here, dial."

"What do I say?"

"Just sound delighted. That will make it impossible for them to offload their crap. You need to persuade them that this incredible opportunity, which, by the way, they aren't paying for, means a second degree from a distinguished university."

I puffed. "You don't know them."

"From what you've told me, I don't want to know them. But if you don't ring them yourself, I will."

I took a long breath and dialled, putting the phone on speakerphone. My mum answered.

"Hi, Mum, it's me."

"Hello. What's the matter? You never ring in the daytime."

"I have news."

"Oh?" I sensed anticipation. My stomach clenched.

Yvonne nudged me. "Good, go on," she hissed and spurred me on with a nod.

"I've found a placement on a training course. To become a language teacher."

The line was still, apart from the sound of her breathing.

"Where?"

My mum's tone had changed. She suspected something. How was that possible?

"In ... erm ... the course is at York University." My brain spiralled. I reached for the bottle, but Yvonne put her fingers around it, holding on tight. She shook her head.

"Phillippa, it's your father. What did you say?"

"Hi, Dad." My trembling voice went up an octave. "I've been accepted at a teaching course in York, England. It starts in September." When I looked at Yvonne, she gave me a thumbs-up sign.

I tilted my head back and mouthed "thank you".

My dad puffed into the receiver.

"You said you wanted to join my company."

"Dad, it was *you* who said that." With my free hand, I pointed at myself. Was this what *standing up for yourself* felt like?

"If you do that, young lady, if you go off to England, you're no longer a daughter of mine."

I struggled to gather myself.

"Dad?" I shouted.

Yvonne tilted her upper body back, watching in horror.

"You heard me: If you go off to England, Phillippa, you cease to be our daughter. Your mother and I will disown you, and you will be on your own. It's your decision what you do next. Goodbye."

He slammed the phone down.

Shaking, I replaced the receiver and pressed a fist to my open mouth.

Yvonne's chin had dropped. There was a moment of silence. My eyes burned as they filled with tears. I covered my face with my hands before clutching fistfuls of hair.

"Oh my God, you think he means it?" Yvonne said.

What had he said? *Cease to be his daughter?*

"He can't mean it. You took him by surprise." She tried comforting me.

"You think he was just caught off guard?" I wiped my face with my hands, ran my sleeve along my nose and sniffed as I remembered the condition on which they had allowed me to go to Surrey for a year. My eyes filled up. I shrugged. "I wish I had your optimism," I sobbed. Yvonne knelt, hugging me.

"How can they be so heartless, so unkind? They should be filled with pride. And realise this is a logical step for you."

I gasped. My face contorted, my shoulders quaking. I struggled for air.

"Shhh, I will make you a cup of chamomile tea," Yvonne said.

I clenched my teeth and nodded. The muscles around my heart went into spasm, forcing a quivering sound with every breath. I watched my friend take a mug from the shelf, put a tea bag in, and fill the kettle. Her movements appeared to be in slow motion.

After the first hot sips, the doorbell rang. I leapt up.

"I'll get it," Yvonne said.

I rubbed my hot, swollen eyes.

There was shuffling in the hallway and the sound of my sister's voice. As Sandra stormed into the room, I suppressed the urge to spread my arms, pleading for her to console me.

"Sandra, what are you doing here? I've just spoken to Dad…"

She raised both hands, her palms facing me. "That's why I'm here." Her sullen frown did not predict what I wished for: that she had rushed across town to share in my disbelief, to draw up a plan to bolster me in my cause and appease our parents.

I rose, my knees shaking. Sandra pushed past me. Her head held high, she marched into my room. Yvonne and I followed.

49

"This is mine. This too. Where's my camera?" She bagged a couple of books that she had given me. Disorientated, I looked around the room. She followed my gaze and discovered the camera on my desk.

She snatched it and turned to leave, Yvonne and I diving aside for safety.

"Ah, I think you won't need this anymore. You obviously think you can just swan off like that and be happy without us. Well, if I'm not good enough for you, neither is all this."

She spat the words with a sarcastic smile and emptied the porcelain jewellery box she had given me for my sixteenth birthday.

Before she stepped through the front door, she turned around and stabbed me with a cold stare. "Oh, and by the way, it was Harald's idea to have you be godmother. I was against it from the start. I told him you wouldn't take it seriously, and you've proved me right."

She left and banged the door on her way out.

Yvonne took a step back before rushing through the kitchen, grabbing the bottle of Tequila, and hurling it at the front door. As the pieces of glass scattered around the hallway, I collapsed on the floor, wailing.

7

Within half an hour after Sandra had plundered my room, a halo of tiny, flickering lights manifested in front of my right eye, limiting my vision. I reassured Yvonne this was a typical course with migraine accompagnée, something she had never experienced. It took me five days to recover, each one marked by a vile headache, spent in bed, the curtains drawn to block out the daylight.

When I regained my appetite, my clothes were sagging on my body. Sitting at the kitchen table, feeling weak, I ate a slice of dry toast, sipping tea to wash down each bite.

Yvonne had disconnected the phone in the first few days of my being unwell. "I thought another verbal assault from your dad might push you over the edge," she said.

"I should be used to this," I gulped. "I should have known they'd react this way."

Although Tom maintained a detached view, he showed sympathy towards my misery. "Time to stand on your own two feet. Your family will come round. But don't put your life on hold for them. Take charge of your destiny." He was the second generation to study in his family and had grown up in an academic household. "You deserve to follow your dreams."

"Why does it have to be such a struggle? Why can't they be happy for me?" I turned to Yvonne and raised my shoulders. "They claim they want me to be happy, but ..."

"Happy on their terms," Yvonne nudged the plate in my direction. "Here, try to finish that."

"You have a tough job, Pippa, taking the lead," said Tom. "It can't be easy for your parents to accept this need to continue your studies in England. They might perceive your independence as a threat. But you will pave the way for generations of Olbigs to come." Despite the pathos in Tom's voice, I sensed his message contained a truth I couldn't grasp.

"I've been paving my way for quite a while, Tom. You should have been there when I got my A-levels. Another milestone, another drama."

"Why? What happened?" Yvonne hunched over. "You haven't told me about that."

"That's because it was embarrassing, just horrible." For a moment, I paused. Was it safe to share with them?

"Go on, what did they do to spoil your excitement this time?" Yvonne squeezed my hand.

"We all went partying that night to celebrate. A friend's brother gave us a ride home after midnight. He dropped me off last."

I felt nauseous as I recalled the twitching of the dining room curtain as we pulled up outside my parents' house.

Yvonne held her arms in the air as if to surrender. "You should have seen me when *I* knew I'd passed. I got so drunk, it was—" she choked, and before she could continue, Tom interrupted her.

"What happened, Pippa?" His voice sounded gentle, like he had observed the scene that unfolded in our hallway that night.

"An avalanche of metal crashed into me in the hallway. Knives, forks, spoons, and ladles clonked and skipped across the tiles around my ankles. I hopped from foot to foot as if I'd stepped into a snake's nest."

"What?" Yvonne stopped laughing. "Did they empty their kitchen drawer at you?"

"It was their present for my degree. A sterling silver cutlery set."

Tom and Yvonne stared at me in silence. I saw Tom's head move from side to side.

"The sound was awful. Metal clunking off the marble. And above that, my dad's shouting. He demanded to know who the guy in the car was."

"Did you not try to explain?" Tom asked, and I cringed.

"As always, I was dumbfounded at their reaction. My dad stood rigid, frothing at the mouth, and my mum, in her pale-yellow nightgown, just looked on."

I took a deep breath and averted my eyes.

"So instead of saying anything and aggravating matters, I picked up the pieces and carried them upstairs to my room." I recoiled as I remembered my dad's words echoing up the stairs. "If we ever find out you've been fooling around with a boy, young lady, the money tap turns off!"

"And … the next … morning?" Yvonne spoke the words as if she were treading on ice.

"Ah, you know …" My eyes pricked, and I cleared my throat. "It just got swept underneath the carpet."

"Let me guess: you got the silent treatment?" Yvonne said.

"Uh-huh." I nodded. I had confided enough.

There was silence. Then Tom said, "That sounds traumatic, Pippa, really it does. But it's in the past. At the moment, take one step at a time."

In the following weeks, the knot in my gut tightened each time I opened the post box, only to stare into the empty, dark space. At least there had been encouraging correspondence from York, instructing me when and where they expected me in September, a few weeks off. I stuck the letter up on my wall. As downbeat as I was after the massive fallout, knowing they expected me at "The Main Hall of the University of York" filled me with an excited thrill.

Ursula had urged me not to contact my mum, dad, or sister. "It's their turn to apologise, Pippa. If you don't stand your ground now, you never will."

With lectures finished, I worked more shifts at the car dealership. I could do with the money, and the banter with the sales staff was an encouraging diversion since none knew of my inner turmoil. To them, I was the *brave student about to embark on an adventure*. "A girl like a Swiss army knife," they called me, "handling a busy switchboard, serving perfect coffee whilst getting her degree and moving to a foreign country."

With a mixture of dread and hope, I watched the revolving doors turn, but my sister never showed up. I realised she had less trouble living her life without my presence. I imagined the six of them, my *family*, ignoring my absence, with her firstborn making up for the gap at her table.

The degree ceremony at Cologne University took place on the first Friday afternoon of September. I photocopied the invitation and posted it to my parents' address.

Ursula protested. "Stop torturing yourself," but I refused to heed her advice.

Tom showed compassion. "It can't be easy for you. It's not in your character. At least you tried everything in your power …"

"Well, not everything. I could cancel York and give my family what they want," I said.

Yvonne raised her arms in surrender. "I give up, honestly, I do."

Urs tutted.

"Maybe they are waiting for an olive branch." I justified myself. "I can't imagine my mum *not* being upset with what's happened. She'll be devastated to miss my ceremony."

"Whatever their answer is, it will give you clarity," Tom said.

My parents' reaction arrived in a large brown envelope. It contained my letter, unopened. There was a note attached with a paperclip. It read:

Your services as godmother to our first grandchild are no longer required.

That was the clarity that Tom had referred to. It was not the outstretched hand I hoped to receive. I was their *daughter*. How could they be so cruel?

September came, and Yvonne was moping around in the apartment by midday on Friday, shifting from leg to leg, peeking at the door. Then Tom let himself in, followed by Ursula. He carried a bouquet and a bottle of champagne in one hand. Urs had a big shopping bag in hers.

"Hey, what's going on?" I asked. "I must get ready …"

They grinned and it dawned on me.

"Hang on, you can't …" I exclaimed.

"Yes, we can. Friends are the family you choose yourself." Tom beamed and handed me the flowers. My eyes welled up.

"Right, take that off," Ursula said, tugging at my baggy T-shirt.

"I beg your pardon." I laughed, stepping back. She pulled a dress from her bag. The soft fabric unfolded as she held the gown in the air—a long, white summer dress with a colourful print of fantasy flowers and butterflies. The shoulder straps were wide, and a soft second layer of sheer textile covered the bust. I touched the delicate material, holding its skirt open wide.

"It's gorgeous," I said, looking at the tiny, pink label on the collar, *Oilily*.

"Wow, exclusive. Are you wearing that today?"

"No. You are, Pippa. Put it on. I bought it last week, so it's not been worn."

The dress fell wide and loose, the material caressing my naked legs, cool and silky.

Admiring whoops filled the kitchen as I entered, having changed into the stunning garment in my room. I put my hair up with a clip and wore silver earrings, a Celtic knot with an aquamarine.

"Are we taking the tram?" I asked.

"No way," Urs said with mock disapproval. "A taxi is awaiting you downstairs, Madam."

The assembly hall hummed with excited voices. I recognised several people sitting on the grey upholstery. Some graduates wore jeans and T-shirts, leggings, or casual summer dresses. The row of chairs on stage was empty. A young woman tapped the microphone and put papers on the off-centre wooden podium. Two large flower displays decorated the stage on either side, marking a pair of steps to enter and exit.

I hesitated at the entrance and studied the scene.

"Am I not overdressed for this occasion?"

Ursula pinched my hip.

"Ouch," I shoved her with my elbow. Yvonne positioned herself on my other side, joined by Tom.

"Ready?" Tom leaned forward and nodded at Urs and me.

"You bet," Urs said and linked arms with me and Yvonne. My friends by my side, I marched up the middle aisle to sit in one of the front rows. When the university staff entered the stage, the audience clapped.

"Who is that?" I heard Tom whisper to Yvonne as Professor Werther appeared, dressed in tweed slacks held up by braces and an oversized matching jacket. Her hair appeared platinum underneath the stage lights. After speeches, she read the names of the graduates and presented us with our degree certificates. Yvonne cheered when my name was called, followed by a roar and enthusiastic clapping by Tom and Ursula. When I turned to walk down the steps, I saw my friends giving me a standing ovation.

Yvonne helped carry my luggage downstairs, where a taxi was waiting, the engine running. I wiped my moist palms on my trousers. Yvonne had pushed the suitcase through the door into the cool stairwell when I grasped her arm. "Wait," I said, "I need a wee."

"Again?" She replied and looked at her watch. It had just gone six thirty in the morning. My train left at seven.

With a flutter in my stomach, I handed my luggage to the driver, who swung the heavy items into the boot. My heart pounded as I reached for Yvonne's hand to sit next to her in the back seat. The artificial smell of air freshener, mixed with the warm morning air, filled the cab.

As we pulled away from the house, I watched the sun's reflection in the windows and front doors sliding past. The shop owner on the corner placed an advertising board on the pavement. He lifted his hand as our eyes met. The indicator ticked while we waited at a traffic light. My mouth turned dry. I sank into the seat with a deep sigh when the driver turned the corner. Yvonne squeezed my hand. "Excited?" she asked, and I nodded, scanning the streets outside.

We met the others at the central station. Jackson's tail-wagging increased as we approached Urs, who stood by the ticket booths. She made a loud "Ha" sound. We hugged, and the dog's nose tickled my knee.

"Oh, come here, my lovely Jackson." I crouched, burying my face in his coat.

"Something tells me she'll miss the pooch more than us." I heard Urs laugh.

"There you are," Yvonne shouted, and we turned to the crowd of travellers rushing around the station hall.

Tom waved both arms like an air traffic controller and worked through the swarm.

"Thank God I'm not too late." He sounded relieved, kissed Yvonne, and patted Jackson on his head whilst nodding to Ursula and me.

"Hi, all set?" He gazed at the backpack resting against the side of the ticket counter, next to the suitcase he had given me. "You'll look like a giant tortoise with this on your back," he joked.

Ursula giggled and grabbed my holdall. "Time to go?"

"Yes," I replied, my voice shaking. "What am I doing?" I asked.

"Emancipating yourself, my dear," Yvonne said, imitating holding a pipe to her chin.

Tom looked quizzical.

"Forget it." I waved him off and picked up my rucksack.

My friends tried to insist on carrying my luggage, but I refused their offer. "I need to handle this for the rest of the day; I'd better get used to it."

"What time will you get there?" Tom asked.

"This afternoon," I replied. "I'll call Yvonne when I get a chance."

As the escalator bore me up to the platform, my heart raced. My stomach churned with happy excitement, doubt, and fear of the unknown. I bit my lip and turned round to Tom and Yvonne, who stood on the steps behind me. Tom wore his usual grin, but Yvonne pouted and pulled a sad face.

Ursula walked up the stairs with Jackson hobbling ahead, trying to overtake the strangers in front.

The train stood ready. I inhaled the sharp smell of tar. A metallic voice through the loudspeaker informed us that this was the train to Brussels.

I reached into my coat pocket and pulled out my ticket. A one-way trip to Dunkirk, from where I got the ferry to Dover. After that, a six-hour train journey to York via London.

"Have you got everything?" Urs asked in the schoolmarm voice she used for such an intimate moment of farewell. I looked vacantly at other passengers, wondering what to say.

"Guess this is it." Yvonne held her arms out wide, and I fell into them, squeezing her tight with a loud sigh, breathing in a whiff of patchouli.

"Argh, I hate goodbyes," I said, struggling to disguise my emotional and mental confusion. "You must all come for a visit."

I took a step back, looking at my friends. Ursula's eyes appeared red. Yvonne pressed her fist against her chest whilst Tom stared at his hands.

"Try to stop us," Ursula said, putting her arm around Yvonne's and Tom's shoulder. A pang of regret shot through my veins. I would miss their camaraderie.

A whistle blew, and Jackson barked, startling a couple of passengers who'd entered the train behind me.

Yvonne and Tom picked up my luggage and pushed it into the carriage whilst I held Ursula by both hands.

"Don't go sentimental on me," she said, her eyes tearful. She pulled me close. "You're doing the right thing, you know. Trust your instincts," she whispered before I got on the train.

"Thank you," I said as I stood in the open door, my chin trembling.

Ursula dug into her pocket and passed me a tissue before the doors closed. My friends jumped up and down, waving their arms in the air. Jackson, tail wagging, howled his farewell. Their bodies became smaller as the train picked up speed until they disappeared. I took a deep breath and closed my eyes, my body moving from side to side to the rhythm of the motion, the one-way ticket in my pocket.

Had I irretrievably left my family behind?

Germany 1970

8

The midwife placed the newborn baby in Waltraud Olbig's arms. The edges of the mother's lips drooped. Her runny blue eyes scanned the bundle of white terrycloth towels.

"A girl?"

"Yes, Mrs Olbig, you have a delightful daughter. A remarkable child. The doctor and nurses said …"

"My husband had hoped for a boy so badly."

"Do you realise what today's date is? The Feast of the Holy Innocents. This cannot be a coincidence. All the staff said so: she is a special child. Very delicate."

A distant smile illuminated Waltraud's face. The child's head shimmered porcelain blue.

"She reacted intensely to the light in the delivery room. Her skin is so tender, you'll have to take extra care of that. And look at her eyelashes: this little one is a redhead. They're exceptionally sensitive."

Waltraud buried herself deep into the pillow. Exhausted, she succumbed to a slumber, savouring the baby's heat radiating into her chest.

The next day, the green VW Beetle raced over the Emscher bridge.

"Careful, Karl, she's asleep." Waltraud hunched over from the back seat and touched her husband's shoulder. "Could you not have picked a different route? With fewer potholes?"

"I wish you'd stop moaning. I am going above and beyond to bring you home, and you're complaining because of a few bumps. There are roadworks the other way. You don't want to be caught in a traffic jam, do you?" He straightened his neck and hurled her a steely look in the rear-view mirror. "I promised my mother to collect Sandra before teatime."

His wife flinched at the mention of their firstborn daughter. Being an only child himself, Karl had hoped he'd continue the Olbig line with a son and hadn't hidden his disappointment when she gave birth to a girl. Waltraud peered at the row of buildings sliding past. Winter drizzle had blackened the brickwork, transforming the grubby exteriors into depressing, blotchy surfaces.

The car pulled up outside the four-storey block of flats. This area had been lucky to escape the Allied bombers a quarter of a century before. The mineworks had shrouded any surviving stone in a veil of grey. Dust and soot had corroded the crevices of mortar. The curtains hung, tired and drab, through the gritty glass of the downstairs windows. Higher up, they appeared lighter in all the dreariness.

Karl opened the driver's door to confirm his distance to the road. He slammed it shut and jerked the gearstick into reverse, steering into the kerb. With another jarring movement, he forced the gearstick into first and adjusted the car to the right.

"Karl, can we go inside, please? I need to lie down." His wife clung to the baby in its blanket.

"You don't want the car to be damaged by that idiot from number three, do you?" he murmured, rotating his head to check for obstacles. "One thing's clear: he never earned that money for a new Ford working as a miner."

Waltraud sighed as she waited by the entrance. She rested her temple against the central windowpane. With the tip of her shoe, she aimed to uncoil the heavy linen cloth covering the grid used as a doormat. Endless footsteps twisted the polluted rug each day. Still, she was the sole tenant who washed and wrung it out each morning.

She sucked in the damp air of the entrance and, stabilising the baby in one arm, held on to the railing to climb up to the third floor. Karl followed, having retrieved the newspaper from the metal letterbox. Upstairs, he planted Waltraud's bag in the cramped corridor of their apartment and opened the door of the nursery.

As Waltraud entered, the smell of washing powder tickled her nose. The half-open door cast a cone of light on the blue wallpaper and the colourful patterns of an oriental carpet. Waltraud lowered the sleeping baby into the wooden cot.

"Let's go into the kitchen. I'll change her later," she said, leaving the door ajar.

Karl Olbig's newspaper covered a third of the table. He turned the front page.

"They are still going on about Brandt falling on his knees in Warsaw. A bow would have sufficed. For all I care, he could have wiped away a fake tear." Karl looked at his wife and smirked. "I tell you one thing for sure: I'd never get on my knees. For nothing and nobody." The paper scrunched as he turned the page.

Waltraud blushed.

"We have to think of a name, Karl." She touched his arm.

"What if we call her Bernardine? Bit of a boy, bit of a girl." He grinned.

"Bernardine? But that's a dog."

"So what, Waltraud? She should have been a boy!"

"I was just getting used to *Phillip*, after my dad. Isn't Philippine a girl's name?"

"That's an Asian archipelago. Bloody hell, Waltraud. Your general education ... did you ever pick up a book in your life, or were you too busy chasing your mother's fat ass?"

Silence. Except for the tentative crackle of a newspaper.

"I'm certain Philippine is a name. Why don't you ask at the town hall? Surely they know." Waltraud defended herself. "Register her today, Karl. Who knows if they're open during the holidays?"

Chair legs screeched across the kitchen floor. Her husband sighed.

"All right, I'm off. I'll pick up Sandra on my way home."

"Oh, by the way. Guess what they said at the hospital? That she's an exceptional girl. She's …"

"Bloody hell, Waltraud. Don't tell me you fell for that nonsense. That's what they tell every new mother in the delivery room. To make them forget the pain. All babies are the same. I advise you not to share that hokum with anyone … people will laugh at you!"

The door slammed shut, followed by silence.

9

With lips pursed Karl stood at the counter of the registration office.
Get your ass into gear, woman.
He scowled.
Did I say that aloud?
The official tidied up her paperwork and pored over the text. "Father's name?"

"The father is here, standing right in front of you!" He couldn't help his cynical tone. He loathed ignorant thickheads who asked the obvious. How often did he have to put a colleague in their place and point out the error of their ways? It was a waste of effort.

Sweat gathered on the inside of his collar.

His eyes were met with a stern expression. "Not every man who registers a child puts his name on the birth certificate. We can't just take that for granted. So please, Christian name and last name?" The clerk's tone was unimpressed.

Bloody civil servants. Lazy and stuck up. Does she realise I pay her wages and pension?

He clenched his molars with a groan.
"Karl Olbig."
"Thank you. Full name of the child?"
"Phillip."

"Mr Olbig, if I understood correctly, you wanted to register a daughter." The clerk leafed through the papers with a furrowed brow.

"Oh, damn it, yes, of course."

A blush rose from his neck. Beads of sweat trickled along his back. Utterly wet, his shirt would be soaked through in just a matter of minutes.

"Phila … Philom …" he stammered. What had Waltraud conjured up? She was constantly coming up with special requests, nothing straightforward. How it pissed him off!

"Philippa. Philippa Olbig is the child's name."

"Double P, one L?"

"Excuse me?"

"Is it Philippa, with two Ps and one L, or two Ls and one P, or vice versa?"

"Two of everything. Or not? Yes, two of everything."

"Middle name?"

"None. Is that it?"

Unimpressed by his edginess, the woman completed the rest of the form, ticking a box here and there, then shoved the sheet across the counter.

"I wish your young family the best, Mr Olbig."

Stupid cow. As if I didn't have my wits with me. I'd have loved to shove that pencil right up her fat ass.

On his way to the car park, he slackened his tie from his dry throat and tugged at the clammy shirt fabric that stuck to his skin. It was time to drive to his parents' house. His mum would be as disappointed to hear about the birth of another daughter as he was.

Hedwig Olbig spotted her son's car before it reached the yard.

She wedged her chest through the kitchen window.

"Yoo-hoo, Karlchen! What is it? A boy?"

"Bloody hell, Mother. Come downstairs and open the door!"

"All right, all right. No need to be so prickly…" She closed the window and padded across the room, fumbling in her apron pockets.

"Otto, where's the key? Karlchen is downstairs."

"It's open." A voice called from the bedroom.

His wife had already hastened to the ground floor. Racing up to the door, she dried the moisture from her eyes with the corner of her apron.

"Mother, how many times have I told you not to call me that?"

"Yes, yes, all right …"

"No, Mother, nothing is all right. You don't know how stupid it sounds. The entire street can hear you. Why don't you utilise your brains for a change?"

"So, what is it?"

"Yes, yes, it's fine. It's a girl, not a boy. A girl." With his fingertips, he tapped the soft body of the sixty-year-old into motion. The woman turned and clambered the stairs in front of him.

"Oh boy, a girl," she said.

"Have you got a beer for me?" Karl asked.

"Of course. Cold, as you like it. Come in. Your father wants to hear everything." She panted for the last few steps. "Well, well, another girl." Her hand reached for the door handle.

"And from the looks of it, she'll be a redhead," Karl said.

Hedwig Olbig winced, cupping both hands before her mouth and twisting.

"Let's hope not!" she said.

"We'll have to wait and see, Mother. I suggest you pop around next week and see for yourself. Maybe things will look different. We can but hope."

10

A tear trickled down Hedwig's red cheek as she stooped over her new granddaughter's cot.

"Why cry?" Otto nodded his balding head at his wife. "The child looks healthy to me." He turned towards Waltraud. "She's stunning, love."

Waltraud's watery eyes shone with modest pride, and Otto nudged her with his elbow. "Well done."

The older woman dabbed her nose with the back of her hand. "No, it's not that … It's just that she doesn't resemble any of us. She's so fair-skinned, and the hair … It's so unfamiliar. How did Sandra respond to her?"

Waltraud's cheeks blushed. "My grandpa's beard was red. Yet me and my sisters turned out brown-haired," she said.

"Take no notice, Waltraud," Otto whispered, and Waltraud bit her lip. "She still can't forgive you for having snatched up her precious son." His thick, grey beard shook as he suppressed a giggle.

"Mother, you are acting like we have a cuckoo in the nest." Karl's forehead shone red with sweat.

"No, no, Karlchen." Karl cleared his throat as she referred to him by his pet name. "I'm not saying that at all." Hedwig turned to her son, who crouched on the carpet, stacking wooden blocks, to the delight of his daughter Sandra. "But Sandra here, she's unquestionably one of us. Look at her dark complexion."

Hedwig tilted her chin toward Sandra. The toddler's soft, brown curls had taken on the same shade as her father's.

"Waltraud, you must see that, too." Hedwig brushed a black lock behind her ear. When she was younger, she had made a few heads turn.

When the toddler heard her name, she kicked her leg against the multicoloured tower, leaned on her podgy hands and lifted her bum. Karl pulled her crunched-up dress across her padded bottom. Sandra clutched a piece of wood, wiggled her arms and, wobbling forward, fell into her grandma's arms.

"That's right, Sandrachen. Come to Granny. My firstborn grandchild."

She tickled the child's belly, and Sandra gurgled.

"Firstborn, firstborn, firstborn!" Gripping the girl's waist, Hedwig Olbig lifted her to the rhythm of her words. Sandra shrieked with delight, her dark curls bobbing and her milk-chocolate eyes shining.

"Let's leave Phillippa to sleep." Waltraud held the door open and beckoned the others to exit. Shaking his head, Otto winked at his daughter-in-law as he passed her on his way into the kitchen. He reached into a nylon bag. "I hope you like it. I saw it when she dragged me into town to do Christmas shopping. Hang it in the window. Pippa will love it when the sun reflects off it."

Waltraud smiled. "Thank you, Dad," she said and unfolded the creased wrapping paper. A little glass bird emerged with a thin cord attached to a tiny eyelet.

"She said it wasn't practical for a baby," Otto added.

"It's perfect." Waltraud smiled and put her hand on the old man's arm. "Thank you."

"Karl, Hedwig, come on," she called over her shoulder.

Her husband got to his knees and brushed off his trousers. "Come on, Mother," he said.

"Aw, your mum wants us to go," Hedwig muttered, giving Sandra a knowing look. The toddler leaned back and held her arms out wide. Her grandma stabilised the child's back with her hand. "Careful, sweetheart." Sandra arched her back and dropped her wooden toy onto the baby's cot. With a clonk, it bounced off one spindle.

Hedwig exhaled as the piece landed next to Phillippa's head.

"Baby gone!" Sandra screamed. "Baby gone!"

"Hush, Sandra, hush," Hedwig felt heat rise in her neck. Clutching Sandra, she lowered her body and squeezed her big hand through the narrow grid, retrieved the piece and hid it in her pocket.

"Want baby gone," Sandra repeated, lashing her hand into the air.

The baby's face contorted, and a muted squeal escaped its tiny mouth. Pippa gasped for air and let out a scream. Tears emerged from underneath her eyelids.

"Come quick, Sandra. Before we get blamed."

11

"Spider leg, knotty-knee, flatty-foot, wobble-toes," Karl murmured to the beat of his steps. Waltraud hurried to keep up with his long strides while Sandra panted. Her mother's hand clutched her wrist.

Karl glared at his youngest daughter's legs, which bounded a few metres ahead of her family. Her snow-white cotton socks had slid off, drooped and crinkled around her ankles.

"Dad, take it easy, please." Her father took no notice of Sandra and continued whispering his self-created melody.

"Honestly, Karl, do we have to hurry after her? She knows the way. Let her run," his wife huffed before she lifted her chin to project her voice. "Trust me, child, you'll stumble and spoil your brand-new dress."

Pippa did not yield, and neither did Karl. Unperturbed, he kept singing, matching the syllables with his melody. The girl hopped along the pavement, her ginger pigtails bobbing, as she did most Sundays after church, oblivious to being her dad's eye-catcher. She kept her gaze on her shoes, extending her gait to watch the sunlight reflect on the glossy surface decorated with tiny bow ties.

She angled her head to the ground. "Cinderella shoes", Grandpa had called them when she had unveiled the box to him in the summerhouse.

"You've done well, Waltraud. Get the children quality items, no matter the cost. Going for a bargain comes with more expense." Those had been Otto's words when his daughter-in-law returned from shopping with her offspring.

"… leg, knotty… wobble …" Pippa heard her dad sing louder and louder, but she was mesmerised by her new footwear. The burgundy surface glimmered in the sun. When she had drawn the sugar paper out of the box that sheltered the precious buy, she held it to her face and breathed in the aroma of leather.

During the service, her mum had nudged Pippa several times, as she was so engrossed in admiring her feet that she forgot to stand for prayer.

"Karl, keep your voice down, please. There'll be tears."

Karl ignored Waltraud's request and chuckled as he raised his voice with every word.

Sandra craned her head. "Is she crying? Why is she crying, Mum?" she asked, her brown yes gleaming.

"She will be if your sister ignores where she's going, Sandra. That's why." Waltraud rushed alongside her husband.

As her dad's rhyme became more distinct, Pippa slowed. She narrowed her eyes into the sun.

"Spider leg, knotty-knee, flatty-foot, wobble-toes."

Pippa swivelled her head mid-movement. "Dad, stop it."

Karl grinned and shook off Waltraud's hand, which tugged his sleeve.

"Mu-um?" Pippa added with an air of anxiety.

"Karl, don't. She'll get upset again and …" Her plea spurred him to sing even louder.

Pippa's face reddened, and her eyes sparkled. "Dad, please stop it…" Her trailing foot got stuck on the corner of an uneven paving stone. She tripped headfirst, one arm outstretched, and hit the ground with a shriek.

"Now look what you've done," Waltraud exclaimed and she sprinted towards her daughter, seized her by the shoulders and rolled her over to sit on the pavement. Tears rolled down Pippa's contorted face.

Sandra bent over to examine a severe cut on her sister's leg. "You're bleeding," she said and turned her grin into a compassionate grimace.

Pippa lifted her knee. Blood emerged from the wound and trickled along her shin.

"Ouch, Mum, it hurts …" Pippa wailed as Waltraud knelt.

"That's what you get from not being mindful. How often have I told you to watch where you're going?"

"Mum, it was Dad …" Pippa implored.

"Ha, of course, it was me. Did I push you over?" Karl did not try to conceal his mocking tone. "Serves you right for not doing as your mother said. Did you see me push your sister?" He turned to Sandra, who looked up at her dad and smiled at his irony.

"Will she get a scar, Mummy?" Sandra placed her arm around her mum's neck.

"I guess so," Waltraud replied. "Get off the cold pavement, Phillippa, before you catch a bladder infection." She extended a hand for Pippa to balance herself.

Pippa stood and wiped the blood before it reached her socks. She froze. Two long scratches ran across the tip of her left shoe.

"Oh dear, there they go, your brand-new shoes," Karl heckled. "How much of my hard-earned cash did you spend on them, Waltraud?"

His wife spat into her embroidered cotton handkerchief and buffed over the damaged surface.

"Honestly, Phillippa, Dad is right. I knew you were too young for them. Why can't you be like Sandra? She's so flawless."

Sandra leaned into her mother and smiled at her troubled sister.

12

The ruby liquid poured into the measuring jug. Spellbound by the glossy bubbles that rose to the surface, Waltraud missed the scale line. The doctor had prescribed 150ml, or was it 100? Never mind.

She matched the top rim of the burgundy content with the indicators. Another 50ml wouldn't harm.

When her GP had suggested this nightcap for Pippa to gain weight, her parents were astounded when the child took to the drink without difficulty. But no matter what, it had no effect: the girl remained slim for her age. It did, however, reduce the incessant pleading for a puppy before bedtime as she drifted off within seconds of taking the final sip.

A dog. It must have been Otto putting those ideas into her head. A dog, of all things. Her daughter was so different from her elder sister, and her bond with her grandpa did not help.

With a sigh, Waltraud grabbed an egg from the fridge. She tapped the cold shell against the edge of the jug. Crack, the fragile barrier surrendered to the pressure and Waltraud's thumb broke the yolk. She flinched and with a scowl wiped her fingers on her apron.

Next, she scooped a tablespoon of sparkling sugar into the mixture.

"Ah, well," she mused and added another one to compensate for the extra 50ml.

Holding the container at an angle, she whisked the content until purple foam built on the surface. The fork scraping and ticking against the side of the metal container, it would not be long before Pippa ventured into the kitchen …

13

"You ought to be ashamed of yourself! Are you aware what this behaviour is known as? Un-grate-ful! Don't we supply you with everything you could desire?"

Waltraud angled her upper body out of the kitchen window. The wind tugged at her hair. She carried on shouting. "But no, Madam continues to be unsatisfied. A dog. Madam desires to have a dog."

With a flurry of arm movements, she let out a shrill laugh, her face crimson with anger. "I've had enough of this foolishness! Get into the house immediately, Phillippa!"

Pippa shivered. The chilly evening air had seeped through her clothes. She repositioned a small layer of gravel off the ash-grey yard with the tip of her shoe.

"Your lips have turned blue. You'll come down with a cold, I promise. Put an end to the fuss and come inside."

"I want a dog!"

"You'll suffer from a sore throat and disrupt our sleep with all your coughing. I'm done with this. You're embarrassing yourself!"

"I'm waiting for Dad … and when he gets here … we'll head to the animal shelter." Pippa's voice broke. "You gave your word."

"Phillippa, for the final time. You're not old enough for the responsibility whilst you're at primary school. Who takes care of it? Will you take a dog out in the middle of the night? In the rain or snow?"

Pippa carved zig-zag lines in the stones with her foot. Her hands hung low by her slender body, and her braided ginger pigtails dangled, frayed, alongside her face. She wiped a trail of mucus from her upper lip with her sleeve.

"I'm just coming in …" The words made her larynx ache, resulting in a squeak. "… if I get a dog … you promised."

"Now you listen to my words, missy. I guarantee you one thing: you're going to have your bottom smacked if you don't come to your senses!"

Pippa's hands clenched into fists, her teeth clenched, and her toes curled into the tips of her shoes. In time, her parents must surrender. Her father's car would pull up, and he would say, "Come on, sweetheart, hop in. We're heading to the pet shelter."

The green VW Beetle trundled onto the driveway and into the yard. Pippa's heart pounded against her breastbone. She sprinted towards the garage door, where her father would park. She had to reach the vehicle before he got out. Positioned at the passenger side, Pippa waited, wanting him to beckon her into the car.

Karl stooped over the dashboard and craned his neck to look at the house. His wife raised her shoulders, shaking her head. It was a familiar scene, and Karl redirected his attention to narrow his eyes at his daughter. With a moan, he unfolded his tall body out of the car and shut the door with force.

"Not this dog nonsense again," he said and without a sideways glance, he marched towards the house. Pippa struggled to keep up with him and clung to his leather briefcase as her dad marched on.

"Do I need to jog your memory why we can't have a dog? Why can't you get it into your stupid head?"

Face low, Pippa observed her feet moving forward whilst, in the periphery of her watery eyes, her dad's large brown shoes walked with wide steps.

A sensation flooded the girl, as if she were vanishing with every move, as if the outline of her body were dissolving alongside her ragged pigtails. Cotton wool filled her head, and she felt a tight noose around her neck, forcing her voice box inwards. She strained to swallow as Karl turned the key in the front door lock.

14

Pippa stared up at the first-floor window. They said Grandpa had bought the property on the outskirts of town after a lucky lottery win. Details remained sketchy, as with most Olbig family stories.

The outside was indigo blue. "Polack blue," Karl had yelled. "Father, do you sincerely want to paint the house polack blue?"

"I said blue! The house shall be blue!" Otto could not be talked out of his preference.

"Bloody hell, Dad, switch on your brains, will you? How is that supposed to look? There are no blue buildings on the entire street or town. You're making a fool of yourself. And me as well, for that matter!"

No argument would sway his father. Karl watched the painters on the scaffolding, shaking his head, as the original grey walls merged to match the dark summer sky—the two-storey house, the extension, the garage.

"Waltraud, I told you he's from a trailer park," he said, and his wife tugged one corner of her mouth, squinting at the renovated property she was to share with her in-laws.

Pippa was intrigued to find out Grandpa had traveller blood. It explained why he differed from the rest of the family, and was unconcerned with rules and conventions. But above all, it demonstrated the bond between her and Grandpa.

For Pippa herself came from the circus. That, at least, was how the adults accounted for her fiery hair.

"Mum and I were at a funfair … During a show, they placed this infant on a table in the middle of the ring … The circus trainers led a big bear in, with saliva oozing out of its mouth from hunger—the way it licked its lips. Mummy gripped my side and pleaded with me: 'Karl, quickly, do something before the bear mauls the child!' I sprang up and hopped across the seats to the front …" Karl spoke with mounting volume, jabbing the air and shoving imagined obstacles out of the way with his elbows, "… grabbed the crying child and fled the tent as fast as I could." He paused to let the dramatic effect of his story settle. Then continued, "This, Phillippa, is how you came to be with us."

"But I was born in the hospital, wasn't I?"

"No, you weren't. We got you from the circus. Just look in the mirror!"

"But Mummy said …"

"Oh yes, Mum … She took you to the hospital afterwards. We examined you to ensure you didn't have a disease, rabies, or something."

Karl loved telling this story, and every time he did, Pippa felt the mockery in her core, as if the bear himself was dancing on the inside of her gut.

England 1992/1993

15

The bus door closed behind me, and with a puff of diesel exhaust, the bus drove off. My journey ended here. At last.

As my grip around the holdall straps loosened, it fell to the ground with a muted thud. The canvas had dug into my skin. I clenched my swollen fingers into a fist to stimulate circulation and switched hands, but at this point, the pieces of luggage felt equally heavy. Squinting, I looked up to read the signpost. "University of York, ½ mile".

I thrust out my jaw and blew a strand of hair stuck to my face. My lips tasted salty. I started moving. The wheels of the suitcase bumped across the cobbles. Pulling the squeaking plastic wheels across platforms, steps, and manhole covers, it surprised me that they remained intact. In the past ten hours, I had become accustomed to the jerky rocking back and forth of this bulky monstrosity. I squared my shoulders—less than a kilometre to go.

My surroundings were a welcome distraction from my exertion. The manicured gardens of the Victorian houses, built from golden-brown sandstone, outshone each other. Symmetrical, trimmed box hedges framed clouds of blue hydrangeas. Lawnmowers had left vast, gleaming swathes on the grass, creating a checked pattern like a chessboard. My chest tightened as I remembered the Sundays when my father scolded me while trying to teach me the moves of the individual pieces. *The bishop can only move diagonally. For heaven's sake, when will you get it? How stupid are you?*

Symmetrical green spaces became visible behind the houses, which were growing fewer. The setting resembled a landscaped park. What was the name of that botanical garden we visited as children? I felt overcome by a depressing nausea. Now, of all times, I was so close to reaching my destination.

Another sign read, "Main Hall." I followed the path up a slope. A young man in multi-coloured baggy trousers skidded towards me on a skateboard. I froze and pulled my luggage close. The wheels of my suitcase sank into the grass verge.

"Wow, excuse me, you all right?" he shouted with a broad beam as he rolled past. I watched him disappear down the incline, turn his head and raise his hand in a casual wave. Smiling, I freed my Samsonite from the dirt.

Everything looked so different from Cologne University. Various buildings were dotted across the landscape, none higher than four storeys. *Without them, you'd think you were walking across a golf course.* A group of students sat on the green. A girl leaning on her elbows, face turning towards the sun, sent a melodic laugh into the air. Then, a male voice, followed by more hilarity. Men in white shirts and bright ties, carrying briefcases, and women in summer skirts and sandals occupied the wooden benches. Some were reading, others were having a picnic. The facades seemed historic, or were they new builds made to look old? White blocks of stone set off the corners of the Main Hall. A wide staircase led to a broad entrance portal; two imposing columns supported its roof.

I pulled the crumpled registration letter out of my pocket. Sure enough, this was it.

Exhausted, I dragged myself up the last few steps to the entrance and pulled open the heavy door. At last, I could drop my backpack. No sooner had I freed my left arm from the strap than gravity pulled its twenty-five kilos to the floor, its momentum unchecked, taking some hair with it. "Ouch," I cried, massaging the back of my head.

"Hello, you must be …" The friendly voice belonged to a grey-haired lady whose blue eyes glanced at me through silver reading glasses. She was studying a sheet of paper clutched in her fingers as she approached with quick strides.

"Olbig. Phillippa Olbig." I stretched out my sweaty, aching hand.

She moved her glasses onto her head. "Do you need help with your luggage? I bet you've had a long journey."

Before I could answer, she pulled a walkie-talkie out of the pocket of her dark blue trousers, put her glasses back on her nose and turned some knobs. We listened to the crackling silence. She smiled at me again. Her brow furrowed into little wrinkles. How friendly he was. She wore cotton trousers and a chiffon blouse and made a dull, staid impression. Mum and Dad would have liked her.

The walkie-talkie's murmur turned into a rattle. I heard a male voice, and her gaze lingered on my luggage.

"Yes, quite a lot. But with the two of you, you'll manage," she said into the mouthpiece.

After she finished talking, she showered me with information. "One of our senior students will help with the bags and show you to your accommodation. This is the main building. There's a map over there. Look, do you see the lake? Behind it is Alcuin College. We have a lovely room for you. Some colleges are very modern. Take James College, for instance. They only opened it in 1990."

The sound of footsteps followed from the stairs. "That must be him," she said, and within a second, a tall, dark-haired young man stood before us.

He's just Yvonne's type. At six feet four inches, his striped polo shirt accentuated his broad shoulders. He introduced himself with an outstretched hand and then turned to my luggage.

"If you're ready, I'll show you to your room," he said. "Let's go." He swung my backpack onto his shoulder, lifted the bag off the floor and grabbed the suitcase.

"Hang on, let me take something," I shouted and hurried to catch up. Leaning against the door, his boot pushed the door open.

Despite him carrying my heavy load, I struggled to keep up with his pace.

"Here we are," he said, putting my luggage down and taking a deep breath. We were standing in front of a two-storey building with a flat roof.

"This is Alcuin College. More students will be arriving this weekend—some international ones, like you. I think you're the first. If you have any questions, our caretaker, John, will gladly help."

"So, where is this Language Centre?"

"Back the way you came, and then on the left there. See?" He stretched his arm to point to a group of smaller houses. "You can't miss it. Just follow the signs. You'll see. This campus is a tiny village. Everyone knows everyone."

He reached for the door, but this time, I was quicker and opened it for him.

The linoleum floor of the entrance hall smelled of fresh polish. The ceiling was low, and the light was dim. I blinked to adjust my eyes and followed my guide to a counter where an elderly gentleman in a tired grey suit was reading the newspaper behind a glass window.

"John, hello." The two men exchanged familiar smiles.

"This is Phillippa. She's moving to 204. Phillippa is from Germany and starts her teaching degree on Monday."

"Welcome, Phillippa. I'll be here most of the time. If you have any questions …" the gentleman said.

"… John has the answer to everything. And what he doesn't know, he'll find out for you," the young man continued.

"Thank you. That's very kind," I mumbled as my parents' voices echoed unfiltered around my head. *Good grief. All this fussing around like bees around a honey pot. You mark my words: men are just after one thing.*

"It must have been a long day." John had got up and stood by a wooden board hung with keys. "There you are. This one is yours. I'm afraid there's no lift, but I'm sure you'll manage. After all, your young legs are designed for it," he said with a cheerful smile.

Spider legs, I recalled my dad's rhyme and froze. *Was this innuendo?* The man was old enough to be my grandfather.

As we walked towards the stairs, my guide pointed out various rooms either side. There was a laundry room, a television room, and a lounge.

I followed him through a narrow, dark corridor upstairs. Around the corner, he stopped. "So, here's your new domain. This is the absolute best room. The bathroom and kitchen are opposite."

He turned the key, pushed the door handle, and, with a motion of his arm, invited me to enter.

"What do you reckon? Did I promise too much?" he asked.

"Oh, this is great. It's huge." Excited, I stepped to the window. In front lay the lake with a tall fountain in the centre. Behind it were the red walls of the Main Hall.

"I'm glad you like it. You'll see, we're a friendly community. Everyone will be happy to help," he said and added, "You'll want to let your parents know you've arrived safely. There is a phone booth next to reception."

A pang rushed through my stomach. I inspected my fingernails, thanked him and when he had gone, leaned against the door.

On the wall to the left was a sink. The wardrobe and bookshelf were made from varnished wood. A pile of folded sheets and covers had been placed on the bed. The entire right-hand side comprised an enormous picture window with a near-enough unrestricted view across the campus. *It's incredible to think this is where I will live in the coming year.* I pressed my leg against the desk to measure its weight. Gathering myself, I leaned in and, with a deep huff, pushed the wooden table from the wall to the window. The panorama was worth the effort.

It didn't take long to unpack my suitcase and hang my clothes in the wardrobe. I rummaged through the backpack for my souvenirs, with which I decorated the empty shelf and bare walls: a few books and a heart made of red clay. With particular care, I felt for my little glass bird in the holdall. Wrapped in the doily, it had survived the journey unscathed. I attached its ribbon to the curtain rod. From there, it had a pretty view of the lake, with the fountain stretching into the sky.

At the bottom of the rucksack was a large envelope of photos. I dumped them on the carpeted floor and looked at my menagerie of memories. There was an open packet of Blu Tack in the desk drawer. I rolled and kneaded the little pieces between my fingers and pressed the sticky mass onto the back of the pictures. Then I arranged them on the wall. The result was a colourful collage of the people I had left behind. Urs positioning herself in front of a billboard of the Cologne cable car, Yvonne pulling a funny face in our kitchen, Tom wearing silly sunglasses, me lying in the grass, fighting off a playful Jackson who was licking my face. Family pictures taken on my dad's birthday.

Looking at them, nobody would presume the tension that was hiding behind those strained smiles. The last few weeks had confirmed that my family dynamics were harsher and more troubled than average. I found it hard to accept, but my friends were right: it was time to set boundaries.

"Be the master of your destiny," Tom had said.

"If you don't put your foot down now, you never will," were Ursula's words.

Yvonne called it 'emancipating yourself', referring to Professor Werther's feminist stance.

Looking at their happy, carefree faces, I smiled. "Thank you for rooting for me," I said. "I wouldn't be here if it were not for you." I then collected a handful of heavy, thick pieces of change from my purse, and it was time to let my friends know I had arrived safe and well.

16

The kettle hummed as I dug through the kitchen cupboards and found an open pack of Earl Grey. Perfect. The hot drink tasted delicious. Wisps of warmth rose from the cup. Drawing in the aroma of bergamot, I stood by my window and breathed on the little glass bird.

"Did you sleep well?" Tap, tap, tap, as it brushed against the windowpane. The lawn shone dark green in the morning sun, and the sky was cloudless, blue as a children's storybook. Colourful figures walked along the grey paths, dressed in shorts, T-shirts or summer jackets. They carried books under their arms or had linen bags dangling at their sides.

My rumbling stomach reminded me I hadn't eaten since yesterday, except for a few biscuits. I finished the tea, put my purse and keys in my denim jacket, and headed outside.

A summer breeze welcomed me as I took the narrow path alongside the buildings. Music sounded from the open entrance of the Language Centre. A woman's voice sang to The Proclaimers and footsteps stomped along to the staccato rhythm of "I'm Gonna Be (500 miles)" The singer emerged in the doorway. She was a lady in her forties with medium-length blonde hair, dressed in neat blue jeans and a pink and white striped T-shirt.

"Good morning. I, erm, I was passing by and erm …" I said but didn't get any further.

"David, you won't believe it. She's here! Phillippa O is standing right in front of me!" she shouted across her shoulder.

The music stopped, and a man appeared behind her. He had striking silver-grey hair, kind, steel-blue eyes, and a prominent birthmark on his cheek.

"Indeed! Phillippa, how nice to see you." He emphasised the last word and flung his hands in the air.

My eyes shifted back and forth between the two. "But I haven't introduced myself. How do you know…?"

"You don't need to," David explained. "Yes, we recognise you from your photo. Dear me, that's astonishing. Come in, and I'll explain."

I followed him into an office, where he offered me a chair. Leaning forward, I spotted a letter of application on his desk and inspected the upside-down red-haired woman in the passport photo. Sure enough, it was me. David saw my frown.

"We've been searching for your submission for weeks," he explained. "Your name is on the list, but … I'll be frank … we lost the paperwork. I'm sure that gives you a terrible impression of us. But it's the truth. Your folder fell behind the filing cabinet."

He hit the metal chest of drawers beside him as if greeting an old friend. "And just as she plugged in the radio, Gill spotted a tiny corner of paper …" Squeezing thumb and forefinger, he imitated the movement. "Well, your application, of course."

He continued, "And not ten minutes later, you're standing here in the flesh. You couldn't make it up!" His eyes alternated between me and the picture. "Unmistakable!"

"What a coincidence! So, I'm accepted?" I asked.

"Of course you are! Presumably, you received the letter we sent to candidates before the course?"

I nodded.

"I'll make coffee. You must tell me about yourself. It saves me reading the documents," he said with a laugh. "Do you have time?"

"Yes," I said as my stomach rumbled.

David was overflowing with enthusiasm—his honesty in admitting the misplaced papers was disarming.

"Gill, will you have a coffee with us?" he asked his assistant.

"No, I'd better get going. The weather is just so lovely. I promised the kids I'd take them to the beach," she replied.

"Ok. Thank you again. I couldn't navigate it all without you," David said.

"Nonsense, Dave. These things can happen to anyone. You're only human!"

"That's right, thank goodness," David exclaimed with relief. "Good job the mice didn't eat Phillippa's application."

The two laughed and hugged each other goodbye. I observed in awe. No accusations. No recriminations. Mea culpa—even if the milk went off in our house, there had to be someone to blame.

"So, Phillippa, how did you discover us?" He leaned forward with curiosity.

Without hesitation, I shared about my great love for England, my year in Surrey, the music of the Beatles, the works of Dickens and the Brontës, which had all left a deep impression.

"That's excellent! You are a loyal ambassador of our kingdom! And erm, did they just let you go, or will they miss you back in Germany?"

I stammered, "No. There's … no one…"

"Well, even better." David ignored my reluctance. "I'm sure you'll make friends here." He looked at my empty cup. "More coffee? Is it good? I believe there are two aspects the English must master: making coffee and speaking foreign languages."

"It's fine, thank you. But I need to go. I want to explore York," I said.

"Yes, this weather makes a tour of the city walls splendid. And, of course, you must visit the Minster." David's eyes twinkled as he spoke.

After saying goodbye, I followed the sloping path, inhaling the sweet scent of summer blossom. It didn't take long before I reached the famous fortifications that had protected the city for centuries. From there, one had an excellent view of the rooftops and flourishing gardens. A line of people queued at the entrance to the Minster, and I decided to postpone the visit for another day. *After all, I can go whenever I want*, I thought and my heart leapt with joy.

On Sunday, my flatmates joined me. We would share a bathroom and kitchen for the coming year if no one left the course prematurely. David had spoken of a drop-out rate of up to ten per cent. That didn't allow conclusions to be drawn about the student's academic ability, he explained. Instead, it was mostly a personal motive that forced a return home. With the best will in the world, I could not imagine any reason for returning.

The studies matched the environment where they took place. It was like a stroll through harmonious parkland. We learned how the English school system works, dealt with the curriculum, and devised lesson plans, the aim being to convey the joy of learning a foreign language to our future pupils as light-heartedly as possible. If this community resembled a family, it was not one as I knew it, full of reproach, envy, and criticism.

However, making new friends proved hard, contrary to David's prediction. My Spanish flatmate spent most of his time reading in his room. Outside of lectures, I met him in the kitchen when he rushed back to his room. He smiled, blushed, and wished a *good-e-morning-e* before disappearing. The French girl, Magali, spent more time in our kitchen. *Magali patisserie*, the others called her, when the scent of warm, sweet cakes wafted through the corridors and into our rooms. Skilfully, she mixed and kneaded the dough and her cakes tasted as delicious as they looked.

As I sat at the kitchen table, watching her measure flour, salt and raisins, an uncomfortable memory from the past overcame me. I had often observed my mum and Sandra bake on Saturday afternoons. They sent me to my room once they spotted me watching from the doorway. I was distracting them, they said, and that, being all fingers and thumbs, I had no talent for baking.

I once asked Magali if I could help with one of her intricate-looking desserts.

"Ah, bien sûr," she replied, passing me a rolling pin. I did my best to guide the wooden tool across the pile of dough that Magali had placed on a bed of soft white flour. I had watched the buttery substance give in to her tender and regular movement, spreading itself across the table to form a smooth surface. Now, though, the mixture resisted my handling. Cracks appeared in the blend, and when I tried reshaping it, deep lines on its surface revealed signs of a fractured structure. My frustration rose with memories of past failed efforts. I applied more pressure, which resulted in the flattened dough folding itself around the rolling pin. The combination of flour, eggs and sugar would not bend to my will, whichever way I tried to handle it.

"Let me," Magali said with a sympathetic smile and took the rolling pin from me. The wood shone with grease, and as she sighed, I sensed I had overworked the dough and spoiled it.

"Sorry," I said, "not one of my fortes."

"Non? I thought the Germans were experts at homemade cake," she said. "I bet you make a lovely Black Forest gateau."

"I never had time to learn. My mum is a superb baker, though, as is my sister," I said.

Magali shrugged her shoulders and unpicked the dough that I had left sticking on the worktop.

The exchange echoed through my mind as I sat on my bed that evening. How often had I compared my home situation with friends at school? Nowhere were the rules as ambiguous. I cringed when my childhood friends pointed this out: *How come they allowed your sister to go to dance lessons but not you? Your parents are awful.* By the time I was fourteen, I had stopped inviting classmates to my house. So many friendships had bled dry.

I looked at my wall of photos. How lucky I was to have met Yvonne right at the beginning of my second year at uni. How were she and Tom getting on, living under one roof? I looked at the picture of Jackson and me and tasted the summer grass in the back of my throat.

I scraped my change into my hand and went to the public phone at reception. As he saw me, John lifted his head and greeted me with a wave.

Ursula answered right away. "Great to hear from you, Pippa. I'm sorry I haven't written. I was so busy." The words came hastily and with an accentuated apologetic tone.

"Me too," I replied. "There's so much to take in."

"Lucky you: a new start, new place, new people. Tell me, how are they?" Ursula rushed her words.

I was not sure to whom she was referring.

"Well, the lecturers are friendly and …"

"Hang on a moment." Ursula interrupted me. "Jackson, stop it, sit … sorry, Pippa, you were saying?"

"How is my favourite dog?" I asked.

"Well, he's been naughty. He needs a walk. In fact, I had just put him on his lead as the phone rang," she said.

"Oh, don't let me keep you. Where are you taking him?" I tried to sound indifferent.

"The river. It's lovely and sunny. He'll enjoy a paddle. We both will, I guess," Ursula said.

"Ah, that sounds wonderful." I forced a smile she couldn't see.

"Glad to hear you sound so well," she said. "I'm sorry, I have to go."

"Can't be helped. I'll ring another time," I promised and hung up. With her loyal dog by her side, I doubted Ursula missed my company.

Turning my back towards John's workstation, I replaced the receiver and cringed when the change dropped into the metal opening with a clatter.

I dialled Yvonne's number. Tom picked up.

"Yvonne just left, doing the shopping. I wasn't allowed to join her. It's our four-month anniversary, you know …"

"Oh, congratulations," I stammered. *That's quite an achievement for her, indeed.*

"I'm tidying up the flat. Do you want me to pass on a message? Can she ring you back?" Tom asked, and I could tell I was holding him up.

"No, it's all right. I will ring back another time. Say 'hi' from me."

"Ok, I'll tell her you called. Glad you're okay."

Was I? Did I do such a good job, giving my friends the impression that all was fine with me when I didn't know what to do with myself outside of lectures?

Weekdays, filled with seminars, became my favourite part of the week whereas Saturdays and Sundays left me empty, with a highlight being a shy greeting with my flatmates or conversing with John. He had a bar stool placed by the window of his booth, and was happy to chat with the students. John knew everyone by name and, for many, became a surrogate family. Whenever I went to my letterbox in the hall and returned empty-handed, he averted his eyes, and I felt a sense of gratitude for his discretion. The pain of my parents, and in particular Sandra ignoring me, cut deep.

"Time for a cuppa?" John would then ask, offering a welcome escape from my growing loneliness.

17

While my flatmates socialised with students from their own country, I kept to myself. I hid my growing sense of loneliness behind a strained, frozen smile, missing my friends and even my family back home.

As I woke up early one Saturday in late September with a piercing awareness of isolation, I dreaded the weekend. It had just gone seven and nobody was stirring. While I envied the others' lie-ins, I could not drift back to sleep despite having no reason to leave my bed. My thoughts turned dark and morbid every time I closed my eyes. *If I was to die here in my room, would anyone care? Who'd miss me?* I craned my neck from my pillow to look at the little bird in my window. Its glass body mirrored the morning light. *You will, won't you?* I cringed. *I'm holding an internal dialogue with a lifeless ornament.* Were these signs of depression? *Fresh air might help me come round.* I jumped out of bed to splash my face with water.

Outside, I tightened my cotton scarf and sunk my hands into my pockets. The lake rippled, and the fountain danced in the autumn wind. My earlier thoughts had left a stale taste in my mouth. I wandered around the grey seminar buildings when I spotted a poster in the students' union headquarters window. *Film night: Peter's Friends—Saturday, 7 pm.* That was tonight. Why not? It would be a welcome distraction.

A queue of people had formed at the entrance, and I hesitated. *It might be too late for a ticket.* I was lucky. The row of heads in the cinema was dimly visible. I strained my eyes to spot a free seat. At last, a gap in the row.

"Excuse me. May I …? … Sorry … Could I just …" I mumbled, pushing past people until I reached the vacant chair.

"May I sit here?" I asked into the darkness.

"Sure. I beg your pardon … hold on," a gentle male voice whispered. The dark figure removed a coat from the chair, and I sank into the soft cushion in time for the film to begin. It was a story about relationships, trust, betrayal, and death.

As the credits rolled by, I caught a deep sigh from the man next to me. Soon, people shuffled towards the exit, and we, too, merged into the crowd. I stayed close enough behind him to pick up a musty smell from the thick fabric of his jacket. He was a few inches taller than me.

"Are you still there?" he muttered in a hushed tone across his shoulder.

I giggled quietly and tapped him on his back.

"Phew." He gave an exaggerated sigh of relief.

Am I flirting with this stranger? I imagined Yvonne's approving expression and pressed my lips together to suppress a grin as we stepped outside. He stopped under a streetlight.

"Hi, I'm Chris." His smile formed a tiny dimple on his cheek.

My heartbeat soared as his striking brown eyes met mine, his mouth curving into a mischievous smile. The long, green, vintage army coat emphasised a straight posture. He was clean-shaven, with the light enhancing his cheekbones.

A gust of wind whisked a strand of hair into my face. As I attempted to brush it behind my ear, it got caught in my earring. Tilting my head, I fiddled to untangle it. He watched with patience.

"I'm Phillippa, Pippa. Nice to meet you," I said with a strained grimace. "Ouch, bloody thing," I muttered under my breath.

His lips parted as his smile widened, and little wrinkles appeared next to his brown eyes. His shaggy, dark hair was long enough to be tied into a short ponytail.

"Here, allow me." He moved closer. I withdrew my hand as he liberated me from my predicament.

"Do you fancy a drink? I've arranged to meet some friends." His accent appeared posh, but he had an air of unpretentiousness.

I dithered. "Just like that?"

"Let's go." He handed me his arm. I hooked up, and we strolled into the bar next door. A few hands shot in the air, signalling us to a table.

"This is Don, Ian, Eleanor and Simon." Chris introduced his friends.

"Hi," I said.

"And you are?" Eleanor glared at me.

"I'm Phillippa. Nice to meet you."

The five lived in the city and were in their final year of university. I twisted the edge of my scarf in my lap, listening to them chatting, comparing lecturers, literature, and foreign travel.

"What do you think of our country?" asked Don. The group stopped chatting. Chris rested his chin on the palm of his hand. He leaned forward, fixing me with his dark eyes.

"Well, there's …" I began.

"And what do you Europeans think of our monarchy?" Eleanor interjected, laughing.

I described my love for this country, where everything, just everything, differed from what I grew up with, from bathroom taps to queuing.

"What about the food? Chips with salt and vinegar?" Ian grimaced. "Or do you have a finer palate? Beef Wellington? Blue Stilton and port?"

"Ian's posh, don't you know?" Simon smacked his friend on the back. "It's a typical public-school dinner, Beef Wellington." He laughed.

I shrugged. "What do you mean?"

"What and how you eat is a dead giveaway of your class," Simon joked.

"Well, take our famous cheese sandwiches, for example," Chris said and grinned. "One could argue that these symbolise a secret code for how sophisticated one is. Sliced cheese is a no-go for high society. The cheddar must be grated!"

"Honestly?" I asked.

"Yes." Don assumed a severe expression. "And the bread has to be white, without crusts, and cut into four equal triangles."

"Indeed." Mimicking an elegant accent, Chris hoisted his glass to his lips with his pinkie stretched out at an angle.

"But the crowning glory has to be our famous cucumber sandwiches," Eleanor said, and laughed.

"Yeah, she's got a point, Pippa." I was startled as Chris referred to me by my nickname. "If you can perfect the skill of making a proper cucumber sandwich, you'll go places!"

"What do I have to do?" I laughed. The group had affected me with their mood.

"Darling," Chris drawled. "You must peel the cucumber meticulously—as thin as possible. If there is an insufficient amount of cucumber left, you'll merely make it to the local council. If you remove the peel without trimming an excessive amount of the flesh, you can make it all the way to Number 10."

The others laughed, but Chris's eyes stayed locked on me as he raised a drink, his eyes twinkling across the rim of the glass. "Are you sure you want to dwell amongst us deranged folks?" he asked.

Yes, I did. Now, more than ever. Beaming, I nodded.

The group proceeded with their banter. I detected an increasing connection between Chris and me as his gaze held mine from across the table. Unnoticed, it had become closing time. The friends were in no rush despite the bartender calling "last orders". Another twenty precious minutes ticked by. *He hasn't asked for my room number.*

We got up to put on our jackets. Chris leaned into me as I draped my scarf around my neck, whispering, "Watch out for your earring."

Eleanor poked him in the side. "Come on, dreamer, get moving."

"You guys go ahead. I'll catch you up," he replied. The others raised their hands in farewell as they left.

"Is anything the matter?" I held back a grin.

"Well," he cleared his throat, "I'd love to see you again."

I turned to the windowsill and studied an empty flowerpot, feeling my heart pounding in my chest. Chris took a step towards me.

"Come on, don't make this so difficult for me." He clutched the ends of my scarf with both hands and tugged me closer. "Where can I find you?"

At last. My pulse accelerated.

"Alcuin, room 204." I struggled to sound aloof.

Don tapped on the window, indicating for us to join them. "We'd better go," I chuckled.

"Finally! Chris, are you coming?" Eleanor shouted from the path outside.

"Yeah, yeah, I'm on my way," he said. "See you, Pippa."

"See you," I called back, as I turned around and walked home.

By mid-October, we had wrapped up most of our academic training and were looking forward to news of our teaching placements. Every day, I dashed to the post box next to the reception, fiddling with the metal lock to check for mail. Despite forwarding my new address on arrival there had been no response from Germany.

I blamed my family's silence on the postal service's sluggish pace and geographic distance—excuses to mask the mounting awareness that I might not hear from them again. I should have realised: an Olbig never broke his word.

On top of this disappointment, Chris had not been in touch either. Had he asked for my room number out of politeness?

"Hey, Pippa, take a look at this," John exclaimed one day and waved an envelope. "I was just about to put it into your mailbox!"

I examined the sender's details: The Department of Education.

"Good news, I hope." John gestured for me to take a seat outside his booth.

With a reluctant sigh, I tore the letter open. John watched, drumming his fingers on the counter. My eyes skimmed over the sheet.

"So, where are they sending you?" John asked.

"Fulford!" I peered at him. This school had an outstanding reputation, and jobs were popular.

"That's wonderful, Pippa! Congratulations!"

"I can't wrap my head around this." I felt my skin glow.

"Well, I'm not surprised. Any school will be keen to have you!" John gave a sly wink and nodded. "Fulford! Boy, oh boy …"

18

Within a few days, all students received news about thei respective teaching placements. The seminars were filled with apprehension. What could we expect in this new phase of education?

To celebrate our progress, the Language Institute arranged an informal gathering in the library's hall, a large room above the walkway with a view of the campus from an elevated position. Expansive windows provided an unobstructed view of the grounds below. Early in the evening, the lecturers welcomed us with bubbly and orange juice. With glasses in our hands, we listened to David giving a speech.

"I'm sure I speak for the entire staff when I say how thrilled we are with you."

His colleagues nodded. Gill stood by, smiling.

David continued: "Working with a new intake of students is always enjoyable. But this group ..." His eyes glided across the room... "impressed me particularly with their cooperation, perseverance and general enthusiasm."

He peered through the crowd and continued: "This is an important point in the course, as you will soon put your teaching skills into practice and become an asset to your respective schools!"

Gill applauded, followed by the rest. We raised our hands and clinked our glasses. David tapped a spoon against a bottle. Tink,

tink, tink. The sound echoed through the hall. "Before we open the buffet, let me add something," he announced. "We've prepared a personal message for each of you. After all, we're a bit like a proper family. We will now hand them out."

I felt the hairs on my arms rise: a proper family! Sitting by the window, I studied the white envelope. My name was written in an elegant hand. Inside, it read:

Dear Pippa, How lucky that Gill turned on the radio that day! You are a wonderful, warm person and already a responsible young teacher. Your students will love you. We wish you all the best for your personal and professional future.

My gut clenched. If only I could show this to Mum and Dad! Deep in the pit of my stomach, a cocktail of pride, sadness and shame boiled to a turbulent storm. At any moment, one of these feelings would overwhelm me and shatter my steady facade. Like an arrow, a sharp pain bored its way up through me. I clenched my teeth and clutched my glass. *No tears, please.* I spun around and stared at the people walking below us.

Amongst the passersby, I caught sight of a familiar-looking figure. The man's coat swayed to the rhythm of his hasty steps. He shielded a bouquet against his chest as he manoeuvred past the pedestrians. *Wasn't that...? Yes, it was Chris*! I pressed my palm against the window.

Come on, look up! I tried to summon his gaze. Once he was level with the library, he would vanish underneath the building. I crossed over to the other side. Too late, I saw the billowing jacket disappear into the darkness. My heart burned.

David was chatting with some students. "We're just saying how quickly time has passed." He sought to draw me into the conversation as I approached. "Since it's half-term, have you got any plans, Pippa?"

"David, I'm afraid I must dash. Something came up. It's been a lovely evening. Thank you for your kind words."

"Shame. I wish you an enjoyable break. And the card: we meant every word!" He gave me a quick hug before I hurried downstairs.

Where had Chris run off to? Why was he carrying flowers? I shuddered. *Blast! I forgot my coat!* I rushed back upstairs.

David laughed at me. "Changed your mind?"

"No, forgot my jacket," I said, waved, turned, and left.

Outside every lit-up bar and seminar room, I peered through the windows. No sign of him. As I entered the entrance hall to Alcuin, the door to the TV room stood ajar. John was watching an evening soap. When he spotted me, he patted the seat next to him.

"Are you coming to join me?" he asked. "There's not much on, though. The problems of these people … makes it easy to forget your own."

"Hi, John. No, I must fly. Bye," I answered and ran upstairs.

When I turned the key in the lock, I noticed the little note jammed in the door frame.

Do you remember me? Peter's Friends. Fancy a cucumber sandwich?

The message was scribbled in tiny letters. Butterflies buzzed in my belly, and my heart soared. At the kitchen table, I smoothed out the little scrap of paper. The kettle hissed. Then heavy footsteps sounded above the noise of bubbling water. With a click, the kettle switched off and Chris appeared from around the corner.

"Finally, there you are!" he cried.

"I, erm, I just, erm, got home," I stammered.

He took a step forward and kissed me on the cheek.

"These are for you," he said, handing me some colourful tulips.

"My goodness, you're freezing! Did you walk here from town? Flowers? They're beautiful. But why?" The sentences gushed from my mouth.

"I'm sorry I didn't get in touch sooner, Pippa. But I've not been in York much since we met. I've stayed with my family in Oxford a lot."

I looked at the tip of my shoe.

"May I?" asked Chris, taking one of the mugs. "Are there any tea bags left?"

We took our mugs and went to my room. Chris stopped at the doorway, his glance sliding over the walls, the shelf, the photos. He stepped closer, sipping the hot drink.

"Your family? And that one: friends?" he asked.

My silence didn't seem to bother him. He stood by the shelf. With fluid moves, he stroked the spines of the books. His eyes smiled before his mouth did.

"*Ansichten eines Clowns? Die Legende von Paul und Paula?* Your favourite novels? Best travel companions, aren't they?"

All rhetorical questions. He wore brown, unfashionable trousers and a jumper knitted from thick wool.

His eye caught sight of my glass bird. He tapped it and smiled.

"Let me see if we have a vase anywhere." I had moved towards the door when he placed his mug on the bookshelf and grabbed my arm.

"Come over here for a second, please. I'm not very good at this." His confidence seemed to fade.

"What are you not good at? Reading German?" I asked, trying to lighten the situation.

He drew me close, my head pressed against his shoulder. The jumper scratched my cheek. What would he do next, and how would I react? Chris kissed my hair. Then his grip loosened.

"The vase?" he reminded me.

"Yeah, right, I'll check what I can find in the kitchen," I said.

His presence confused me. I rummaged through the cupboards. As I returned with a carafe, Chris sat at my desk and studied the photos on the wall. Meanwhile, I placed the flowers in the water.

"Who are these people? Tell me," he asked and reached out to me.

I took his hand, and he embraced my waist. With a simulated nonchalance, I placed an arm on his shoulder.

"Well, that's me there, obviously."

"Cute." He smiled.

"And this is my sister, but she looks different now."

"What do you mean?"

"She's pregnant. She must be much rounder by now."

"When did you last see her?"

I pictured Sandra yelling: "The camera is mine too!"

"This summer, before I came here," I answered.

Chris pressed his lips together.

"Hmm, hmm," he hummed. "And that's Pa and Ma?"

I nodded.

"What's going on with you guys? You say little about your family. Do you prefer not to talk about them?"

"I, erm, they resent me for moving abroad. I never fit in with their plans for me. I'm not so …" I searched for words.

"Boche." Chris completed my sentence, looking at me with a smile. "Oh, don't be offended, please. Here in England, we respect anything German. Boche—it's a compliment."

His explanation made me chuckle.

"Yes, that sums it up nicely. I'm certainly not Boche. Rather, the black sheep."

"The scapegoat? It takes guts to take the unusual path."

He pulled me onto his lap and took my face in both hands. Only a few inches separated us. He seemed to draw a map of my forehead, nose, cheeks, lashes, and mouth. Close up, I saw his pupils move over every millimetre of my skin.

"May I?" he whispered.

"May you what?" I asked back.

"Kiss you?"

"Don't let me stop you."

He pressed his lips against mine. I felt his soft hair in my palm. With a deep sigh, he pulled my body closer to his. Gently, he stroked my head, touched my skin, my shoulders, and moved his hands down to the side of my breasts. I remembered what the senior student had said on the day of my arrival. *The whole campus is a village. Everyone knows everyone.* I broke away from the embrace. Chris smiled; his eyebrows raised.

"Is there a boyfriend back home?" he asked.

"No, that's not it," I said.

"Moving too fast for you?"

"Maybe. What you said back then … about being the scapegoat."

"Honestly, Pippa. I noticed it in your eyes. There's a lot of sadness. Shall I leave?"

"Maybe we should stop, yes. Perhaps another time?"

I got up and leaned against the wall.

"Listen, do you like dancing?" he asked, studying my face.

"Dancing?" I cheered. "I love it!"

"Any plans for tomorrow night?"

"No, nothing. I can't remember the last time I danced."

"Fine, I'll pick you up at ten."

Excited, I jumped up and down and clapped. Chris laughed as he got up and laid his hands on my shoulders.

"I'm so glad I found you. See you tomorrow."

"I'm looking forward to it!" I said.

Laughing, he ran along the corridor. When I had closed my door, I rushed around. What had just happened? I had finally, finally seen him again. And then this? I placed his mug against my lips and pinned the little scrap of paper to my photo wall. I smiled at the faces of my parents, Sandra, friends, and familiar landscapes from back home. In between, I read his handwriting. All was well with my world.

19

"I'm so sorry you're staying behind," my Spanish flatmate said melodically, as if he might break into song.

"Someone has to keep things running on the home front," I said and winced. *That's something my mum might say.* "Have a *très bon* time."

"A bientôt." Magali waved, holding a box of homemade biscuits under her arm before they both disappeared down the stairs.

Finally. I turned the radio up high and joined in with the chorus of "Don't You Forget About Me". I bobbed through the kitchen, sang to the ducks on the green, back through the hallway, straight into John.

"Someone's in a good mood." He cupped his hands in front of his mouth like a megaphone.

Shit. I rushed to lower the volume.

He rubbed his ears. "That's better." We both laughed.

"Anything to do with the young fellow who dropped by yesterday?"

"Yes, that was …" I stammered.

"Chris, isn't it?"

My chin dropped.

"You know him?" I asked.

"He lived on campus, later moved to the city." The corners of his eyes tightened. He nodded at the vase. "Hence the flowers."

"Bit old-fashioned, don't you think?" I said and cringed as I half expected a lecture, which I was used to back home.

"No, Pippa, Chris is a gentleman. He's from Oxford if I remember correctly. He'll go far one day." John squinted. "And what about you? Are you staying for the half-term? Saving your trip home until Christmas?"

"Oh no, I'm skipping Christmas this year. To be honest, my departure for England caused quite a storm."

"I see." He studied my face and shook his head. "Ah well, if you were my daughter …"

My eyes pricked as I thought of Grandpa. John reminded me of him.

"Anyway, Chris is a great guy. Will you see him again?" he asked.

"Yeah, tonight. We're going dancing!"

"Oh, we used to dance, my wife and I." He imitated holding a waltzing partner and swayed from side to side.

"Come along," I said and laughed.

"Goodness, no. All that wiggling about like puppets with their strings cut," John said.

I shrugged and laughed.

"Enjoy yourselves," he called from back to the hallway. "Pippa, if you need me at any time, you know where I am."

"Thanks," I called after him.

By nine o'clock, I was dressed in black leggings and a matching top that fell over my hips. Just before ten, I heard the familiar sound of heavy footsteps. I jolted, then froze—not too eager. My heart was pounding. Silence. He was on the other side of my door. I drew in a deep breath and exhaled through my mouth.

A knock. *Wait.*

"Hang on." *One, two, three, four*, I counted before opening. Chris propped his arm against the doorframe.

"Wow, you look stunning," he said and drew in a sharp breath.

"What you see is my wardrobe for all occasions: theatre, concert, weddings, even funerals," I said and twirled around with a childish giggle.

"And, not to mention, perfect for Millers, the best nightclub in Yorkshire," Chris said.

"Seriously, Chris! Can I go like this? I'm not into this dressing up and stuff."

"How refreshingly uncomplicated! You look fantastic. Come on, there's a taxi waiting."

After a short drive, the car dropped us at the end of the pedestrian zone. I surveyed the dingy street.

"Where are you taking me?" I looked at the shady buildings.

"Trust me." He grabbed my hand.

Within a few steps, we arrived at a plain door with a peephole in the middle of the pane. Chris knocked, and a tall, burly man opened. He scrutinised us, mumbled something from under a thick moustache, nodded and led us down a spiral staircase.

Stifling heat burned my face. As I shuffled through the crowd I bumped into a woman. Cold liquid spilled over my hand.

"I'm sorry." I took a step back.

"No worries. All in the game," she replied with a shrug and disappeared into the crowd.

There was space by the wall, and I moved over to get my bearings. The primary source of light were the illuminated cabinets behind the bar. A man took orders, pulling pints at the same time. People shouted conversation into each other's ears. I stood on my toes and caught heads bobbing up and down to the music.

I felt a stare and caught Chris's face by the bar. His lips moved.

"What?" I mouthed, shrugging my shoulders as I worked myself over to him.

He tugged at my collar and pointed behind the bar. I jiggled my shoulders to let my jacket slip down. Chris waved to the barman, pointed, and gestured. The barman nodded and let the jackets disappear behind the counter.

The music boomed. I shuffled my feet, glaring at the dancefloor like a preying cat. "It's raining men"—there was my cue. I pushed into the crowd, but Chris clenched my arm. He raised a hand in a drinking gesture. My lips touched his ear.

"White wine," I shouted before I broke free to dive into the swarm of dancing people. In unison, we swung our arms at the chorus and spun around. Adrenaline rushed through my veins.

I closed my eyes and let the beat move my body. When I looked up, Chris leaned against the wall amongst other spectators, holding two drinks. He lifted a wine glass to his chin without taking his eyes off me. With my arms stretched out, I formed a path back through the crowd. My lungs burned as I caught my breath. I took a few sips.

Chris pressed his mouth against my ear. "You're a good dancer."

I held the cool glass against my temple.

"Come on, join me?" I shouted.

He put his mouth close to my ears. "No, you go. I'd rather watch."

I placed my hand on his cheek, shifting it to the side. "Why did you bring me here?" I replied, my hot breath rebounding from his skin.

"Got a feeling you'd like it." He grinned.

The D.J. played "I Will Survive"—another of my favourites. I pushed the glass against his chest. He placed his hand over mine. We were close, like the night before. I pressed my lips together and gave him a mischievous smile. The dance floor was shaking. Singing the first lines, I left him to hold the glass.

It took three more songs before I returned to him.

"Letting go of pent-up energy, right?" he asked.

I gathered my hair, which was stuck to my neck. Chris pulled me close and blew against my neck. I tilted my head and stretched my chin forward into the minute breeze.

The vibration of a bass guitar filled the room. "I believe in miracles". I put on a theatrical pout. He loosened his grip and nodded in the direction of the dancefloor. My mouth met his before I mingled with the dancing crowd.

Midway through the song, Chris enveloped my stomach with his hands from behind. Spooned like this, we swayed to the music in perfect harmony. Chris's breath bit into my sweaty skin. "Let me be the one to take your clothes off tonight," he whispered.

I spun in his embrace. My lips grazed against his neck and tasted his salty skin. He tugged me closer and nestled his face into my hair. His lips left my skin burning, but I still felt goosebumps on my arms and a shiver running down my spine.

"I do want you," he said.

I turned my face and pressed my mouth on his.

A trumpet introduced the next song. Chris threw his head in the air. "How to spoil a perfect moment," he laughed as the crowd joined in with the Village People.

"Let's go somewhere quieter." I brushed hair from my sticky face. Chris knew a wine bar nearby. We sat by the window opposite each other.

"Glad you loved the place. Watching you dance is like …" He searched for words.

"… Aerobics?" I finished his sentence.

He gave a loud laugh and leaned across the table far enough to reach my arms. His hands held my elbows, and his face turned serious.

"You are exceptional; do you know that?" His brown eyes seemed darker than before.

"Not everyone would agree with you on that one." I cleared my throat, avoiding his eyes.

"Well, you are. You are bright, good fun and a crazy dancer," he said, and I blushed.

"Crazy, yes. That's more like it," I said, thinking of my father calling me 'irrational'.

"I don't mean it like that. I mean in the sense of passion. And I believe you are more than that, too—empathetic, for example."

"Empa-*what*? Pathetic? My dad would certainly agree with you on that one." I laughed with a nervous edginess.

"Well, Miss Olbig, you can take it from me. You're a good dancer, clever, and kind. You're all that to me."

I winced at the mention of my family name.

"Chris, what's going on? Are we flirting?" I coughed.

"I think we've passed that stage, don't you?" He straightened his spine and leaned against the back of his chair. Our hands touched, and he laced his fingers through mine.

My heart pounded. I freed my right hand and emptied my wineglass in one go.

"Wow, careful," he said.

"Shall we go?" My confidence would not last long. "I want to see where you live."

He gave me a puzzled look, then replied, "Come on, let's go."

Outside, he hailed a taxi. Resting my head on his shoulder, I closed my eyes. Every time the driver changed gear to take a corner, our bodies shook closer. *Let me be the one to take your clothes off tonight.* My legs felt light. Was it the wine?

Chris raised a finger to his mouth as he opened the front door. "Don is still here. The others have flown the coop." He gestured for me to enter.

"Where's the light switch?" I giggled as I stumbled into the hallway.

Chris laughed and covered my mouth. "Don't shout," he chuckled.

"Oops, sorry. I think I'm a bit tipsy."

"The second door is my room. The bathroom and loo are at the far end," he said, turning on the light.

I shimmied up the stairs, holding on to the bannister, singing "You Sexy Thing" in a subdued voice.

There was a fluorescent bottle of mouthwash and fresh towels on the shelf. Resting my hands on the sink, I leaned into the mirror's reflection. My fringe was stuck to my forehead, and my face was blotchy. I had a quick pee and then counted the doors back to his room. Chris came up the stairs with two large mugs in his hands. The caramelised smell of coffee seemed wrong, somehow.

"I'm afraid we don't have any milk," he said, extending one arm to me.

"No wine either?" I said and hiccupped.

We both laughed.

"Well, yes, there is. I just don't want you to think I would take advantage of the situation. I don't want to get you drunk," Chris said.

"Not to worry, I already am." I grinned and flopped on his bed.

Chris gasped.

"I'm joking," I said.

"Phew," he exhaled.

"I just think you are cute when you are like this," I explained.

"Like what?" He sat down beside me. Resting on one arm, he brushed a sticky strand of hair to one side.

"Like you really care about me."

"That's because I do."

With my finger, I traced along his chin.

"I like being with you," Chris said.

"I liked what you whispered into my ear back there," I replied.

Minutes later, we were naked, clothes still warm, creased up around us.

"I don't have anything here, if you know what you mean," he whispered.

"I do know what you mean. We must be careful, then." I breathed into his ear as a wave of warmth washed through my body.

20

Chris's breath blew against my nape, warm and fleeting in the dark. I glided my hand across the mattress until my fingertips touched his skin, and a tingling shot through me.

A church bell chimed, the echo lingering in my ear. I shuddered, and my chest stiffened as I recalled the final words my dad had yelled through the phone. My heart felt solid as I ruminated. Even with a barrier of water between us, my stomach cramped as I looked back.

Since I was fourteen, my parents had warned me about boys' intentions. I recall one evening when a girl from my school was over at my house, eagerly anticipating a Friday night disco. Her father was waiting in the car, the engine running. As I approached the landing, I overheard my father questioning my friend as to when the 'party' would end. I hurried down the stairs to spare her any embarrassment. "Bye," I yelled across my shoulder and rolled my eyes.

"Madam, not so fast," he said, his tone indicating trouble. "Come here and turn towards the light."

I felt heat rising to my neck like an ink blot on paper. "Dad, please. We need to go," I said, trying to keep my voice steady.

"Well, you'd better remove that nonsense from your face," he replied, handing me a cotton handkerchief.

"Please, Dad," I pleaded, as tears began to well up in my eyes. He opened the door, allowing my friend to leave.

My neck ached as I tried to hold back a sob. I used the dry cotton to wipe away my makeup until the mascara was gone, and a grey shadow circled my swollen eyelids.

Chris and I spent the half-term break getting to know each other at a more relaxed pace. The daylight softened my approach from the first night, and we both agreed to take things slowly. It was reassuring to learn that Chris hadn't been with many girls before me. We talked about our favourite books, music, childhood memories, smells, and food. Chris preferred soul music over jazz, savoury food over sweet, and Lao Tzu over Lacan. He had a cosy terraced house with a bathtub, one of the few luxuries I had missed since arriving in York. I relaxed in the water while Chris cooked in the kitchen, where the clattering of pots and pans combined with the radio playing to create a symphony of sounds. Chris was a talented cook, and there were no limits to his creativity. One of his specialities was ravioli with smoked mackerel in a sticky cheese sauce—a true delicacy. After eating our fill, we'd snuggle in the dishevelled bed, shoulder to shoulder, contented and full.

Towards the weekend, I began to feel anxious. Chris's housemates would soon return from their autumn break, and I was worried about how they would react to finding me at their kitchen table.

"What if they don't like me?" I asked Chris.

He turned from the sink, holding a plate and washing-up brush, and gave me a quizzical look.

"Are you happy?" he asked. I nodded.

"Well, so am I. Surely, people who care will be happy for us," he said.

He passed me a tea towel, and I dried the dishes as we talked.

"Pippa, I don't understand why you worry about what others think of our relationship. We're adults and not causing any harm, are we?" he said.

I replied that I wished I had been raised the same way as him, not always having to keep a relationship a secret.

"That approach might have worked in the past. But at what cost? Trust me, the others will adore you. I've no intention of living a double life," he said.

I felt terrible for ruining what I hoped would be a new beginning.

"Look, if you need more time, we can wait a few more weeks," he said, smiling.

"No, you're right. We're not teenagers," I replied, trying to sound cheerful.

Chris poured two cups of tea and gestured for me to sit at the table.

"I guess this is serious," he said. "Our relationship, I mean."

"It's scary, but lovely." I laughed. But then I noticed something was troubling him. "Chris, do you need more time?" I asked.

He hesitated, then replied, "We should use better protection."

I cleared my throat and rolled the edge of the towel between my fingers. "I know, we need to stop taking risks. It's an accident waiting to happen."

"I can get more …" he said, but I interrupted him. "No, I don't like those things, let alone trust them. I'll find a doctor and get a prescription for the Pill."

Chris exhaled with a sigh, then leaned over and kissed me.

Later that afternoon, I called Yvonne. I hadn't told my friends about my new boyfriend, fearing I might spoil it. 'Jinxing it', as Yvonne called it, when one of her relationships ended before it had even begun.

"Well, you're a dark horse," my friend shouted into the receiver. "How long have you known him? Six weeks?"

"No, not even half that, to be honest," I said.

"Still, long enough to get serious. I mean, you two are … you have …?"

"Yvonne, please!" Talking about my love life was more accessible with a bottle of wine and candlelight to hide my blushing face.

"All right, all right. But tell me, what's he like, this Chris?"

"He's wonderful. He's gorgeous, tall, and handsome, and he has this amazing, cute smile when his eyes glint and the corners of his mouth hardly move," I gushed.

"That's how he looks at you? Madam, he's a keeper. That look is a tell-tale sign he's blind to everyone else. Take it from someone who knows," Yvonne insisted.

Her determination to convince me of Chris's genuine intentions made me giggle. Men were her favourite topic, and she had enough experience for me to trust her implicitly.

"I know, I know." I tried to calm her enthusiasm. "He's special, and the feeling is mutual."

"Quite right. I can't wait to meet him. Will you bring him over the next time you visit? Or perhaps Tom and I can come and stay with you. Easter, perhaps?"

"Yes, we'll see. I won't make any plans before I have a job here and am settled. But yes, by the looks of it, this could be it," I answered before ending the conversation.

Ursula reacted to my news with a more critical mindset. Had I met his parents? How long had he been single, and did I know his ex? My friend wanted to know everything.

"Urs, everything is fine here. He's wonderful, and despite not having known him for a long time, I trust him."

"Well, just as long as he's not on the rebound. If he hurts you, I'll come over myself and …" Urs huffed.

"Stop it, please." I laughed. "I can look after myself. Speaking of which, I must hang up. I need to make an appointment at the GP for, you know what …"

"Of course, you'd better do that PDQ. And give him my love. Tell him your best friend is ecstatic that he floats your boat."

After I had made myself a cup of tea and mulled over my conversations with my friends, I leafed through the telephone book and called the local clinic. A few days later, I got an appointment, a date that confirmed to me that my relationship with Chris was serious.

December came, and Chris devoted every day to the philosophy department, working on his thesis. No matter how absorbed he was in Asian theory, he abandoned everything whenever I stopped by.

"Hi, Miss Boche, how was your day? Were the children well-behaved?" he joked when we sat with his fellow students, who welcomed the distraction.

During this time, I got to know his mentor, Naomi. She was a young Japanese woman with a research position at the institute. Whenever I overheard them absorbed in conversations, I felt like a stranger, lost in a foreign land.

Chris was skilled at drawing me into the conversation.

"Naomi, are you familiar with German literature? Pippa has an entire shelf of it. Had we met earlier, I'd have read Nietzsche instead of Nishida."

At weekends, he took the time to have breakfast with the household before settling behind his desk.

I admired his dedication. As Chris poured tea into a large mug to take back to his room, I enjoyed clearing the table with the others. We'd sit on the squeaky wooden chairs, engaging in conversation.

"I doubt I could deal with a class of smelly adolescent children," Eleanor said.

"They're not that awful," I replied. "Most of them are lovely and polite. And if anyone misbehaves, I assign them to detention."

"That never panned out for me as a kid," said Don. "It's a miracle I made it to uni."

"Yeah, Don, I can picture you at school! Enough to make you think twice about having children, don't you agree, Pippa?" Eleanor laughed.

I could imagine that he'd been a cheeky pupil, I said. But did that stop me from wanting to start a family? I shook my head vehemently and swallowed hard. Little did they know how often my dad had stressed I was unfit to be a mother.

21

"I hope we're not late," I said.

"If we are, where's she going to go? She'll wait for us by the entrance. Stop fretting and enjoy the view," Chris said, putting his hand on my knee. My stomach jumped as he took a speed bump without braking. The taste of bile burned the back of my throat. I held my breath, closed my eyes, and leaned against the side window before I blew out.

"Oh, sorry, is it my driving? I'll slow down." Chris sounded concerned.

"No, please, Chris. Keep your eyes on the road and your hands on the wheel. I don't trust these winding lanes, where I can't see around the bend."

Without another word, he did as I asked. I had been on the Pill for two weeks. The doctor warned me I might experience some nausea and urged me to call should it not subside within a few days. It had—until we hit those bumpy roads.

Chris chuckled. "How long ago did you last see your friend? What's her name, Your-salad?"

I slapped his thigh. "Stop it," I laughed. "It was in September. When she saw me off at the station." My eyes followed the single-track road, which descended into a village of limestone and redbrick houses. Chris adjusted his speed. "Her name is Ursula. Please don't call her 'Your salad' when you meet her."

"I wouldn't dream of it. I'm looking forward to meeting one of your friends."

So was I. When Urs announced her visit for a mid-week break, I thought she was having me on. But when she told me about her travel itinerary and the arrangements she'd made for Jackson, I realised she was serious.

I spotted my friend as we approached the extensive car park outside the ferry terminal entrance. Her dark green winter coat matched the crumpled hat. Urs stood beside her small holdall and squinted as she peeked into every passing vehicle.

"There she is. I can see her. Flash, Chris, flash the lights." I bobbed up and down on my seat, undoing my seatbelt.

Chris scanned the area, pulled the indicator's lever, and beeped the horn simultaneously.

"I'm so excited," I said. Chris pulled up next to my friend, whose face lit up as she spotted us. I flung the door open and got out. Screeching, we hugged, both swaying, laughing, and sobbing with joy.

"You made it. It's so good to see you." In her tight embrace, Ursula's scarf muffled my voice.

"Same here, same here," she replied, kissing me on the cheek before releasing me. "Wow, you're beaming. England suits you." Ursula grinned as she held my shoulders. She turned her head to face Chris.

"Hello." He stretched out his arm. "I'm Chris. I'm pleased to meet you, finally…"

Before he could finish, Ursula let go of me and put her arms around his waist. "Oh, come here and hug me. I'm Ursula. Thank you for picking me up. I'm so happy to meet you."

When she let go, Chris pulled up his eyebrows and gave me a wide smile. I giggled, and as he winked, I knew he'd like her. I loved him for that.

Ursula and I shared the back seat on our way back to York. While she updated me on life in Cologne, Chris watched us in the rearview mirror, wrinkles of joy framing his eyes.

"So, Jackson is staying at Yvonne's, is he?" I asked.

"Yvonne and Tom, sweetheart, Yvonne and Tom. The two of them are inseparable." She stressed every syllable as she spoke the last word.

"Aww, poor Jackson. Do they ever get out of bed in time to walk him?" I asked.

Ursula winked. "It's good practice for them …" She stopped and grinned.

"What? Are you telling me they are thinking of …" I gasped and opened my mouth in disbelief.

"That's exactly what I am telling you. The pitter-patter of little feet will soon echo around that flat." She nodded before adding, "if you ask me."

"You've decided, have you?" I laughed.

"Come on, Pippa. You should see them. They're tied at the hip. Tom only applies for jobs in Cologne. The guy could live anywhere, but all he does is dote on his beloved Yvonne."

A pang of jealousy shot through my veins, and I swallowed another wave of sickness. "There in the distance, those are the spires of York Minster," I said to distract her, and we spent the rest of our journey admiring the historic buildings as we approached the city.

After Chris had carried my friend's bag up the stairs and into my room, she took his hand with both of hers and shook it. "Thank you for picking me up. And thank you for looking after my dear friend here."

Chris reached out and drew me in close.

"She's an extraordinary lady," he said, kissing the side of my face. "Right, you two, enjoy your time, and if you need anything, call me."

I walked with Chris to the end of the corridor, and as I came back, Ursula stood by the window, admiring the views.

"What a special place, Pippa. No wonder you love it here." She pointed her head to the door. "And he's breathtakingly gorgeous and so well-mannered. Does he have a twin brother?" she joked.

"I am so glad you approve. Yes, he's amazing. I just hope it lasts," I said.

"Why shouldn't it? He adores you. He struggles to keep his eyes or his hands off you."

Ursula inspected my room. She stopped in front of my wall with photos and tutted. "Oh my God, did you not have a more flattering one of me? This one is lovely of you and the dog … hang on, is this your sister? Why do you have pictures of your family here?" There it was again, that schoolmarm's voice.

"I, erm, I guess out of loyalty," I stammered.

Ursula froze, her gaze hovering in space. I turned. "What is it, Urs? What did I say?"

"Nothing. It's just that …I'm not sure I should tell you. Oh, forget it." She waved her hand at my photo display, then focused on me.

"Urs, you can't do this. You can't be all mysterious and then expect me to *forget it.*"

My friend pressed her lips together and took a deep breath. She let the air escape through a tiny crack.

"Promise me you won't go crazy." She pushed her chin forward and creased her eyebrows like she had been caught breaking someone's favourite mug.

"Urs, please, tell me." My heart was thumping in anticipation.

"Well, I visited my folks not long ago." She carried a look of guilt.

"Ah, I see." The blood rushing through my head sounded like an ocean. "You met my parents," I said, trying to sound matter-of-fact.

"I bumped into them all. Sandra, your brother-in-law, your parents, and another elderly couple. No idea who they were."

"It was probably the in-laws," I explained.

"I didn't know where to look. I was shopping with my mum, and there they were, outside church."

I gulped and lowered myself onto a chair. A wave of dizziness washed over me.

"Church?" I asked.

"Look, let's just forget it." Ursula tried a cheerful voice.

"No, no. There's more, isn't there? Did they say anything?" My voice quivered.

She hesitated. "Argh, I am such an idiot. I wish I hadn't mentioned anything. But yes, your mum said they had an appointment with the vicar—for the christening."

A shockwave flashed through my body. I looked at the floor, chewing the inside of my cheek.

Ursula sat beside me and took my hand, but I withdrew my arm.

"Don't be mad at me. It's them who are cruel. They don't deserve your loyalty." Ursula gave a deep sigh. "Please don't torture yourself. You'll spoil all the good you have found here."

"Easier said than done, Urs."

"Please don't be upset, Pippa. It just annoys me how they get to you. And do you know why that is?"

I shrugged.

"It's because you would never do that shit to anybody. You'd never be so cold, so cruel." Our eyes locked briefly, then Ursula zoomed in on the little piece of paper between the prints. "Peter's Friends," she read. "What's this?"

Relieved at the change of topic, I told her about the night at the cinema. Ursula kept nudging me, interjecting, "Oh, I say," and "So happy he floats your boat." We both laughed.

Her approval did not fade once we'd spent time with Chris and his housemates.

One evening, she joined me in Chris's kitchen, where I was preparing drinks.

"I admit I was worried about you loving your new life more than life with us. You're so fortunate with all of this." She paused and looked at me, her eyes intense. "You *are* happy, aren't you?"

My grip around the kettle tightened as I started filling cups, the tea bags swirling to the surface. Urs leaned forward and gathered the hair hiding my face.

I put the pot down.

"Yes, I am. In a way, I feel lonely, though," I said.

Ursula jolted, pointing towards the door to the living room.

"Lonely? You have this amazing guy, a ready-made group of friends and a house with a bathtub thrown in. How can you be lonely?" Ursula sounded exasperated.

"Well, I mean, you all have a family. Parents, I mean …" I stopped, and Ursula squinted.

"Do you miss them?" she asked.

"Hm." I nodded, swallowing. "I can't believe they just dropped me like that—all of them. So much remains unsaid."

"And that will never change. No matter how long you wait, they will never give you closure."

"That's it, closure. That's what I want."

"You might as well wait for the dead to bury themselves," Ursula huffed. "Get a shovel and start digging, Pippa."

I chuckled. "If you say it like that …" I stepped forward and hugged her. "Better stop fretting, eh?"

"Too right, Pippa. They've done enough damage already. You're so lucky you escaped their constant criticism." She placed the cups on a tea tray. "Come on, lover boy will wonder where we are."

Ursula spent a few days with me on campus and in town. She loved the city, and I made an excellent tour guide.

"The history, Pippa, you inhale it everywhere," she exclaimed in awe as we strolled arm in arm down the cobbled streets.

While I was at school, she ventured into town by herself and, at tea time, enthusiastically described the market, the Minster, and the street artist she'd watched outside the Viking Centre.

Before she had to leave, she visited Fulford School with me. When we entered the classroom, the kids bombarded her with questions about life in Germany. She showed them photos of her dog and explained her work, and when the students asked to visit, we joked about organising a language trip to Cologne. The children listened with wide eyes as Ursula told them about the cable car that took passengers across the Rhine to the zoo, river cruises along the vineyards, and old castles. A lump formed in my throat. I pressed my hand to my breastbone and sighed deeply but could not fill my lungs. When the bell rang, the class thanked Ursula, some asking her to write her name on their exercise books.

My mood dropped the closer her departure came. "I'll miss you. Promise you'll bring the others next time," I said.

She studied my face before she replied, "Maybe I will come here and find myself a handsome gentleman like your Chris. And sure enough, my money is on the happy couple Yvonne and Tom having their honeymoon here."

We laughed and set off home, ready to pack my friend's bag for the next day.

22

"Let's go away to the coast. What do you say?" Chris asked, raising his eyebrows.

"But York is so charming right now, so festive," I pleaded.

"If you call 'crowded with tourists admiring shop windows dressed up in tacky tinsel' festive. Do you know Whitby? Scarborough? Come on, Pips. Let's have an adventure."

"What about your family? Won't they expect you to celebrate Christmas with them?" I asked.

"It's my nan's big birthday in January. She'll be ninety. We agreed I'd travel to Oxford then instead."

It would be my first year without singing carols by the tree and eating Mum's special turkey recipe. Chris's idea sounded tempting. He told me he'd hire a car and pick me up in the morning.

When I pulled the travel backpack from under my bed, my stomach churned as I brushed the dust off its cover. "You're going on holiday, not back to Germany," I tried to encourage myself. With a deep sigh of relief, I gathered clothes and filled my cosmetic bag with a toothbrush, deodorant, and a strip of contraceptive pills.

The following day, Chris pulled up in a small, white Micra. I clapped my hands and skipped to the door, reaching for the driver's handle.

"Hey, Miss Continent, if you want to drive, be my guest." He laughed and raised the key in the air, ready to throw it at me.

"I wouldn't dare," I replied. Chris stored my bag in the boot. I walked around the vehicle to let myself glide into the passenger seat.

We left the town and took the main route north, guided by large roundabouts. Then we followed signs for Whitby until we saw an exit sign: "Coast. Panoramic route".

Chris turned, and we found ourselves on a narrow, winding road that conformed to the hilly landscape, descending, only to then climb steeply. Grey stone walls separated broad fields. Sheep braved the winter chill and grazed in the barren meadows. Pillars of smoke rose from farmhouse chimneys.

As we neared Whitby, Chris told me of the monasteries' dissolution. The old walls of this cathedral were famous for their spectacular location above the cliffs, next to the graveyard of St Mary's Church.

The fishing village welcomed us with its patchwork of uneven rooftops in various shades of auburn, covered in a layer of frost. Straight columns of smoke rose from chimneys. The narrow, quiet main road led us to the harbour square. Chris pulled into a parking lot and turned off the engine. "Here we are. It doesn't look busy, thank goodness. Let's find a place to stay, shall we?" he said, and we stepped out of the car.

Fishermen busied themselves around the harbour, maintaining their boats, calling out to each other in heavy Yorkshire accents. Their voices echoed through the chilly winter air.

The smell of smoked fish lingered. Seagulls screeched above us and searched for leftovers in the bins. I inhaled a whiff of diesel mixed with seaweed. Boats, many decorated with colourful fairy lights, bobbed on the water. I leaned against the railing to let the spectacular view of the town with its crooked houses sink in.

We crossed the harbour bridge and turned onto a steep pedestrian street. The shop windows were adorned with Christmas decorations, and every door carried a wreath with red ribbons, pine cones, and miniature bells.

"Watch your footing on the cobbles. They can be slippery." Chris shifted his bag up on his shoulder and offered his arm. I grasped his hand and slowed down, distracted by the display of large bay windows with their sparkling array of jewellery. Most of the ornaments were decorated with polished, black stone.

Chris explained that jet stone had, next to the Abbey, become another trademark of the town.

"It became popular via a rather sad story," Chris said. "When Prince Albert died, Queen Victoria wore Whitby Jet jewellery. You know, she mourned him all her life, never wearing anything else but black following his death."

A shiver ran across my arms. I shuddered. "How sad," I whispered, "and how beautiful, simultaneously."

Chris ran his hand across my back. "You're shaking. Let's drop our luggage off, then come back and maybe do some shopping later."

"Great idea." I took his hand, and we continued until we spotted a "B&B" sign on a side street.

Yes, the landlady said she could offer a room for one night. With a friendly smile, she led us up the stairs to our room.

From our little cottage, we reached another landmark of the historic fishing town: the steep steps to the abbey. Moving up, we stopped and turned around to admire the view that opened across the town, with the beach, cliffs and patchworked landscape to the north.

Children counted aloud as their parents watched their steps with care. "Eighty-seven, eighty-nine, eighty-eight," said a little girl, wrapped warmly in a pink woolly hat and matching scarf, who stopped in her tracks as we met her, one step apart. Her eyes opened wide, and she smiled. "I can count to a hundred," she said, lifting her hands and spreading her fingers, wrapped in white gloves.

"Can you now?" Chris smiled widely. "How many have you counted so far?"

A woman bent to the girl and put her hand around the thick, padded coat.

"Eighty-nine, eighty-nine," the girl chanted.

Chris let go of my hand and put his arm around my waist, pulling me closer.

"Clever girl," he said, ruffling the fluffy bobble on the girl's hat. "Enjoy your day." We both stepped aside, letting them pass.

"Thank you, you too," the woman replied, and we heard the tiny voice continue, "eighty-seven, eighty-five …"

The higher we climbed, the more often I had to stop to catch my breath.

"Just a few more before we reach the top," Chris encouraged me, nodding toward the abbey. He turned the sleeve of his coat to read his watch.

As we reached the gothic ruin, we stood on tiptoes, looking over the vast wall that encircled its grounds. The sandstone remains looked unaffected by the admiring visitors, some of whom were wearing headphones, listening to recorded information, while others huddled around a guide, their heads shifting between speaker, historical artefact, and the booklets in their hand. The view through the central arch onto the sea mesmerised me.

After visiting the Saint Mary's Church graveyard, we linked arms and took a small country lane down the hill. After another couple of turns, we ended up in the same shopping lane as our arrival. It was getting busier, with people making last-minute Christmas purchases with festive wrapping paper sticking out of their bags.

Chris held the door to the jewellery shop open. A string of bells swung from the ceiling, announcing our entrance with friendly chimes. The small space was cramped with cabinets, all displaying black stone set in silver in various sizes, shapes and forms.

As I moved between the shelves, I felt Chris watching.

"Do you see anything you like?" he asked.

"It *is* gloomy, isn't it?" I whispered.

"Well, yes," he said. That was the purpose—to reflect Victoria's deep grief. But she made it fashionable, inadvertently."

"I can see that," I said as I saw a pair of teardrop-shaped earrings set in a silver cluster.

"They're beautiful," Chris said, his mouth touching my hair. He wrapped his hands around my waist.

"Excuse me, can we look at those teardrops, please?" Chris turned to the saleswoman.

The lady shuffled her heavy body across, navigating between the glass displays.

"Oh, they they'll suit your girlfriend to a tee," she said, winking at me as she fiddled for the key. After opening the cabinet, she placed the set in my palm. "There you go. Do you ever wear your hair up?"

I held one pendant against my earlobe and looked at my reflection in the display cabinet's mirrored back.

"Would you please gift-wrap them in Christmas paper for me?" Chris asked the lady before turning to me. "They're exceptional."

"May they bring you only tears of joy," the lady said as she passed the box to Chris.

Chris suggested we have an Indian meal, which I had never tasted before. I was surprised by the number of Asian restaurants in this small town.

"How do you choose one over another?" I asked.

"Pay attention to the music," Chris advised. "If you like the sound of the place, you'll like the food."

As we entered the first restaurant, an eager waiter intercepted us.

"Table for two?" He held out the menu.

Chris looked at me. "Darling, listen."

"Table for two?" The waiter repeated.

"Hold on a sec, I'm talking to my wife," he said and we both chuckled.

Chris pointed his finger towards the speaker in the ceiling and spun it in a circle. "Honey, what do you hear?"

"Abba," I snorted.

Chris grabbed my hand and pulled me out the door. Laughing, we fell into each other's arms.

"I … I am sorry for the poor guy. What must he make of us?" I struggled to speak and imitated Chris's hand gesture: "Honey, do you hear that? You're impossible."

"I know, but you love me for it." Without waiting for a response, he headed for the next restaurant.

"Passage to India. Now that sounds more authentic." Chris sprinted ahead and held the door open. "Sounds good. What do you reckon?" he asked.

I passed him and entered. Inside, I heard the swift, vibrating tones of a string instrument.

The food tasted wonderful. We ordered poppadoms with various dips. For the main course, I chose a mild curry, while Chris tried a spicier one.

"Have you celebrated Christmas this way before?"

"Usually, I'd be singing *Silent Night* by the tree right now. Though it hasn't been that harmonious back home for a long time. And afterwards, we'd unwrap presents. Our tradition is to exchange gifts on Christmas Eve."

"Speaking of presents, I have something for you." He rummaged in his trouser pocket and produced the small jewellery package.

I played along. "For me? Oh, my goodness." I slapped my hands in front of my face. "I've got nothing for you. You should have warned me."

In the candlelight, the precious teardrop-shaped earrings shone, the light reflecting on the delicate facets.

I put them on, then took Chris's hand. He lifted it to his mouth and kissed my fingers.

I wiggled my head in small movements. Chris beamed from across the table.

"Watch out, try not to get entangled. Do you remember?" he said.

"Don't remind me, that was so embarrassing." I grinned.

"You were lovely. Black suits you, by the way."

I lifted my hair from my neck and turned my head back and forth.

A muffled sound introduced the waiter, who pushed a trolley over the thick carpet. With nimble moves, he cleared away our hors d'oeuvre dishes, replaced plates, and covered the table with bowls of steaming food.

23

"Enjoy your meal," the waiter said, smiled and left.

"Pips, there's something—" Chris began, but he was interrupted.

"Hello, you two. What a coincidence." It was Naomi. As she moved closer, she placed her hand on Chris's shoulder. He blushed.

"Erm, hello, Naomi. What are you doing here?" Chris asked with a flat voice.

Without giving her a chance to answer, Chris rattled on. "Pips and I are celebrating Christmas together." He reached across the table for my hand and winked.

"That's wonderful. I have family visiting from Japan," she said and smiled at me.

She turned to Chris. "Now that I've bumped into you, I keep meaning to ask: have you posted your—"

"That's so typical of you, Naomi. You're never off duty," Chris interrupted. He gave her a stern look, his eyes darkening. "I'll get back to you at the beginning of the year, alright?"

"You do that," she replied. Her gaze shifted from me to him. "You have so much potential. Never forget that."

Chris tore off a piece of naan bread from a basket and handed it to me. "Here, you must try it." Then he turned to Naomi. "Have you eaten yet?"

"I can tell I'm disturbing you," Naomi replied with a grin. "I'll leave you to it."

With a little farewell wave, she returned to her family.

Chris leaned back in his chair and exhaled.

"I feared she'd never go. Sorry, Pips," he said and rubbed his forehead.

We changed the subject and spent the rest of the evening discussing my affinity with England and his for Asia before turning to our families.

"It's harsh of them to give you such a brutal ultimatum: stay in Germany or be disowned," he said.

"I know. I never thought they could be so cruel. And the irony: I know they would love it here," I said, feeling my eyes sting.

Over the next few days, my handsome guide showed me more highlights of North Yorkshire. Hugging, we braved the icy wind and struggled along the outstretched seafront of Scarborough, warming our frozen bodies with hot chocolate by the open fire of the castle café.

The landscape became more desolate inland. The higher we climbed, the harsher the expanse of the moors. Signs warned of snowdrifts and roaming sheep. The idea of getting snowed in here with Chris appealed to me more than it scared me.

We stopped at an isolated pub, an ancient building which had once served as a tavern for shepherds and coach passengers. The thick stone walls had few windows, and the architecture pointed to harsh and hostile winters. The entrance led to a narrow porch where hikers could leave their muddy boots, walking sticks, and bulky backpacks.

A second door opened into the bar, and the weeping sound of a violin filled the room. My eyes adjusted to the dim light, and I spotted the musicians sitting by the fireplace among the other guests.

"Watch out, don't bump your head." Chris pointed to the beams on the ceiling.

We dropped onto a worn-out sofa, which was too low for the table in front.

The melodic folklore captivated us. The group sang jolly drinking songs or played sad melodies on small metal flutes. Melancholic tunes of unfulfilled longing and painful love rang out. I sighed and leaned against Chris. He suggested we stay for the night and got up. I watched him chatting to a man behind the bar. Minutes later, he placed a key with a wooden tag on the table. "Sorted," he said, smiling, and put his arm around me.

After last orders, we carried our luggage into our bedroom. My feet sunk into the thick, dark red carpet. A canopy of embroidered linen was suspended over the bed. A renovated stable door led into the bathroom. Fluffy towels lay ready on the edge of the bathtub. Honeymoon suite, no doubt.

My heartbeat woke me up in the middle of the night. Boom, boom, boom! It pounded in my chest. I stared into the black space above me, careful not to move whilst keeping my breathing shallow. Boom, boom, boom, it thumped, unchanged. A band of pain wrapped itself around my temple, tightening with every breath.

Chris lay snuggled close to me. I released his embrace and pushed my legs out of the bed. My feet touched the soft rug, and I crept through the darkness into the bathroom. Nausea rose, and saliva ran along the inside of my cheeks. Had I eaten something to upset my stomach?

Sitting on the toilet, I searched through my cosmetic bag. There must be an aspirin somewhere. With shaky fingers, I opened the little zip on the inner lining. What was wrong with me?

When I spotted the strip of contraceptive pills, I winced. No, it was impossible. My cycle was regular, and my next period was due at the end of this week. End of the week ... today was Friday.

I felt queasy, as if I had caught myself in a lie. Where was my notebook, the little calendar where I marked my menstruation? Had I left it at the college?

"Oh, shit," I whispered into a towel pressed to my face. A jackhammer was busy breaking through the top of my skull.

Had I not waited long enough for the contraception to work? Could it be that...? I cursed myself. *You stupid, stupid cow, how could you be so reckless? Keep calm. Nothing is certain. You often have migraines before you get your period. Don't go crazy!*

When I put my head back on the pillow, the jackhammer reached my eye sockets. I clenched my teeth and took a deep breath through my nose. Chris nestled against my spine, his hand on my chest.

I was glad to see the grey morning light shimmer through the window and told Chris I had a splitting headache.

"I won't be able to eat much, but maybe a coffee will help," I suggested, and we made our way to the breakfast room, where the strong aroma of bacon and scrambled eggs hit us.

He pulled up a chair. "Have a seat. I'll fetch the coffee." He wrinkled one brow.

He bit his lip as he placed the cups on the white tablecloth.

"Poor love, you look white as a sheet. Maybe the wine last night?"

I managed a weak smile.

"Do you want to go back to bed?"

I needed to find my notebook and shook my head in slow motion.

"No, I'd rather not. Honestly, I want to go home. I am afraid this won't be over in a couple of hours," I said. "Maybe we should have been more careful, Chris."

Chris studied my face. Before he could reply, I raised my hands and shook my head. He nodded, then said, "Fine, we'll head home. And we 'll catch up on the rest of the tour
another time."

24

"There you are." John raised his palms. "Had a pleasant trip?"

"Yes, Pippa learned all the lyrics to 'Whisky in The Jar'. You should have heard her."

I managed a drained smile, grateful for Chris's distraction.

"I'll go on up," I said in as trivial a fashion as possible.

"Are you ok? You look …" John asked, but before he could finish, Chris broke in. "How are things here? What did we miss?" I heard his voice fade as I hastened up the stairs.

Back in my room, I discovered my notebook on the desk, stashed it in my waistband, and dashed to the bathroom. There was still no red smear on the inside of my underpants. Perching on the toilet, I flipped through the calendar.

November. My cycle started at the beginning of the month. December: I held my breath. "Concentrate," I told myself, counting the days from my last period.

My brain buzzed. Numbers and lines flitted before my eyes and refused to be caught. Confused, I started over. Another recount was of little use other than to confirm the obvious. In numerical terms, I was four weeks overdue.

A knock on the door startled me, and I dropped the notebook. With unsteady hands, I gathered it up.

"Are you alright, Pips?" Chris sounded worried.

I opened the door.

"Do you want me to get you an aspirin…?" He spotted the notebook in my hands.

"Oh," he gulped. "I take it you're not planning our next trip?"

I bit my lip, trying to stop my tears. In vain.

"Shhhh, come here. It's okay …" Chris hugged me tight. "It's alright, it's going to be alright."

"No, it won't! This can't be happening. It just can't!"

"We don't even know that yet. Let's go to my place. Tomorrow, we'll get a test."

Still half asleep, I placed one hand on my abdomen the following morning. Was there a tug? Did I feel my uterus tightening? Wrenching cramps had tormented me every month since puberty. Now that I wished those pelvic pains upon me, my insides remained relaxed.

With Chris breathing deeply and regularly, I sneaked into the bathroom. The toilet paper I pressed between my legs stayed clear. I gasped. We had thrown caution to the wind. Ever since being with him, my body was in constant arousal. I refused none of his advances, as it was impossible to restrain myself. And yes, we had not consistently used alternative protection before I started on the Pill. I still pined for him amid this desperation.

When I returned, the bed was deserted, and the house was silent. I went to the kitchen, where the only noise was from the coffee machine, which coughed and prattled, filling the room with a spicy bouquet of warm toffee. I watched from the table as the black liquid dripped into the pot.

"Where have you been?" I called absentmindedly when I heard the door latch.

Chris rubbed his hands and pulled a chair towards me.

"How are you? Any … news?" He drew air quotes with his index fingers.

"No news." I imitated his gesture.

He placed a paper bag on the table. In blue letters, it read "Boots Pharmacy".

The test brought certainty. A sense of vertigo washed over me as I stared at the two blue lines. I held on to the sink to let the wave of dizziness pass—another one … and more. The surges were replaced by a lightheaded pressure as if someone had blown up a helium balloon inside my skull. Leaning on Chris, I struggled back to bed and sat staring at my toes.

"Look, love …" Chris placed a hand on my knee.

"Don't." I cringed, a burning discomfort pinching behind my eyes.

Chris grabbed my shoulders.

"I'm sorry," I whimpered. "I don't know what to do. I'm so scared."

"We," Chris insisted, "we'll get through this. I am with you all the way."

"He's a keeper", Ursula had said. This might prove her right or wrong.

"Whatever you decide to do, I will support you. We're together," Chris said.

For the next few days, I stayed in the house, staring at the walls until my face was smudged and my throat sore from crying. I asked Chris to get two other tests. Although I prayed for divine intervention, both showed the same result.

New Year's Eve passed unnoticed. Before midnight, Chris had called his family and a few friends, exchanging traditional good wishes.

"Are you going to ring Ursula or your other friend?" Chris asked.

"No. I can't face them. I must come to terms with this in my own time," I said.

How I had looked forward to welcoming the future with Chris. I envisioned making plans whilst admiring the fireworks. Instead, everything was on the brink because of our negligence.

I remembered Naomi's words, "You have so much potential." "He'll go far," John had said.

I imagined my father's bellowing voice. "What an embarrassment you are. Do you have any idea what you are doing to us?"

Sandra also interfered with my thoughts. "Well, Sis, too bad. Don't count on Mum and Dad to support you as a single parent!"

Single parent—my goodness. We were only just beginning our adult lives. A family? Now? Impossible. What about his studies? What about mine? The image of little Vincent in Susanne's arms flashed by my inner eye. Not only didn't I have parents like her, but I also had less than half her courage.

Morning sickness set in from one day to the next, announcing itself with increased salivation. When I crouched over the toilet bowl, Chris gathered strands of hair from my face with one hand and rubbed my back with the other, soothing my discomfort.

A week into January, it was time for him to return to university.

"Are you sure I can leave you alone?" I still had a few days off and wanted to hunker down at his place.

"Of course, no problem," I replied.

Chris placed a cup of herbal tea on the kitchen table before he left. I stirred the drink and watched the liquid ripple and rotate.

I heard the letterbox cap rattle, and something slithered across the hallway tiles. It was an envelope with unfamiliar stamps and red postmarks addressed to Mr. C. Jones. It was from the University of Nagoya, Department of Humanities and Sociology. I held my breath. My knees felt disconnected from my legs. With the letter in my hand, I returned to the table and stared into the teacup.

"Only me! I forgot a couple of books that I need to get back today," Chris shouted through the door as it slammed behind him. His messy hair glistened as he stormed in, and his smile waned as he saw me.

"What's wrong, Pips?" He put his bag on the chair and squatted in front of me. Crisp winter air surrounded him.

"You're white as a sheet," he said.

I looked at the envelope. He followed my gaze.

"Shit!" He read the sender's address.

"I didn't open it, I swear," I exclaimed.

"What if you did? It doesn't matter. I wanted to explain, but…"

"Then this happened!" I smacked my fist against my belly.

Chris pulled my wrist away. "Don't do that, Pips."

"Are you leaving for Japan? Please tell me. Things can't get worse," I sobbed.

"I applied months ago. Before we met. It's a PhD."

"Is that what Naomi referred to in the restaurant?" I asked.

Chris studied me, frowning. We both remained silent for a moment.

"I wanted to tell you myself." He stroked my hair. "I'm sorry."

"Don't be. We couldn't have known that we'd meet …" My last words were drowned out by sobbing.

"… and fall in love." He lifted my chin with one hand, and our eyes met. "And that's why I'm not going."

"Now, don't get sentimental. I can't stand that in my condition." I forced a smile, as tears ran down my face.

I got to my feet and set about clearing the dishes. Chris stood, shifting his weight from one foot to the other, watching my every move.

"Chris, it's fine. You get your stuff done. I'll tidy up here. It helps me think."

"Let's talk tonight, Pips," he said, with a soothing voice, taking the envelope from the table and sliding it into his pocket.

"Alright. If anyone asks, tell them I got the flu," I replied, turning on the tap above the sink.

By the time I'd tidied the kitchen, cleaned the bathroom, and made the bed, my head was calmer. I reached for the phone book and looked up the number of the local Medical Centre.

"How can I help you?" an obliging-sounding voice on the other end of the line asked.

"I'm pregnant," I said.

Silence.

"Unplanned," I added.

"I see. I can schedule you at the Family Planning Clinic. Would Thursday next week at 2 pm be convenient for you?"

"Yes, that's fine."

25

"The nurse will compile your data. Then, the doctor will speak to you and explain everything else." The receptionist forced a smile. "Please, take a seat." She raised her chin towards a row of chairs by the window.

I pondered on the "everything else" while I waited.

Then, another nurse asked me to follow her into a consultancy room.

"First, I will ask you a couple of questions," she said warmly. "Next, I will take your blood pressure and weigh you. After that, the doctor will talk to you about everything else."

That expression again.

She passed me a translucent plastic jar and pointed towards a door.

I took the container and entered the small toilet room. As the jar warmed up, I wondered again about "everything else." How did you say what I had come for?

As I returned to the room, the nurse stood by the toilet door. She took the container, disappeared behind a partition made from bookshelves, and returned.

She noted my date of birth, address, occupation, and family status.

"Would you hop on the scale, please? I will measure you at the same time."

I obliged.

She pushed the slider until the metal pressed on the crown of my head. *If only she could squash me until I disappeared.*

Had I put on weight? I lifted my shoulders and shook my head. Had my waistband been tweaking, or was that my imagination? My blood pressure was healthy.

"When was the last time you had your period?" she asked.

My face boiled. Like a school kid caught cheating, I put my notebook on the table. With clammy fingers, I turned to November.

She scribbled something on her form, looked at the calendar, flicked back a month, then forward. Pressure built up inside my abdomen, pressing up against my stomach. I bent my head to count the carpet tiles.

She stuck her head through the crack of the door to the room next door and passed the papers into the obscured space. A voice murmured something.

"The doctor is ready." She held the door open. "All the best," she said as I stepped past her.

I had expected a white coat. Instead, the woman wore a purple blouse with a name tag pinned to her chest. *Dr. E. Patterson.* She held the forms her assistant had filled in.

"Hello, I'm Phillippa Olbig." My voice was constrained.

She stretched an arm to a chair in front of her desk, furrowed her brows, and flipped through the papers.

"How are you feeling?" she asked.

My eyes burned, and my chin trembled. I took a breath, and she moved a box of tissues towards me.

"I know it's tough. Take your time." She spoke with a soft voice.

My vision blurred. *Did I notice pity in her voice?*

"It just shouldn't have happened to me. I've hardly been here a few months ..." I pressed a handkerchief against my eyes.

"Hm, hm," she repeated as I wept and outlined the last few weeks. My shoulders shaking, I caught my breath.

"And the child's father? Do you not think your relationship is stable?" she asked.

"Not really," I stammered. "He's ... he's got ... I can't pin him down with a child. He has so much potential."

"Do you have family here?" I jolted as she spoke.

"No, I left everything behind," I said, adding, "and I can't go back."

"Phillippa, we can help you." Her tone triggered another crying fit, "That is if you decide to have the child."

"As a single mother in a foreign country? How will I manage?" I took the handkerchief from my face and looked at her with burning eyes.

"Will your family not support you?" she replied.

"You can't imagine what they're like. My dad is choleric, and my mother is utterly submissive. They'd kill me if they found out." My voice shook, and my eyes stung.

"I'm so sorry to hear that." Her words brought on another stream of tears.

"No, they must never, never, never find out. All that counts for them is what the neighbours think. For them, I'm the biggest disappointment anyway." I trailed off to brush my nose on my sleeve.

She studied the paper and said: "I estimate you are late seventh week. An examination will tell us the exact term. You are early enough for an abortion if that's the option you chose."

So that's what it was called.

"I must. There is no alternative."

"Discuss it with the child's father. Maybe you can talk to your parents after all." She tilted her head as she spoke.

"Impossible. My parents have refused to speak to me since I left Germany." I broke down, my shoulders quivering. "How … how … do you think they'll … react if I … arrive home with this?" I struggled to breathe.

The handkerchief covering my face, I listened to the sliding of a drawer. "We'll help you," I heard the doctor say.

I wiped my eyes.

"Look, Phillippa, you will find all the information about a termination here. Take a few days before you decide. We have time."

Her voice was like a warm towel hugging my body after an icy rain shower.

"I will first examine you and write my report. Later today, one of my team will contact you to arrange an appointment at the hospital."

My chin dropped. She paused for a moment.

"The law requires a colleague to give a second opinion and you to be seen by two doctors."

The examination verified her suspicions—I was at the end of week seven. While I tied my shoelaces, she filled out the paperwork.

"Here in the UK, an abortion is possible up to week 24 if the child's health or that of the mother is at risk. That includes the emotional health of the mother." She tilted her forehead and raised her eyes. "If carrying the child full-term poses a greater psychological risk to your mental health than an abortion. I think we can assume that in your case."

When her words reached my ears, they echoed, distorted, like the broken announcement through a tannoy.

The appointment for the second examination was not for another two weeks. An agonising fourteen days of cells dividing in my belly to form a tiny human being.

No one suspected the change in my circumstances. As a proper Olbig, I had become an expert in covering up and was inventive in hiding my condition. I explained my absences at school as stomach upsets or migraine attacks and blamed my shortness of breath on a lack of exercise. Meanwhile, my appetite grew, and I imagined feeling a slight bulge on my otherwise flat belly. It was easy to conceal with baggy tops. My pinching bra straps reminded me that my body was changing. A little person was forming inside me—a new life in my hands.

Wide and lazy, the river pushed through the middle of York. Chris and I had gone for an afternoon walk.

Despite it being the middle of winter, tourists lined up at the steps to the bridge, laughing as they lingered to embark on a river cruise. No one suspected my dilemma, the crisis developing in my life.

"Look at those happy families," I said, lifting my chin to point in their direction. I sunk my hands into my winter jacket.

"They look happy, but I'm sure they have their own worries and problems." Chris sighed, putting his arm around my shoulder.

"Pippa, if you choose to have the baby …" He hesitated.

"Good grief, Chris. I can't have it, but I sense it wants to live. Every day, I feel it growing. Yet I can't, I mustn't."

He pressed his lips together, eyebrows raised.

"What did you have in mind?" I snapped. "You're going to quit your studies, give up your future, and get a minimum-wage job around here?" I twisted around and waved my hands at the illuminated neon sign of a grocery shop.

"I could ask my parents …" he said.

"No, no, Chris," I interrupted. "Honestly, you'll go abroad shortly. Just like I did last year. It's a once-in-a-lifetime chance. That's what you're studying for. Just because I've screwed up doesn't mean everything stops here for you, too."

"You have screwed nothing up, Pips. We're both responsible for the baby."

"You're so remarkably unscathed. Life's been nothing but good. That's precisely why I can't do this. I don't want to be the one to take this from you," I said.

"I can see you're frightened of your family's reaction. But you've put them behind you. They have no influence, no power over you anymore."

Chris's words confirmed that he could not comprehend something he had no experience of. He was unfamiliar with a hostile family climate, and no conflict of loyalties tormented him. No shame churned his stomach, and no fear crept up his spine. He did not know how years of put-downs and petty gripes had eroded my confidence.

I looked across the river at the jetty. A child sat on a young man's shoulders. The queue shuffled towards the "Yorkshire Rose" ticket officer. If I had this baby, it left me with one choice: moving back home just as they wanted. But as a single mother? Impossible.

It was pointless trying to explain my parents' anger to Chris. For a few moments, I hung on to my thoughts.

"I'm scared," I said. "Pure panic. They'd kill me."

"But *my* family will come to terms with it," Chris replied.

"Ha, don't count on that. They didn't fund your studies for nothing."

"Listen to yourself. You sound like your parents," he said. I cringed. "The bottom line is that I'm their son, and they will support me regardless of what I do—and you too."

"Chris, I'd lose them for good if I did that. It might seem insane to you, but I hope this break in contact won't be permanent. After all, they are my family."

From his point of view, I understood him. And still, the pregnancy would wipe out any faint chance of reconciliation in one fell swoop. I was not strong enough to pay that price.

"You are so accommodating to everybody else's expectations. But what do you want for yourself? What do you feel?" Chris asked.

I shrugged. "Empty." Numb, I could not access any emotions other than fear and despair. I was breaking the family doctrine that I had been instilled with from an early age: you shall honour your parents.

26

I agreed for Chris to join me at the second specialist's appointment I asked him to wait outside until the doctor had examined me and he nodded.

The idea of the two of us gawking at an ultrasound screen of pixelated shadows, tuning in to the heartbeat hungry for life, seemed unbearable.

After the ultrasound, I dressed behind a curtain in the corner.

"May the ... well... the father ..." I felt my cheeks heat.

"I'll fetch him while you finish getting dressed," the doctor replied.

A door creaked, followed by footsteps. I pushed the curtain aside, and Chris hugged me with clumsy rigidity.

"You alright?" he asked.

My heartbeat raced, and heat spread up from my neck. I evaded his gaze. I wasn't sick. I was pregnant.

The doctor motioned for us to sit in front of his desk. Chris grabbed my hand with clammy fingers and placed it on his thigh.

"Miss Olbig, I estimate you are in your tenth week."

He watched me over the tops of his reading glasses and then peered at Chris. Was he hoping for a hint of paternal joy? Chris's fingers squeezed mine.

"I have decided ..." My battle to find the correct word was agonising.

"You told my colleague that you did not want to carry the pregnancy to term," the doctor said. "And your decision remains the same?" He turned to Chris, whose hand I now crushed.

"Yes, it does," Chris said. I welled up.

"The termination will take place here in hospital. You will go home the same day." His voice took on a matter-of-fact tone. I exhaled audibly and leaned back in my chair.

He reached for the phone. I looked out of the window. The barren branches of the trees stood out black against the watery sky. *Winter is not over.*

"Can I ..." A lump in my throat pushed on my vocal cords. I coughed. Chris turned to face me.

"I want to think about it a bit longer. Can I?" I asked.

"Absolutely. You have ..." He studied the notes. His head made minute, brief movements.

"... a few more weeks. But let me caution you. The further you advance into the pregnancy, the greater the risk of complications after an abortion. Your hormone levels are changing by the day. The decision will not become easier as time proceeds."

His gaze shifted between us. "But of course, take the time to review everything." He handed me an envelope. "Here you will find more details. What to expect before and after the termination."

He reached for the phone and pressed a number.

"Yes, I have an appointment for Miss Olbig, termination, tenth week," he said into the receiver.

My heart pounded.

He ended the call and told me they'd expect me in two weeks. He rose and said goodbye with a firm handshake.

On the street, the spicy aroma of wood fires burned in my nose. Columns of smoke ascended straight from the chimneys like blown-out candles. Chris walked me back to the university and appreciated my wish to be alone for the rest of the day.

The college entrance hall was empty. John sat in the back room of his office. Laughter rang out from behind his counter. He was watching a quiz show on TV. Relieved to steal past him undetected, I tiptoed up the stairs.

A roller coaster had been racing through my head since leaving the hospital and would not stop, despite lying on my bed. I turned onto my side, pulling up my knees and embracing them with both arms—foetal position. An icy shiver ran down my spine. Soon, the child's body would curl up in the same way. How could I rob it of the opportunity to experience the world? To never know Chris's tender smile, never feel my protective embrace. Never would my hands hold, my lips kiss, my voice provide comfort.

I swayed. *My child, my dear, dear child, I'm desperate. I want to meet you, watch you take your first breath, and hear your first cry. But I can't. I just can't. Please, please forgive me.*

Footsteps echoed in the corridor, accompanied by the sound of clattering dishes, blended with laughter. A door clanged before it was silent. I got up and looked in the mirror. Had I been crying? Smudges of mascara had left a shadow under my eyes, and my skin appeared grey.

"You need to get out, distract yourself," I told my ghostly image. There might be an evening show on TV.

This time, I did not slip past John. He stood in the hall, studying the classified ads on the noticeboard.

"Hi, Pippa, look, someone's searching for a … Hey, are you feeling OK?"

Looking alarmed, he took a step back and scrutinised my appearance.

"Excuse me for saying so, but you look dreadful. What's the matter?" he asked.

My jaw quivered.

"Come, child, sit down. I'll put the kettle on."

I let myself drop onto a seat.

"Are you and Chris having a row?"

"No, John, it's much worse. Please don't ask. I can't tell you!"

"But Pippa, who else are you going to tell? Something is troubling you. That much is obvious!"

My cheeks burned. My lips tasted salty.

"Is it to do with your parents? Because they still haven't contacted you?"

"They never will unless I return home. Maybe it would be for the best if I did." I sobbed, and my shoulders shook.

"What do you mean? You want to go back to Germany?"

"No, John. It's the last thing I want. That's just it," I bawled.

Shaking and struggling to catch my breath, everything burst out of me. An avalanche of incoherent words, followed by disjointed sentences until I'd flooded John with the events of recent weeks.

He poured us both a cup of tea. Listening, he shook his head whilst stirring his spoon, pensive.

"I can't decide, John. I have no clue what to do!"

Daylight had died out. The ceiling lights lit up the interior of the hall.

I tried to explain my father's dominance, how he accepted nothing that differed from his views: our rigid upbringing and the iron rules at home.

"There were so many taboos," I tried to explain. "My father reigns over our family as if we were his property. And if you defied him, then … well, you know what happens then!" I turned my fingers inward to point at myself.

John lifted his head and held my gaze.

"I don't want to offend you, but your father's behaviour sounds compulsive and narcissistic."

"How do you know these terms?" I widened my eyes.

"Well, I've been working at a university for most of my life. Over the years, students of all disciplines have sat on that stool out there." He tilted his head towards the counter behind us.

"Narcissistic? Do you mean vain and full of your own importance?" I asked.

"Seeing yourself as a gift to others. Which is no problem unless somebody challenges their self-image." John explained.

"John, you amaze me." I leaned back and stared at him. With a modest smile, John shrugged his shoulders and lifted his mug.

"Anyway, how do your parents get on with your sister?"

"Oh, my sister. She knows how to keep out of the firing line. She despises me."

John allowed his chin to drop.

"It's true. She repeatedly told me so, and I have no reason to doubt her."

"Does she have kids?" he asked.

"That's the odd thing, John. She's expecting. I think the baby's due around now."

John studied me before he settled his gaze on the ground. We both held the silence until he continued.

"Whatever label you give this, Pippa, your childhood sounds awful. I'm so sorry for you."

I choked.

"And the irony, John: they have the best conditions to raise a child. Space is no problem. But they would go utterly berserk if they knew…"

He rubbed his chin in silence.

"What if you tried, Pippa? You could see how they react. What if their minds have changed, but they can't admit it? You could make the first move."

"That's unthinkable. The thought itself horrifies me."

A stinging taste of nausea ran up my throat. John could not imagine life at my house any more than Chris could.

"When you meet your sister, your gut may tell you what to do."

I reflected on his words. How often had I envisioned myself facing Sandra with her child in the last few weeks? I imagined carrying her baby in my arms, overwhelmed by warmth and gratitude.

"She'd snarl something like, 'Well, you got that sorted nicely. Gallivanting around England to come here and live rent-free with a bastard.' At me, John."

John frowned.

"This is how she speaks to me. I have known her long enough."

He looked dazed.

"Now, do you see why I'm in such a dilemma? I can't turn either left or right."

"That doesn't sound like a family. More like a dictatorship."

"That's well said, John." I snickered through my tears. "My father can be such a tyrant!"

"I'm so sorry, Pippa. Still, go there. This is your life. You don't have to tell them. If you can't speak the truth, come back in time for the clinic appointment."

"I don't know, John …" I trailed off, letting his words sink in. We looked at each other in silence. He picked a phone book out of a drawer and leafed through it.

"Who are you calling?" I asked, confused.

"The airport. I'll book you a flight."

"You can't. I don't have any money for a ticket."

"I'll lend it to you."

His suggestion made sense. But the walk up to my parents' house would be a long, grim one. Did I have the confidence to do that?

"You may be right, and I owe it to the child to at least exhaust this last possibility."

He held the phone in his hand. "Why are you helping me?" I asked.

"Because your parents, who should be there for you, are not."

He dialled. I heard the line click and the remote ringtone.

"You and Chris are at the beginning of your lives. You need to be entirely sure that there was no alternative. Otherwise, this decision will be too heavy a burden, one you'll both carry for the rest of your lives."

I nodded.

John held the receiver closer to his ear. "Yes, good evening. I would like to book a flight to Germany …"

Germany 1993

27

A cluster of passengers drew me into the arrival lobby. Tourists and business travellers hastened to the baggage transportation belt and disappeared beyond the exit of the entrance hall. My bag swung over my shoulder, its indented shape revealing that I travelled light.

Fellow tourists shoved past me, heads raised, reading information boards, fumbling with passports. A suitcase smacked into my shin. "Watch out," I called at the woman rushing past, but she was gone, foraging in her handbag.

I found a phone booth, dug out my address book and looked up Sandra's number. A rock of shame pressed on my gut. A sense of being caught—I knew it well. My heart pounded up to my neck. I dialled with trembling fingers.

"Lindenthal." A chill travelled across my body. Then a surge of adrenaline made my heart race.

"Hel …" I cleared my throat. "Hi Sandra, it's Pippa."

There was a second's silence.

"Phillippa? Where are you?"

Her voice sounded firm. As ever, my sister embodied complete self-control. My eyes pricked, and I suppressed an impulse to scream into the receiver: *Help me, Sandra, tell me what to do.*

Instead, I pulled myself together.

"I'm here, in Germany. I wanted to see you." My voice trembled.

Through the noise that enveloped me, I picked up her breathing and imagined the look on her face: icy with a furrowed brow.

"Just like that?" Another pause. "Do Mum and Dad know you're back?"

"Can I see you first? I could be there in a couple of hours." I noticed the pleading tone of my voice. It annoyed me.

"All right," she replied after a moment, then broke the connection.

A swarm of wasps buzzed through my stomach, bouncing off my intestines.

Thoughts bobbed around my head like ping-pong balls. I should have holed up in a dark room in York, sitting out the two weeks until the hospital appointment. Why punish myself by coming here? Was this a journey of penance? Had I come to chastise myself for a decision already made?

Then I rang Chris.

"I've arrived," I said.

"Did you speak to them?"

I told him I'd rung my sister first and he wanted to know how it had gone.

"At least she didn't hang up on me. I am off to see her first," I said, as if it were a small blink of hope.

"Love you, stay strong and come straight back if they give you grief." Chris tried to encourage me.

"I will," I said, grateful for his support.

"Promise? I need to hear you say it, Pippa."

"I promise," I said, hearing the last coins fall through, and then the line went dead.

After a two-hour journey, I stood in front of Sandra's apartment building, my knees quivering. Rolling blinds half-covered her windows. Hopefully, Harald was away on one of his business trips. Whatever was going to hit me, I preferred not to have witnesses.

I pressed the bell and turned to the intercom. Nothing. I pressed again. Then Sandra appeared at the front door. Her enormous belly blocked the entrance.

"So, what do you want?" she asked.

"Hello, Sandra. I wanted to surprise you. I'm on holiday … I was wondering … well…"

Her face darkened. "That's typical. You disappear when it suits you. And then you show up out of the blue without a moment's thought. Are you out of your mind?"

My eyes filled.

"Here we go, turning on the waterworks before you even enter the door. Do you realise what you did to Mum and Dad?"

I bit my lip and looked at her stomach. Tears ran down my cheeks.

"Come in. I'd rather you not put on a show for the neighbours," she said, turning and walking to her flat. She hoisted herself up, holding onto the bannister. I guessed she'd prefer not to be in a lift with me.

Once in her apartment, her tone became less hostile.

She offered me a glass of water, which I held with both hands to stop myself from shaking. I sniffled.

Sandra pulled a corner of her mouth up and puffed her breath out through her nose. "Spare me the crocodile tears. You could have thought of that before you waltzed off to England without a word."

Was this the right moment to tell her my secret?

"Can I have a look at the nursery?" I asked instead.

"Sure."

She walked ahead into the baby's room. I took a deep breath. The walls were painted off-white. The pine wardrobe doors squeaked as Sandra opened them. Beige, yellow and green. I ran my hand over the fluffy fabrics.

Everything is as it should be.

"We don't know whether it's a boy or a girl yet," Sandra said, closing the wardrobe solemnly as if it were a shrine. I stepped back.

"The main thing is that it's healthy," I heard myself say and cringed.

Sandra remained distant, but she became more talkative. Harald worked away a lot after a recent promotion. He was in Munich and expected to return the day after tomorrow. Then, he was off work for a few weeks for the birth.

How perfectly arranged everything was. My eyes wandered around the room. *How stupid of me not to bring a present.* Little wooden figures decorated a honey-coloured pine shelf. Silky cushions and stuffed animals adorned a nursing chair. Above it, a picture frame with colourful letters that read, *A grand adventure is about to begin.* I gulped.

"So, what are you going to do? Are you going to see Mum and Dad?" my sister wanted to know.

"May I stay with you for a night? I'll call them tomorrow," I asked with a weak voice.

Sandra squinted with familiar sarcasm.

"Yes, you can sleep on the sofa."

The conversation remained superficial for the rest of the day. We avoided eye contact and skirted around personal topics other than the baby. My sister explained that the baby was in a breech position, and for a moment, her matter-of-factness reminded me of my professor in her tweed jacket.

"Are you worried?" I asked.

"What good is that going to do?" She smirked. "They'll sort it out in the maternity ward when I'm admitted. I can't change the situation."

I winced. As time passed, any attempts to incite interest in *my* life failed. I dropped hints about my journey, work, and life in York. She did not bite, so eventually, I let it go.

"I'm off to bed," she said before the evening news finished, turned off the television and left me in the room, which was illuminated only by the faint streetlight. The table and chairs cast black shadows in the grey. Not once had she mentioned my hasty departure. The argument back then still lingered between us. And yet she took me in. She had always been proud to be the firstborn. I had no illusions. She granted me shelter out of sheer duty.

My sister's voice woke me up in the middle of the night.

"Damn, this place stinks."

Hunching her body, she jerked the window open.

"Sandra, what …" Something was wrong. I flicked on the lamp. Sandra slumped in the armchair, leaning forward, groaning. Her hair stuck to the back of her neck.

"Have you had a shower? You're soaking wet," I said. My voice quivered.

Contorted, she released a low moan. I gasped. Sandra never let on when she wasn't feeling well.

"I'll close the window. You'll catch your death," I said, desperate to be helpful.

"Leave it," she groaned and raised an arm. "Stinks … fresh air …"

I put my duvet around her, prepared for her to lash out. Her face was glittering. Were those tears? I had never seen her cry, and her distress alarmed me.

"Sandra, what do I … what do I have to do? Is the baby coming?"

I glanced from her belly down to her groin. Sandra squealed and writhed, then whimpered.

"I have to go to the hos … pit…" she groaned.

"Shhh … shhh … breathe, Sandra. Breathe … I'll get dressed."

She slid off the chair onto the floor. I shimmied one leg into my jeans. This couldn't be happening. Now of all times. Sandra was the strong one. Could she die? She lay wincing on the carpet. I closed the window while she lay huddled on the floor. She grabbed my hand as I tried to push a cushion under her head.

"Help me. The bag …" She pointed to her bedroom door. I hurried and found a packed holdall.

"Can you make it to the car? Where did you park? Which hospital?" I asked.

She propped herself up on the coffee table. I helped her get up, and she stood, hunching her back.

"Do you want me to call Harald? What about Mum and Dad?" I asked.

"Ambu …" she squealed and slumped on the floor.

28

Sandra held out until the ambulance arrived, screaming and whimpering. Her waters had broken, and when the nurse asked if I was to come along, my sister gave a dismissive wave. After they left, I cleaned up the pieces of broken glass she had smashed against the wall. Then I looked for the car and the front-door keys. Before I left, I called Harald at his hotel. Yes, he was coming on the next flight. But the child wasn't due for another week. Was the early birth my fault? Had I upset her?

By the time I arrived at the hospital, a caesarean section had delivered a little girl. I could see my sister, the nurse said, but the baby had to be monitored in intensive care for a few hours. This was how it ought to be. Everything was done to give the baby a good start in life. Whereas, I had come here still not knowing if I'd let my child live.

Sandra was asleep when I pulled a chair up to her bed. It was a single room—private insurance, no doubt. Her features were softened, her lips parted, and the corners of her mouth relaxed. The pain must have been unbearable. However, Sandra was tough, be it at the dentist or when she broke her arm trying out her new rollerblades.

I looked around for a writing pad and found a brochure from the maternity ward in her bedside table drawer.

I'll be back in the morning. I called Harald. He'll be here soon. I scribbled on the back of the paper and leaned it against a glass.

Back in the flat, I settled into the armchair where Sandra had been shaking in pain a few hours earlier. Wrapped in the duvet, a heavy sadness settled over me. Hot tears burned my cheeks; my nose dripped. *What am I going to do?* My thoughts spun, as if on a roundabout without an exit.

In a state of slumber, I sobbed and felt paralysed by fear. Now, I would see my parents sooner than planned. Harald had offered to make that call. It was dawn, and I wondered if they were already on their way.

I looked out for my father's Opel in the hospital car park. My pulse quickened, yet my chest felt caught in the jaws of a press that narrowed with every step.

Outside the door, I tuned in for voices. Sandra was not alone. My stomach jolted. I filled my lungs with air and walked into the room.

"Ah, there she is," my father announced under his breath. His gaze settled on my shoes.

"Hello, Dad," I squeezed out, my voice shaking. There was a gurgling sound. Sandra was grinning at a bundle in her arms. My mother perched on the edge of the bed, folding a towel in silence.

"Hello, little one." I was overwhelmed with wonder. I walked around the bed to get a better view of the newborn.

"Hello, Mum," I said as I passed her.

She avoided eye contact but murmured a weak "hello".

I knew that expression: head cocked to one side, corners of her mouth sagging. The posture of the martyr, the victim. As a child, I sat next to her in church every Sunday, watching her folding her fingers compulsively, praying, "… and forgive us our sins." I knew I was a dreadful disappointment.

"Congratulations on your first grandchild." I hoped to soften the features of her contemptuous face. Was there a hint of compassion?

"Phillippa, don't bother," my mother said.

To my amazement, Sandra came to my rescue. "Pippa, thank you for last night. If you hadn't been there …"

"Then we wouldn't have had this emergency birth, Sandra." My father interrupted with a shuddering voice, as if to suppress his anger. We turned our faces to him. "Can you do anything without putting on a show? I mean, can't you act normal for once? Turning up here out of the blue…"

I gazed at the baby, blood rushing through my brain. "What are you going to call her?" My voice sounded an octave too high. My dad released a deep groan behind me.

"Liliane."

Trust my sister to choose an alliteration for her baby's name. Liliane Lindenthal, *LL*. How often had she teased me about my initials spelling the German word for "bum."

"Nice," I replied, thinking of the life in my belly. What would I name *my* baby?

"What were you thinking, Phillippa?" my father scolded.

"Karl, not here, not in front of the child." For a moment, I was not sure to whom my mother was referring.

"Do you think there will be a better time, Waltraud? This is a pitstop for her before she'll be off gallivanting again."

He looked at me, a vein pulsing in his forehead. "I'm right, am I not? You come and go as you please, without a care in the world for your family."

Sandra interrupted. "Do you want to hold her, Pippa?"

Before I could react, my mother moved and helped place the soft, warm bundle in my arms. What was I doing here? How could I have thought this visit was a good idea? The baby lay in my arms with a crumpled face and tiny fingers with miniature nails moving as if to grasp the terry cloth blanket.

"You're a natural." Sandra's words tightened my throat.

I welcomed my father's intervention this time. "Stop it, Sandra. Don't put ideas in her empty head. She should get her life in order and find a decent job."

I brought the baby closer to my chest as if to shield it from the toxic air that permeated the room.

My mother grabbed my arm. "Are you coming home tonight?"

Her question hit me like a bolt of lightning,

"For dinner, I mean," she added.

I placed little Liliane back in my sister's arms. "I have to stay for another night," she announced. "Why don't you go?" Her tone sounded comforting. *Perhaps it's the hormones.*

"Home" was hundreds of miles away, with Chris. I avoided my father's eyes. Guilt tormented me at the miserable look on my mother's face. How I longed to confide in my big sister.

"I'm going into town. I have to meet someone," I said, grabbing my jacket and running to the door.

"Think about it, Phillippa. You can sleep in your room."

I hesitated and remembered John's words: "Your gut may tell you what to do". My mother looked at me, her eyes as pale as her skin. I nodded. "Okay, I'll see you later."

The city was hectic, with people rushing from shop to shop. The modern, shiny facades bore a futuristic contrast to the historic buildings of York. The wind whistled hostilely, and I was relieved to disappear into the warm entrance of a shop.

I wavered for a moment. Prams, cots, and oversized stuffed animals surrounded me. I caught sight of shelves of toys and baby clothes and buried my hands between a pile of folded rompers.

"Lovely and soft, aren't they?" A stylish saleswoman approached me. "Are you looking for something for the first few months?" She looked at my belly.

"No, it's not for me." I pulled my coat tightly around me.

"But something for a newborn?" she asked.

She suggested various outfits.

"It'll be spring before you know it. How about this little outfit with daffodils on the front? How old did you say the little one is?"

On the train ride home, I reached for the soft toy I had bought, alongside tiny socks, a romper, and a matching top. As I watched the silvery city pass by, I pressed the lion against my chest. *Maybe I should keep him.*

29

The slate-covered path led me through the immaculate front garden to my parents' house. The irregularly placed stones forced me to adapt my gait, and I could not take the steps in a continuous movement. Tinted glass surrounded the entrance door on either side. In the mirrored image, I prepared a merry smile, tidied my hair, and held in my stomach.

I rang the doorbell.

My father appeared. He spanned the hall with long strides. Separated by the glass, I heard him shout, "Crap. Waltraud, the bloody door is locked again."

My mother, a mixing bowl cradled in one arm, fumbled in her apron pocket. Dad ripped the keys from her hand, his lips pressed together.

"I must continue whipping the cream," she shouted and rushed off.

My father shook his head as he unlocked the door.

Now he would ask if the train had been on time.

"Yes," I replied, "everything was like clockwork."

Our eye contact was as brief as possible.

The jarring of the mixer blared from the kitchen.

"I need to use the bathroom." I gestured and escaped into the downstairs lavatory. I looked at the slight bulge on my abdomen.

"I can't do this to you or me. You must understand," I whispered, sitting on the toilet. This house did not approve of change: every move, sound, and word—the same as ever.

My mum set the dining table with the gold-rimmed china she kept for birthdays and special holidays. She tapped the seat next to me, and I felt miserable.

"I baked cheesecake, your favourite. Karl, would you like a piece of gooseberry tart?" Not waiting for an answer, she placed a sizeable slice on our plates.

"Shall I pour?" I asked, reaching for the coffee pot.

"It's leaking. I'll do it," my mum replied and snatched it to her side of the table.

"I'm astounded our daughter still drinks coffee. I would have thought she'd switched to English Breakfast tea," my father grunted. Mum gave him a stern frown. I inhaled a heavy breath.

"I only just got here, Dad." My courage surprised me.

His eyes flared as he shot me a look stewing with anger.

"You listen to me, Miss High and Mighty. As long as your feet are under my table..."

"Stop it," my mother shouted. "Pull yourselves together and have some cake. I've been toiling all morning to arrange everything; all you do is fight."

She rubbed her nose with a napkin, her eyes red.

"Mum, I'm sorry, but I can't stand his endless criticism."

"Her ladyship *can't stand it*. Was that the reason why you ran off to England? Because you couldn't stand it? And over there? Can you *stand it* there? Let me guess: the English are *so lovely* and fawn at your feet."

He shouted the last sentence in a voice meant to mimic me. Nothing had changed. He could still push my buttons.

"I wish I hadn't shown up here," I yelled, pushing my untouched plate into the middle of the table, getting up and storming out.

"Come back here at once," my father yelled. "Do you have any idea what you're doing to your mother?"

I hurled the door shut behind me and ran upstairs into what used to be my bedroom. Tidy and orderly, everything looked flawless.

Sitting on the bed, I held Barry to my chest. Snot ran out of my nose as I sobbed. Why, why had I come? Pure masochism. I had gained a healthy distance. Why did I agree with this absurd idea? John had no clue how toxic the atmosphere was in my family home. *I wish I'd never got on that plane.*

When my tears eased, I walked around the old flat. The parquet floor gleamed in the winter sun that fell through the curtains. Everything was impeccable. I tried to imagine living there, the baby in its cot.

"I need to tell you something," I said to the silence. "I'm …" I couldn't bring myself to say the word "pregnant".

It's not possible, not possible. Little one, you must understand, I can't have you. Who would want a mother paralysed with fear in the presence of her parents?

There was a knock at the door. "Pippa, please. At least join us and finish the cake."

"Dad needs to shut up, Mum."

"Yes, he will. Come downstairs," she begged and, as I followed her, added, "But he has a point, though."

My father sat at the table, piercing a gooseberry with his fork. I poured myself coffee, catching the drips with my napkin. My parents turned the conversation to the neighbours as if nothing had happened.

"We expect their daughter to get married soon," my father added. "With his job, they'll secure a generous pension for their retirement."

I imagined how he'd talk about Chris. A penniless artist, the eternal student, freeloading off the taxpayer's money. Someone who got his leg over and would dump me when the next *easy* girl crossed his path.

I knew his choice of words and the gleeful tone he used when he talked about couples who didn't fit his bourgeois middle-class image.

Throughout the afternoon I kept thinking of how to escape this house that was so predictable. Then the phone rang—it was Sandra. The hospital would discharge her in a few hours and Harald was on his way home.

"Will you spend the night with Mum and Dad?"

"No, I must get back to England. All the best to you both and the baby."

After I hung up, I dialled Ursula's number.

"Pips, how fantastic! You sound like you're in the other room. Where are you?"

I whispered, "At my parents, I'll explain later. Can I come and stay with you?"

"Take the next train. I'll wait at the station to meet you."

As I returned to the kitchen, my mother looked at me with vacant eyes. The corners of her mouth drooped. My heart ached at the sight. Had she been listening?

I wanted to tell her the truth. But my fear was overwhelming. The news would break her.

30

"I'm pregnant."

My friends looked at each other, aghast.

They think it's a joke.

We sat at the table in what used to be my former kitchen. Here, I'd opened the letter from York University, unaware of the dramatic consequences.

Yvonne broke the silence. "Is that the reason for your spontaneous visit?"

"I *had* to get away from my parents." I hoped they'd spare me having to explain more.

My dad had driven me to the station in total silence earlier that afternoon. My mum was convinced that my premature departure was her fault. I could not persuade her otherwise without admitting the truth. Instead, I left her blaming herself. The only sound at my departure was the thud of the boot closing and my mum, sitting in the passenger seat, sniffling into her handkerchief.

"Did you tell them? Is that why they kicked you out?" Yvonne asked, and I shifted in my seat.

"I had planned to tell them. But before I got the chance, my sister went into labour, and that was it."

Ursula poured herself a glass of wine and stopped mid-movement. "No way. Little Miss Perfect had her baby, and you stood by, hiding your own … pregnancy?"

I nodded, chewing the inside of my cheek.

Yvonne put her hand on my arm. "So, erm, what are you going to do? What did Chris say?"

This was a question I had been dreading since the train journey. Ursula blew a strand of hair from her face and leaned back, sighing, as I described Chris's plans and why I had come to Germany.

"Please tell me you are not bunking off to Japan?" Yvonne widened her eyes.

"No way," I said. "It was England I wanted to move to. And I was so happy when it happened. At last, a dream come true."

Ursula took my hand. "And I, for one, can see why you love it. It's a beautiful place, and the people are lovely—at least the ones I met."

I pressed a tissue against my eyes.

"Aw, come here. You poor thing." Ursula hugged me tight, her hands rubbing my back. I freed myself from her embrace and blew into my handkerchief.

"I don't think I have any tears left, but better not be too nice to me." I tried to joke, but both friends looked at me with serious faces.

"So, your mind is made up?" Yvonne wondered, and Ursula shot her a scowl.

"I guess so. This is the worst timing ever. Do I sound callous?"

Yvonne shook her head.

I turned to her. "You'd be thinking very differently in my situation. You and Tom are planning a life together, whereas I ..." Again, I felt Ursula's comforting hand on my back as I sobbed into a tissue.

We heard a noise from the hallway. "That'll be Tom. I'd better tell him." Yvonne jumped up. She closed the kitchen door behind her. Soft voices muttering echoed in the hallway. Then Tom stood in the doorway with arms wide open. "Pippa, it's so good to see you." He came over to hug me tight.

"Hi, Tom. I guess Yvonne has told you about my predicament?"

"Yes, I'm so glad you're with your best mates here. You must feel desperate."

His comforting rationality made it easy to confide in him.

"Ursula has told us about your Chris. He sounds a top bloke, by the way," Tom said. "And I can understand your dilemma, Pippa. I'm not sure what we'd do if Yvonne got pregnant out of the blue."

Yvonne choked as she took a few sips from her wine glass.

"At least none of you plan to move to the other side of the world. I mean, what would you do, tell me honestly?" I looked at Yvonne, then at her boyfriend.

Tom bit his lip. "Phillippa, you mustn't ask anyone this question. Only you can decide what's best for yourself. But you need to be sure. It's your life, your body, your child. How long have you been dreaming of living in England?"

"Yes, Tom," I replied, "but this changes things. Am I not selfish, not having this baby when I could return and raise it here?"

"Wait a minute." Ursula joined in. "May I remind you that your miserable family is why you left in the first place?"

I winced; she was right. The hostility at home had driven me away. First Cologne, then abroad.

"Yes, I guess … but it feels such a cowardly act, so weak."

Tom leaned forward to catch my eyes. "On the contrary. To me, you come across as a powerful woman." He reached out to Yvonne, who put her hand in his. "As a guy, I might have no right saying this. But this is *your* time to be selfish. Choosing a termination is far from cowardly."

Yvonne and Ursula shifted in their seats. I cringed.

"I haven't decided what I'm going to do, Tom," I rushed to say.

"Well, you should. Because if you wait much longer, the decision will be made for you. One way or another, it's time to take charge."

England 1993

31

That same night, I called the airport and booked a flight for the following day. Tom managed to borrow his dad's car, and once more, my friends saw me off as I waved goodbye before disappearing into the check-in queue. As the plane taxied to the runway, I mulled over the last few days and fell into a slumber until the loudspeaker woke me. "We are preparing for landing and ask all passengers to return to their seats and fasten their seat belts."

When I looked down, a carpet of patchwork made from fields with different colours and shapes, framed by green hedges, was laid out below me. *What a gorgeous welcome.* I imagined myself dropping down onto the soft blanket of grass. I could hardly wait to touch English soil.

I walked through passport control and took the escalator to the station below. Like a fish in water, I glided through the crowds and lined up on the busy platform. Once on the train, I found a seat and closed my eyes. My body surrendered to the gentle rocking of the carriage, and I fell into a semi-sleep. The jolting rhythm woke me as we moved across the sleepers near our destination. Ka-den-ge, Ka-den-ge, Ka-den-ge. Then nothing for a few seconds before the pattern repeated: Ka-den-ge, Ka-den-ge, Ka-den-ge. The rocking turned fiercer, and I had to tense my body to avoid colliding with the person beside me.

We were approaching the end of the line. Ka den-ge, Ka-den-ge, Ka-den-ge, three short syllables that evolved into words in my head. For-give-me, for-give-me, for-give-me. I put my hand on my belly. For-give-me, for-give-me, for-give-me.

The sky in York was milky. I blinked as I stepped out of the station building.

"Taxi?" a stocky man called out, leaning against a car, blowing out cigar smoke.

"No, thanks," I replied and set off. The walk to Fulford was long enough to prepare me for my reunion with Chris. He would be home, writing one of his papers.

Before I rang the doorbell, I stepped back and glanced at the house. How sad the dirty windows looked. Had they ever been cleaned? I pressed the bell and heard the muffled sound of heavy footsteps. Chris opened the front door.

"Pips, my Pips, you're back. I was afraid they'd persuaded you to stay."

He put down his tea, pulled me into the house and hugged me tight. I pressed my face into his jumper and inhaled the musty smell of soap and his warm skin. I had arrived.

"At last," I said. "I'm so happy." The thick wool silenced my voice.

"And me. Come on in. Are you hungry? Let me take your bag. I'll make us something. Tea?" Still hugging me, he slowly turned us in a circle, then let go and placed my bag underneath the coat rack in the hall.

The kitchen smelled of burnt toast. I took in the clutter of used plates, cereal bowls, and teacups piled on the sideboard. A tea towel lay on the floor. Chris stood before me and untied the scarf I had knotted around my neck. "Take a seat. I'll tidy this mess up later." He pulled down the zip of my jacket and slipped it off my shoulders.

I shrugged him off to pick up the tea towel, folded it and placed it beside the worktop. Then, I put the rubber stopper in the sink and turned on the tap.

"Pippa, what are you doing?" Chris rushed to me and took my hand off the tap. "Why don't you sit down?"

"This place needs airing out. It stinks." I pointed to the window. "When was the last time you opened that?"

He placed his hands on my shoulders, pushed me onto a chair and knelt, his hands on my thighs.

"Darling, calm down. What's the matter with you?"

"What should be the matter? I'm tired, and this mess is annoying."

I cringed. Was this me talking? Chris leant back, removing his hands.

"Ah, wait a minute," he said, contorting his face as if in deep thought. He stood and ran into the hallway, returning with my luggage in his hand. He placed my bag on the kitchen table. "So, let's see …" He patted the bag down.

"What are you doing?" I asked, irritated. My joy at seeing him again evaporated.

"Let's see, where are you hiding them? Ma, Pa, Sis?"

"Cut the crap, Chris."

"Yes, yes, I'm sure of it. They're hiding here somewhere." He put an ear to the bag. "Hello, Boche family, you can come out now."

"Please stop acting the fool. I'm tired. It's all been so exhausting." I was too tired to sound exasperated.

"Lie down, and we'll talk in a couple of hours. I'll bring you a cup of tea. It'll help you relax."

He took the pot from the cooker.

"No, I can't sleep. I'm far too wired. I want to call the hospital and confirm the appointment."

Chris put the teapot back and looked at me. "Have you told your parents?"

I laughed out loud. "Ha ha ha. *Told?* Not once while I was there did they ask about my life. They can't forgive me for leaving their oh-so-perfect world."

He took my hand, his smile subsiding.

"I'm so sorry."

"It went just as I imagined. I could have saved myself the trip and all the stress."

"No, now you know for sure."

"There's no doubt. Not anymore. I can't have the child." A shudder went down my spine. "I'll call right away. Will you go with me to the appointment?"

"Of course, Pippa. We'll get through this together. Wouldn't you like to lie down upstairs? I'll cook something. Do you fancy ravioli?"

"No. But can I have a bath? And before that, I'd like to call the hospital."

Chris looked at me with soft eyes and nodded. When I stood up, he hugged me again.

"I missed you so much." His hands slid down my side and grazed my breasts. His touch revealed how plump they had become. His grip on my waist tightened as he kissed me.

No, I can't do it, I thought. *He can't enjoy my pregnant body*. I broke away from his embrace. "I'm going upstairs."

"Okay." he cleared his throat.

As I turned the bath taps, I heard dishes clatter in the sink, and I felt a pang of guilt for rejecting him.

With the telephone number scribbled on a piece of paper, I went back downstairs and dialled. "Für Elise" rang in my ear.

Chris rested his hands on the edge of the sink, his gaze focused on a stack of dishes. Waiting for the phone to be answered, I glanced at a pile of books on the windowsill: encyclopaedias, a volume on philosophy, and an unfamiliar title: the *Study Guide of Nagoya University*.

"City of York Hospital, Gynaecology, Jane speaking, how can I help you?"

My heart pounded. "My name is Phillippa Olbig, I …"

Chris put his finger to his lips and left the room.

"Hello, Ms Olbig?" the voice on the phone asked.

"Yes, well … I have an appointment for … erm … for … an abortion. I … erm … I want to confirm it." My head spun, and I held one hand against the wall to steady myself. Trembling, the words fell out of my mouth.

"One moment, please … Olbig … Yes, you are scheduled for Thursday."

"I'll be there," I said, having regained my composure.

My body relaxed as I lowered myself into the water. For a moment, my mind stopped spinning. Instead, I sensed the warm comfort of soft bubbles surrounding me, drawing me in as I became one with this element that engulfed me. From where did I recognise this feeling of being detached from any care in the world? I saw myself in the cable car, with Ursula sitting opposite, the sunshine heating the cabin, and cars moving along the motorway underneath. *A protective membrane.* I shuddered at the thought and put my hand on my belly. *You think you're safe there. You don't know the decision I just made.*

I felt shabby, like a criminal who regrets her deed before she commits it and still knows she will stab her victim. I closed my eyes and disappeared under the water. There was a rustling in my ears. Was this what babies heard inside the womb? If I stayed there, we could die together. A dull knocking drowned out the murmur. I emerged. Chris sat on the edge of the bathtub.

"Hey, is it nice in there?" Was he asking me or our child?

"Mmm," I mumbled. He stroked a few strands of hair out of my face. "You look like a drowned puppy," he said with a smile, kissing my forehead. His gaze slid down my body.

"Please don't look at me," I pleaded, taking his hand.

"So, you've made up your mind." Chris looked at me thoughtfully.

"You have too, haven't you?" I replied, ashamed of my reproachful tone.

He frowned. "What do you mean?"

"The books on Japan. In the kitchen."

"I, erm, well, I can still cancel. It would only be for two years at the most."

"Keep talking," I begged him, slipping under the surface again.

"Maybe you'll join me."

Muffled and distorted, his words reached me.

"We'll see each other when I return to Oxford." It sounded like he'd shouted every syllable through a mouthpiece from another planet.

Me and Japan, me with a PhD philosopher. Chris and I were from alien galaxies. I came up, gasping for breath.

"Well, what do you think?" he asked. Was he really that naïve?

"Honestly, I don't have room in my head for that right now," I replied, more sharply than I'd intended. "I have other stuff to think about."

"Sorry," he said, and I pitied him.

After dinner, Chris accompanied me to the bus.

"See you the day after tomorrow," he said.

"It's a date." I forced a smile, my lips trembling.

The campus grounds were quiet. Relieved that I had not met anyone, I entered the entrance hall. The caretaker's light was on, but there was a note on the counter: "Be right back." Hopefully, John was on duty today. Upstairs, it was quiet.

I put the bag in my room and returned to the entrance hall. John was back at his main workstation.

"I'm glad to see you, Pippa. I'm curious to hear how it went. Fancy a cuppa?"

Warming my hand on the teacup, I spoke about the trip, my stay, Sandra, and her baby. When I told him about the night Liliane was born, he put down his cup and leaned back in his chair, shaking his head.

"That is unbelievable. A week early, as it were, to welcome you."

"You can say that again. I couldn't talk to my sister at all. She'd probably accused me of making this pregnancy up to steal her show."

"My goodness, things are bad between you. And how was it at your parents?"

"The same as before. Blaming me, making me feel bad, and disappointed in my choices. Perfect house, perfect garden, perfect world."

"Perfect Pippa."

"That's sweet of you. But I don't feel like that at all. I just don't fit in back there."

"And yet you seem so enmeshed with that world."

"You're right, John."

I took a sip of tea. That expression made me think. I imagined tangled wool, the impossibility of finding the beginning of one's skein.

"But how do you get out of it?" I asked.

"That's hard. You didn't create this distance for nothing, I guess. That's a starting point."

"Where did you get your wisdom?"

"Oh, you know. In my work, you meet many young people in the middle of their journey. And most of them have a story. It's not often as extreme as yours and your family's, but they all have something. And the ones who say they don't just don't talk about it." He winked at me.

That night, I went to sleep without fear for the first time. I felt an inner conviction that my decision was the right one.

32

Chris nudged me and smiled as he held the hospital door open.

I entered, whispering a weak "thank you."

The acidic smell of disinfectant stung my nose, and my stomach turned. One of the receptionists checked my identity card and took the forms I had filled out. She scrutinised the paperwork, then me, and pointed toward the gynaecology department.

"Are you all right?" Chris rubbed my back as we walked past clinical white doors.

"It must be here, on the left." I increased my pace to escape his attention.

We arrived at another desk where a lady checked the paperwork once more. Satisfied that everything was in order, she showed me to a room. "If you'd like to get changed here, please."

Chris stood by with hunched shoulders as if struggling to hold on to my bag, which was dangling from his arm. I felt an urge to snatch it out of his hand, but then I felt sorry for him. "Like a drowned puppy"—he looked like one himself.

I longed for a hot bath. A folded nightgown lay ready for me. I held it up and watched the fabric fall stiffly like cardboard. Chris turned to the window. Wasn't he just a stranger? It seemed paradoxical that I had got into this situation within weeks of moving to this country. *This situation.* Before long, it would be resolved. Life would be back in balance.

I held the two ends of the shirt behind my back. "Erm," I muttered.

"Here, let me help," Chris offered.

My body turned like a dummy being dressed in a shop window. A nurse came in and placed a cup of water with a pill sealed in plastic on the table beside the bed. "There you are. Take this as soon as you're ready," she said, disappearing again.

I pushed the duvet aside and sat on the bed. The smooth, fresh sheet felt cool where it touched my skin. I would have liked to lie down, pull the covers over my head, sleep, and not wake up until it was over. Over for long enough to have forgotten. I swallowed the pill and waited for my body to grow heavier. Then I pulled my legs onto the bed. Chris struggled to cover me with the crunched duvet under my legs.

"Leave it; it's fine," I muttered.

"I just want you to be okay, Pips. As well as you can be."

"Why should I be better off than my ba—"

The door opened again with a brisk swing, and two nurses pushed in a narrow hospital bed on a shiny frame with thick, rubber wheels.

"Miss Olbig, we're ready for you." They sounded like the announcement of a pilot before take-off. This was not a holiday trip. Did they not know what I was about to do?

One of the nurses held my arm while I stood up. "No need, I can manage," I said and plummeted back against the mattress. My legs had turned to jelly. This time, one nurse on each side moved me onto the wheeled stretcher, where I dropped my head onto the pillow.

"See you in a bit. I'll wait for you." Chris blew me a kiss.

"Mmm," I mumbled, then was rolled into the hallway. The overhead lights hurt my eyes as they passed, like glaring clouds.

I leaned forward to look out of the plane window. The right wing was ablaze, illuminating what was left of the machine's body. People stumbled across the aisle, climbing over seats and screaming. In contrast to the panic around me, I did not move. These would be my last seconds.

Someone shouted, "Recovery position", but my body would not move. I was frozen. As soon as the plane hit the ground, a metal rod drilled into my stomach through the back of the seat in front of me. Dark red blood gaped from the open wound.

"Pippa, hey, are you in pain?" It was Chris's voice.

"Ouch, yes, damn it," I whispered with my eyes closed. "I had the worst nightmare."

"Here, you can have one of these, the nurse said. The doctor will be here in a minute. How are you, I mean, otherwise?"

I opened my eyes to a squint and looked around. This was not the room I had last been in.

"Where are my clothes?" I asked.

"In here," he replied, pointing his head to a modern built-in wardrobe painted a friendly green. A television hung on the wall next to it. Chris sat in a comfortable-looking upholstered armchair.

"Fancy," I breathed, gulping down the painkiller with a glass of water.

"Isn't it? This is the *Boche Suite*." He winked.

"Ha," I pretended to laugh. My stomach tightened. "Ouch," I groaned.

Chris pressed his lips together, and before we could speak, Doctor McMinn entered the room, accompanied by a nurse. She stopped behind him and followed our conversation with a polite smile.

"Ah yes, Miss Olbig, you're awake. How are you?"

I gave a short groan and pulled up my legs under the covers.

"We'll give you something for the pain." He mumbled something to the nurse, who nodded and scribbled on a notepad. "If the pain does not ease within a few hours, take additional paracetamol." His tone was matter of fact. Wasn't he about to lecture me?

"Thank you," I squeezed out.

"My advice is to take it easy for a few days."

Doctor McMinn turned to Chris and said, "Take care of her. Each patient processes this experience differently."

"I will," Chris promised.

"Mary here will explain when you can be discharged." Once again, the doctor turned to me. "All the best." Then he left the room.

Mary stepped up to my bedside with a large envelope.

"Right, Miss Olbig, here are your papers," she explained, "with details about the procedure and possible side effects. You heard the doctor. Everything went well. This is standard information that we give to all our patients. Have you taken your painkillers?"

Without waiting for an answer, she inspected the empty cup beside my bed. "Good, you'll feel better in a minute. Have you been to the toilet yet?"

I shook my head.

"Please let me know when you've been. After that, you're free to go."

I drank the cup of water as soon as she had gone, asking Chris for a refill.

The painkillers were taking effect. My belly relaxed. I filled my stomach with air. My abdominal wall rose and fell without pain. Less than half an hour later, my bladder responded, and I was discharged shortly afterwards.

We took a taxi to Chris's. I had called in sick to the university and wanted to avoid questions from my flatmates. If anyone asked, I had prepared the excuse that I had suffered a severe migraine attack.

Chris put his arm around me in the backseat of the car. I clutched the large envelope holding my patient file.

"Here, let me take it," Chris reached over.

"No, leave it." I pressed it against my chest. Nobody but me would ever see the contents. I would hide it, closed, in a safe place and never open it again.

Just as Chris reached for the key in his pocket, Don flung open the front door.

"Hi, guys. I was about to go into town. Are you not feeling well, Pippa?" He frowned.

I sighed and shook my head.

"She's having a bad migraine attack and needs to get to bed and rest," Chris explained.

Don lowered his voice. "Okay, that's crap. Quiet it is. You have the house to yourselves," he whispered.

"Thank you." I was in agony. What a hypocritical liar I had become.

"By the way." Chris picked up a small parcel from the table. "This arrived for you yesterday." He handed it to me like a fragile fortune cookie.

"What is…?" I took the packet and turned it around in my hands.

From your best friends. I recognised Yvonne's handwriting.

Chris stood by, smiling with curiosity. He pulled one eyebrow. "Scissors?"

"Yes, please," I replied, piercing the sharp blade through the thick sellotape. I placed the contents on the table.

"No card?" Chris asked.

I shook my head and smiled. "No need to."

I found a CD by Annie Lennox wrapped in pink silk paper. I opened the cover and read the song titles. "Little Bird" was highlighted in red felt-tip pen. Next, I unwrapped a box of herbal tea named "Tension Soother" and a packet of paper tissues decorated with dog paws.

"Oh, that's so sweet," Chris exclaimed, picking up and examining my gifts, one by one.

On the bottom of the box, I discovered a square tile made from hardened, beige clay. It was decorated with a drawing of angel wings, and underneath, the writing read: *Pippa, you are loved for being you.*

A deep gasp escaped my mouth. Tears welled up in my eyes.

"Wow, I don't know what to say. I feel bad not getting in touch more," I said.

"That's the thing about friends, love. They don't expect you always to get it all right."

Upstairs in his room, Chris drew the curtains. I hid as deeply as I could under the duvet. Again, I lay in the foetal position with my knees drawn up, hands clasped together as if in prayer. *I'm sorry, I'm sorry, I'm so sorry*—the words echoed through my head. Who was I asking for absolution? I squeezed my burning eyes shut.

Through the covers, I felt Chris's hand on my shoulder. "Shall I make you some of that tension soother?" he asked.

I stopped sobbing for a moment to recollect what he meant. Then I sighed, nodded, and turned my head towards him. Tears rolled down my cheeks.

"Yes, please. That'll be perfect."

He looked at me, worry etched into his eyes, and was about to say something, but I interrupted before he could utter the first syllables. "No, leave it. I'll be fine. I must go through this on my own."

He nodded and left.

As I cried, my whole body shook, the effects of the painkillers wearing off. My abdomen throbbed as if I was getting a heavy period. I didn't want to take any more pills.

You deserve the pain, I thought.

"How are you, Pippa?" Three voices sounded through the telephone receiver.

"Hi, well, erm, I am ..." I wiped my hand across my face and cleared my throat. An image of the revolving doors of the Ford car showroom flashed by. I lifted the corners of my mouth to a smile. "All the better for hearing you all."

I heard sighs of relief at the end of the line. "Thank you all for your parcel. I don't know what to say."

"Nothing ..." Yvonne started, but Ursula took over.

"How are you feeling? Was it ... did it ...hurt?" she asked, and I could feel the anguish in her voice.

Aware that the three were waiting for my reply, I took a deep breath to gather myself.

"They looked after me really well in hospital. I'm feeling a bit sore."

"Poor thing," Yvonne said. "I wish I could be there for you."

"You've done so much for me, all of you," I said with an unsteady voice. "I am still a bit weepy, sorry," I added.

"Don't apologise. We're just glad you are okay." Tom sounded further away.

"Ish," Ursula corrected him. "Okay-ish." After a pause, she continued. "Pippa, tell me to mind my own business … but when is Chris leaving?" She whispered the last words, and I imagined her ducking for cover.

"We still have a few weeks before he goes to stay with his parents for a few days before his flight."

"How are you doing? Do you want us to visit?" Ursula's voice exuded a comforting warmth.

"That is sweet. Yes, that'll be wonderful once he's gone, sure." The thought of them visiting lifted my spirits, and for a moment, I forgot that I was saying goodbye too soon to the man with whom I had shared so much in such a short time.

33

The heavy wooden door gave way to my shoulder and opened with a dark creak. A draught of chilly air struck my face, driving my eyes to water. I dabbed my eyes with the tip of my finger and examined the murky inside of the church; I was alone.

I peered at the plinths along the side aisle. "Saint Anthony was a remarkably modest man," my mum used to point out when she took me to light a candle after Sunday service. "Look for him in a less prominent place." And indeed, here he was. I discovered the statue in a corner, carrying a child. He glanced into the distance, ignoring me.

A cast-iron rack in front carried flickering candles. Most were extinguished; others had not reached half of their burning hours. One was freshly lit. Who might that have been for? I hadn't passed anyone on the stairs up to St Wilfrid's Church that morning.

Holy Anthony—the saint of vanished items. I recalled my mum's hands on my shoulder, pushing me to look closer at the wooden figure, with its gown tinted brown, held by a plain piece of rope and his balding pate encircled by an unbroken receding hairline.

Clunk—my pound coin landed on a bed of change in the iron box. I stood my candle on the far-left corner of the tray and knelt on the cushioned prayer bench.

Anthony looked wretched as he carried the pudgy baby Jesus cradled on one arm. I remembered my mum squeezing my arm before nudging me to perform the same ritual. How rigidly this saint was bearing the Son of God. Clearly, a mother holds her baby closer to her chest. I'd capture it if the little body slid out from under the saint's elbow.

Forgive me, forgive me. The individual flames melted into one mild, milky light.

There was a shuffling behind me, and I peered to the side. A shadowy figure emerged from the gloom. A middle-aged lady with ash-blonde hair sank her hand into a marble bowl of holy water and crossed her chest. With my head bowed, I feigned deep prayer until the sound of her steps faded. When I opened my eyes, I noticed her enter the confession booth at the side of the building.

I could do that. It might soothe my conscience. I tried to recall the last time I practised this sacrament. Our class attended a school service, and they expected everyone to confess. I sat in the pew with sweaty hands, thinking what to tell the priest. When it was my turn, I mumbled something about not listening to my parents. The priest told me to repeat three Hail Marys and the Lord's Prayer. Is there a worthy repentance for having killed an unborn child? How raw-hearted had I become since those innocent school days?

Eager to be gone before the penitent left the wooden booth, I stood up. "I will come back, if I may," I whispered my request, but Saint Anthony continued to gaze into the distance, aloof and indifferent. I made my way to the door. When I passed the bowl of holy water, I dipped my fingers and, with tiny movements, crossed my chest.

"Isn't it a handsome building?" a voice announced behind me. I let go of the worn brass door handle and turned.

"It is," I answered without thinking, adding, "I never noticed you leaving the confession booth."

"You were buried in prayer," the lady whispered, tilting her head toward the sea of candles below the statue.

"Erm," I cleared my throat. *Buried—if only she knew my truth.*

"Something you lost … or some*one*?" A smile creased the skin around her sparkling eyes.

"Neither. It reminded me of home and attending Mass with my mother."

"Oh, yes? Where are you from?" Her insistence surprised me. She was probably in her fifties. The grey locks that framed her face contrasted with the rest of her hair.

What a relief it might be if I confided my sinful deed. Would she judge me, having just been to confession herself? What could she have told the priest? Such a tender, godly-looking woman.

"Germany."

"Marvel …" Before she could finish, I interrupted.

"Sorry, I must go."

"Wait," she said, touching my arm as I reached for the door. "I have no idea what a youthful woman like yourself is doing here. But I want you to know that you're special."

"Thank you." I coughed. "You're very kind."

"Jesus forgives anyone who prays with sincerity."

Was this a trick? Were my parents behind this?

"Look after yourself," she said, letting her hand slip off my coat as I opened the door.

"Thank you. I will," I said and walked out.

What a funny lady that was. Probably one of those holier-than-holy spinsters who never got a man and instead turned to an imaginary heavenly husband. I cringed. This was my dad speaking, not me. John would agree with the stranger, as would David. Only yesterday, he had observed a lesson of mine. "You have what it takes to be a *first-class* schoolteacher. The students hang on to your every word."

"That's because English kids are well-mannered. They'd be nothing else but polite."

"No, Pippa, I meant it. Your charisma inspires everyone around you."

His compliment still bothered me. He did not know how egotistical I had been. Pretence and emotional coldness were the traits I resented most in my family. Now, I loathed myself for revealing these same attributes in myself.

If they all knew the truth, including the good-hearted woman in the church, they'd be horrified: I had killed my child.

34

On my way home, I picked up a local paper, sat in my favourite café and ordered a slice of carrot cake. There was no hurry to return to university or Chris's house. He was in the middle of making travel arrangements, and watching him fill in paperwork, sort through his belongings and offer his study books to diverse alumni filled me with sadness. To distract myself, I spent most days in the library writing essays, compiling summaries of my seminars, and developing teaching materials for my portfolio.

The travel arrangements took up a considerable amount of Chris's time. As my university courses were ending, I spent most days in the library writing essays and compiling summaries of my seminars and work experience at Fulford School. At the same time, advertisements for the coming school year appeared in the newspaper.

Jobs in York were popular, and I did not see myself landing a position in one of the prestigious schools. Instead, I sought posts further afield. After all, there was not much to keep me here once Chris was gone. David assured me that I was in a powerful position. I was one of the few native German speakers in the region and had exceptional references. His praise continued to be tough to take.

"My goodness," I heard my father say. "What is this guy buttering you up for? Can they not find anyone from their own ranks? The barrel must be dry of decent fish."

Quietly, I was saying goodbye to York and bracing myself for a fresh start in an inner-city school where teacher turnover was high, and expectations of candidates were low.

One morning, John waved me over as I walked down the stairs.

"Hello, Pippa. At last. I bet you've not read the job ads today?"

"Not yet. Why?" A tingle shot through my body as John smirked and lifted his eyebrows. He nodded at the newspaper in front of him. As I approached, I spotted a block of text circled several times in ballpoint ink.

"Can I see?" I stood on my toes and leaned over through the window.

"There you are," he said, pushing the paper towards me. "I was about to shove this under your door had you not shown up."

My fingers trembled as I raised the page:

Archbishop Thomas School is looking to appoint a young, dynamic colleague to join the language department, majoring in German. This position is ideal for recruits to gain professional experience at one of York's most excellent schools.

"What do you say?" John shifted his head forward.

"Erm …" I cleared my throat. "They're Catholic, aren't they?" *I could not possibly be this hypocritical.*

"No, no. Anglican. It's the crème de la crème, Pippa. And perfect for you."

I lowered my hands, my fingers holding the paper.

"I don't know, John. Maybe too exclusive?"

"Pippa," John inspected me over his glasses, "never think you're not good enough for them. Who put those ideas in your head?"

I ignored his question. "I suppose I've nothing to lose." I hushed my voice.

"There you go. Take it with you. I've finished reading it."

With paper in hand, I raced across campus to the philosophy department, where I caught Chris relaxing with Eleanor at a table in the cafeteria.

"Hey, Pippa. It's good to see you."

He hugged me and pulled a chair over.

"Come sit with us. I'll get you a coffee. Do you want anything with that? Muffin?"

"No, thanks," I replied, baffled by the urgency in his tone. "Look what John gave me." I unfolded the paper and flattened it out on the table.

Eleanor was the first to react when she read the highlighted ad. "Wow, Archbishop Thomas." She bowed her head. "Your Excellency ..."

Chris put a coffee mug on the newspaper.

"Jeez, watch it," Eleanor hissed, lifting the drink, "or you'll jinx Pippa's future."

Chris bent over the paper, lifting one brow. "Pips, this is wonderful. And right around the corner."

The vast sports fields of the reputable school adjoined the university campus. My eyes veered from one to the other, deciding whether their enthusiasm was sincere.

"You guys are more excited than I am," I said, sipping my coffee.

"Well, you know, you don't get an opportunity like this daily. For us simple mortals, that school is unattainable. To get a job there is a once-in-a-lifetime opportunity," Eleanor said.

"That's right, Pippa," Chris explained. "Until a few years ago, it was a boarding school reserved for the top echelon. I bet you'd get a fascinating look behind the scenes working there."

Eleanor touched Chris's forearm as if she had had an epiphany. "And it's only a few minutes' walk from the house—from *our* house."

Chris's eyes flashed wide. "Of course, *our* house." He echoed Eleanor's emphasis. He turned to me. "Because it's, erm, so our house ..." Chris squinted and tore tiny cuts into the corner of the newspaper.

Eleanor glanced at him. "In a few weeks, we'll be gone. Don's as good as moved out. I'm leaving at the end of the month, and Chris, well ..." She nudged him as if to prompt him to speak.

Putting his hand on my arm, he said, "I'll also be off soon to say goodbye to my family in Oxford."

He hesitated. I wondered when he was going, but my thoughts declined to shift.

"I'm coming back for the holidays, though," Chris continued, "but for a moment, imagine if we didn't pull out of the tenancy?"

He looked at me. What was he getting at?

"Well," Eleanor butted in, "Chris and I were just saying how you could move in. Then everything stays *in the family,* so to speak." She giggled.

I shuddered. "I see."

I pushed Chris' hand off my arm. "In the family, huh?" Heat rose in my neck. "How convenient for you both," I said, and my face tingled.

"Pippa, please don't take this the wrong way," Chris said. "It was purely a thought. I'm sorry. But imagine if you got a job close by ... you could walk to work."

I lifted the mug to my mouth to shield my embarrassment. Was I cruel to insinuate they were taking advantage?

"I thought you liked it to remain *our house.*" Chris took my hand. "Forgive me, Pips."

Eleanor nodded. I managed a weak smile, and she parted her lips to exhale.

I mimed, "Am I too Boche?"

Chris crinkled his eyes and nose, holding his thumb and forefinger a few millimetres apart. *A little.*

"Can I pay the rent on my own?" I attempted a matter-of-fact tone.

"Ha, on the salary you'll be on, sure. And you could rent out a room to make it easier," Eleanor said.

"And, love," Chris winked, "we'd have a landline."

I imagined Ursula and Yvonne visiting with Tom. There'd be enough space to put them up in the house. Careful not to show my sudden change of mind, I hid my excitement.

"But I've still got to apply. Who knows if I'll be considered for the job?"

"The Archbishop would be a fool not to accept *this* particular candidate." Chris put his hands on my shoulder as if to straighten me up. He grinned. With both hands, he clutched my face, pulled me towards him and kissed me on the mouth.

"Well, I'll get to writing my application." My heart beat in my chest, relieved that I had managed to turn my suspicions around.

35

My loose coat danced in the summer breeze. Excited, I stumbled over the entrance steps into the university cafeteria.

"Hey, watch it," a student holding a coffee mug grumbled.

Sorry," I reacted without glancing at her.

I picked up a cheerful voice. "Well, someone's in a hurry." Chris sat at a table by the window, folding his book shut and moving it aside.

"May I offer my congratulations?" He grinned and rose with his arms outstretched.

"You may, Chris. You may." I giggled and ran to meet him. We hugged.

"Great, Pips. What did I tell you? They'd be stupid not to take on such an exceptional woman." He let go of me. "This calls for a celebration. Let's join the others."

Don and Eleanor had settled by a wooden table in the sun outside the student bar. When Eleanor saw me, she jumped off her seat. "You've done it, haven't you? I can tell by the look on your face. Congratulations, Pippa." She ran towards me.

Chris beamed a radiant smile.

"Well done, you. A pint? Wine? Champagne?" Don whooped.

We told him our orders, and he vanished inside.

"Next round's on me," I called after him.

"So, how was it? I want all the details," Eleanor prompted, straining her upper body across the table.

"Awesome," I sought a term to sum up my impression. "Ancient, dark, lots of wood, they use real fireplaces. People were so lovely."

Don balanced the drinks on a tray as he returned from the bar. "So, Pippa, what's behind these ancient walls, unattainable for the likes of me?"

"It's like a Jane Austen novel," I said. "It's a whole different world. I genuinely didn't think they'd hire me."

"Did you have to teach?" Chris asked. "Give a trial lesson?"

"No, nothing like that. But there was a member of the Parents Council and another senior official with a title I cannot recall—someone from the Department of Education. I was nervous as hell. They asked me different questions, requested examples of good lessons I'd given in my traineeship, and asked what I'd learnt from less successful classes."

"That's when you answered, 'there are none', right?" Don cheered.

Chris looked at me with a quiet and sincere smile.

"What is it?" I asked him. "What's on your mind?"

"I am proud of you," he said. I winced, hoping the shudder that ran across my body remained unnoticed. Chris drew me over by the shoulders to kiss my hair. "I knew it, Pips; if you have to be *Boche*, you'll be *Boche*." His grin broadened.

I told them about the day's proceedings and the different candidates I'd met. One man had dropped out after lunch.

"It's weird how it works over here," I said. "After each stage, they asked us if we were still serious candidates. And at one such moment, the guy said he didn't think he'd fit in with the school. What a cheek and so discourteous, I thought. I would have sat it out until the end of the day."

"But why? Being forthright about your impressions and feelings is essential in such a setting. Otherwise, you're wasting not only their time but your own." Don studied me, dismayed, and my gut churned.

With a smile, I recalled what my mother had instilled in me: *Take the low road. Turn the other cheek.* From an early age, shame plagued me whenever I did the opposite and stood up for myself.

"It was an all-day selection process. The people there had given their time. You don't want to antagonise anyone, do you?" I noticed their baffled faces.

"I think Don's right," Eleanor interjected. "Imagine you continue feigning interest in something even though you realise early it's not for you. What if they end up offering you the job to someone who would never take it?"

I felt my face burn.

"Well, my Pippa wanted the job. She came, saw, and conquered the panel," Chris interjected, and I was thankful.

"By the way, can we start moving my stuff to your place afterwards?" Despite my triumph, I was impatient to change the topic.

"Sure. We can shift the lot ourselves. I guess one or two taxi rides, and it's done." His hand patted my thigh as if to reassure me.

After a few more rounds, we left for the college. John was sitting on the floor, his back bent towards us, fixing a socket. As we neared, he turned. With a screwdriver in one hand, leaning on a toolbox with the other, he sighed and stood up.

"Hello, you two. I hope you bring good news."

"John, may I present the new German teacher at Archbishop Thomas School in York?" Chris whirled me around the hall.

"Wonderful, congratulations!" John's eyes sparkled. "I've been thinking of you, Pippa, all morning."

"So that's your secret to success," Chris chuckled. "John's positive vibes."

"Exactly. Looks like I have *you* to thank, John," I replied. "Anyway, that was the good news. The even better news is that I can stay in York. We've come to collect some of my stuff," I added.

"Shame that you're moving out." A gloomy shadow flew across the elderly man's face. "But with your workplace around the corner, I hope you will pop in from time to time for a cuppa." He winked at Chris. "I'll keep an eye on her."

Chris patted him on the shoulder. "Thanks, John, I appreciate it."

Upstairs, I stood by the window and untied the glass bird that had been looking out over the park for the last few months. Wrapped in a sheet of newspaper, I placed it on a box of books.

"I guess that's everything," I said. "I'll do a last check in the bathroom and kitchen."

Chris lifted the crate from the table.

"Everything packed?" he asked as I stepped back into the room.

"Yeah. Let's go."

A taxi dropped us off at my new home. Eleanor had offered for me to store some of my belongings in her room. I didn't want to impose on Chris's space. It was still a fortnight before he'd move out. I heard him walking around the house, opening and closing cupboards and rearranging his bookshelves for me.

"Hey, Pips, can I leave these towels here?" he called from the hallway.

"Yes, that's fine. Saves me having to do the laundry too often." I tried to sound light-hearted.

"Shit. I *had* hoped to pack the washing machine." Chris laughed.

"Hilarious," I chided.

The phone rang.

"Hello," Chris answered the call, still chuckling.

It was silent.

"Mmm, mmm ... is she conscious?" He spoke in a muffled voice.

I froze and held my breath.

"All right, Mum, I'll see what I can do. I ... erm ... I ... yes, everything's packed. Yes, in theory... tomorrow ..."

The receiver clicked, and it was quiet. I sat on the bed and resumed breathing in silence. *This was terrible news.*

"That was my mother." Chris stood in the opening of the door. "My grandma had a stroke. She's in hospital,"

The last word made my stomach jolt. "Oh, is it bad?"

"She's paralysed on one side and doesn't recognise anyone." He moved his hand through his hair before wiping it across his face. "Bloody hell, of all things, this happens—now of all times."

His shoulders hanging, he stared at the floor.

I struggled for something to say. "Your father's mother or your mother's?"

"Mum's," he said. "I ... erm ... I have to go there. Before it's too late."

"What?" My jaw dropped. I gathered myself. "I'm so sorry."

It took several seconds until the significance of this news unfolded.

"What about Japan?" Was there an optimistic ring in my voice?

Chris's face darkened. He tapped his head. "I need to let this sink in." He sighed and crunched his hands into a fist. "Argh, why Gran? She's such a strong woman."

Close family ties were unknown to me. I tasted the grease of bacon and fried potatoes in the back of my throat. Was that all that remained as a memory of my granddad's death?

I put a handful of socks into an old cupboard and pushed a few of Chris's clothes to one side.

"Empty my stuff onto the bed," he said, rummaging through the contents of the dresser with both hands. "I'd better take everything. Who knows ..." He sounded distant, as if his mind had already moved out.

"I'll put the kettle on," I whispered and went downstairs.

The creeping floorboards gave away his pacing in his room. After a while, the sound stopped, and I heard his footsteps on the stairs. He sank into a chair, rested both elbows on the kitchen table and nodded as I placed a mug in front of him.

"So, when will you go?"

He glanced into the cup as if to look for an answer on the bottom of the stained china. "I'll take the first train tomorrow morning. It means I can be at the hospital around ten. I just hope she holds out."

"Tomorrow? That soon." The words escaped before I could capture them.

Chris's chin quivered; he bit his lip.

That means tonight is our last night. The woman was old. Did we have to sacrifice our remaining precious days for her?

"I'll help you pack. I'm so sorry for you and your family." I tried to suppress my trembling voice.

By evening, Chris had packed and carried his suitcases and a rucksack into the hallway.

"Goodness, what's in here?" I tried to push his luggage with my foot.

"Mostly books and paperwork. I'll sort it out at my parents' house."

Why didn't he say *I'll pick my things up later*? The weight of his luggage told me that this exit was indeed final. I had imagined our remaining moments differently. Our bodies intertwined. Scattered items of clothing that could belong to either of us. I had envisioned whispers of *I love you* and assurances of fidelity. Instead, we sat on the bed, drained. Chris was leaning against the headboard with his legs stretched out. I was resting my head against his shoulder. Both of us were worn out. He from packing, phoning, and organising, me from concealing the pain of parting.

"I don't think I'll be able to sleep tonight," I said, taking a big sip from my wine glass before I settled my head on Chris's chest. His heart was a clock, ticking away precious time.

"Hmm," sounded from deep in his torso.

"Do that again."

"Hmm, hmm," Chris murmured. The soothing vibration travelled through my ear. A sharp pain shot through my heart. This is what the baby had felt before I had killed it. I squeezed my eyes shut and swallowed a lump down.

The humming became a melody as he murmured lyrics about a starlit sky.

I pressed my ear against his body. "What song is that?"

"'Vincent' by Don McLean," he explained and continued humming a few more lines before he stopped.

"Keep singing, please," I urged him, like a child begging for a lullaby.

"I don't know all the words. Besides, it's a sad song."

"Even better," I replied. "Come on, please, keep singing."

He whispered the following words, ran his hand over my hair and purred more of the melody before continuing. What was his song about? Who would not listen to whom, and why not?

I slipped my fingers between his. "Don't stop," I urged him in a whisper. "I want to hear the rest."

"… our love… hm hm … true …" he continued to sing and let the song fade out, crooning.

"Just once more," I asked, and Chris repeated the ballad until all the lyrics returned to him. I fell asleep to the image of blue skies dotted with grey clouds.

36

"Shit. Pippa, we overslept." Chris's panicked cry pierced through my skull. The mattress wobbled as he rolled out of bed, dragging the duvet.

"Ouch." I gathered the pillow over my head and patted around in the dark to locate the blanket.

"It's a quarter past five. My train leaves in half an hour. Can you call for a taxi? I must get ready."

Train? Taxi? The words hit me like an ice-cold shower. I peeked and captured Chris's naked body escaping through the open door. Next, I heard rushing water.

A half-full wine bottle stood beside the bed, and an empty one on the desk. I flinched when I saw the bare bookcase, boxes, and crumpled newspaper.

With a groan, I sat up and, with one foot, fished for my jeans on the floor. I steadied myself with one hand on any furniture within reach. What to do? Breakfast? There was no time for that. Coffee was easier. Chris did not drink it on an empty stomach. I felt nauseous and tasted bile in the back of my throat. *Call a taxi,–right?* I took the stairs, clinging to the railing with both hands, and in the kitchen, I shuffled through bus timetables, take-away menus, and postcards pinned to a corkboard by the window. *If he misses the train, I'll have him with me longer.*

"Did you call?" Chris shouted from upstairs.

"Hold on." There was a yellow and black taxi card, and I dismissed the idea of delaying his departure.

"York-Centre taxi office, where to?" a lady's voice inquired.

Nowhere, I thought. "To the station."

"Where from?"

I gave the address.

"What time is the train?"

"At a quarter to six."

"I'll send a driver over straight away."

I replaced the receiver. "On his way," I called upstairs when I heard Chris's footsteps. He ran straight into the entrance hall and grabbed his jacket. My stomach tightened. Everything had happened so soon.

"Shall I prepare a sandwich?" My thoughts whirled through my brain.

"I'll buy something at the station. Thank you. Pips, this is dreadful… Oh, come here …" He stepped forward and hugged me. "I'm sorry, love," he said, and I buried my face in his shoulder, inhaling his scent.

"I'll call you when I get there." He turned to the windowsill, which was cluttered with notebooks and pens. "Let me jot down my parents' number." He tore the edge of a newspaper and scribbled.

"Just in case," he said, embracing me and studying my face. I bit my lip and blinked to stop tears welling up. "Pips, love. Don't be sad. This is not the end. We'll continue where we …"

Outside, a car engine sounded.

"Bloody hell, that was fast."

He pulled my face towards him, kissed me, and dashed to the front door. I stood behind him. Chris waved to the driver.

"Have you got everything?" A feeling of loss and anxiety overwhelmed me: there was too much to say and no time to find the words.

Chris mumbled something and lifted the suitcases in the back of the car. The driver stood close by and closed the boot. I picked up the backpack and stepped out the door.

"Wait there, love," Chris ran up to me, "you're barefoot, and the pavement is wet."

He shook his head with a smile as he took the rucksack from me, ran back to the car, and put it on the back seat.

My heart plummeted: was that it?

"Be right back," I heard him say to the driver before he returned to me. He squeezed his lips into a painful-looking smile.

"Sorry I'm in a rush," he said, taking my hands. "But maybe it's just as well. I hate long goodbyes." He lifted my hands to his lips.

My chin quivered. I glanced sideways and took a sharp breath.

"Pippa, when I return, we'll pick up precisely where we left off."

"Sure thing." I tried to laugh, my voice throaty. "I hope your grandma gets better."

Why couldn't I think of something loving to say? I couldn't care less about an old woman I'd never met. If I felt anything for her, it was anger.

"We have to go," a voice called from the car.

"Go," I said, pretending to laugh. "I need a pee."

"That's how I love you: All Boche," Chris replied with a laugh, kissed me on the forehead, ran to the car and got in.

I watched him pull out the seat belt and fasten it. I saw his hand wave; his lips moved to say a muted "Love you". Our eyes remained locked until the taxi faded from view.

As the front door closed with a thud, I noticed his winter coat on the hook. *The only thing I have left of him.* I touched the sturdy material and recalled the garment flapping in the wind to the rhythm of his pace. I gazed around the kitchen. Had he forgotten anything else? The clock above the refrigerator showed twenty to six. Would he turn up at the station on time? In slow motion, I sat at the table. Every noise made my ears prick up, and listen: was that a car stopping in front of the door? Did I hear footsteps? The minute hand of the clock passed nine. His train was leaving now. Chris's tea mug from the night before stood on the table. I clutched it and brought it to my mouth. Thoughts floated through my head with no context. I was in a void. He was gone.

What am I going to do? Two, four, six, eight—I counted the patterns in the curtain.

A shiver ran down my back. Had I been sitting there for a long time? It was getting on for half past six. All the while, the train carried him further away. Had he reached Leeds? It would be another couple of hours before he could call. There was nothing I could do but stay indoors to wait for the phone to ring. Gathering the limited energy that I had, I crawled up the stairs. My legs felt limp, my mind dazed.

As I lowered my head, I felt something in the pillowcase. A square stood out in the fabric. Chris must have put it there. A book? I reached inside and pulled out a record. The single cover looked aged, the paper faded to a watery yellow, and the corners were torn. I turned it over. Roberta Flack, "The first time ever I saw your face." I had never heard of the singer or the song, but the title sent goosebumps down my spine. How annoying that there was no stereo in the house. Holding the record in one hand, I pulled the covers over me and inhaled the scent of Chris's body.

Ring, ring … I jumped up and ran to the telephone.

"Hello?"

"Hi, it's me. I've arrived safely."

"Chris, it's wonderful to hear your voice. How was the trip? Are you at the hospital?"

"No, she's on a ventilator. I'm about to go there with my mother. We're preparing for the worst. How are you feeling?"

"Sad, I …"

Chris interrupted me, "By the way, be careful when you get into bed…"

"Found it. How am I supposed to listen to it without a record player?"

"Look under the stairs. I'm sure there's one there amongst the boxes."

"All right," I promised. "I'll check later. I miss you here," I added, and he said he felt the same.

After we hung up, I felt an oppressive silence. I stood rooted to the spot and focused on something to hear. Nothing. I perceived a pulsating murmur in my head.

Trance-like, I gathered up the used dishes of the last few days and washed them on autopilot. By evening, I had dusted, cleaned, and tidied the house.

My utensils were on Chris's desk, my books on the shelf, and my jewellery box on the table beside the bed. Seeing our blended possessions comforted me: space was the only thing that separated us. It was a temporary split. I stuck photos on the wall, this time leaving the ones of my family in an envelope in the drawer. The note that Chris had left on my door months ago got a prominent place in the middle. My glass bird dangled in the kitchen window. It would be the first to see Chris return.

There was a lingering hope that he might come back to York before the flight to Japan. I searched his desk for documents he might have forgotten and looked in the wardrobe for essential items of clothing. His next call destroyed my illusion.

"My grandma passed away last night."

"Oh, Chris. I'm so sorry." I aimed for a compassionate tone. My mind was spinning: what did this mean for us?

"She had a second stroke. It was fatal."

"How awful," I continued, feeling no pity. I had never experienced the death of a loved one.

"I'm kind of numb," Chris said, and I had to pinch myself not to shout into the phone, *That's how I've been feeling since you left.*

"Hm. So what's happening now?"

"My mother's taking it terribly. We're all shellshocked."

"Of course." I willed with all my heart that Chris would say he'd cancelled Japan.

"When, er … when is the funeral?" Did he not want me there to support him?

"Next week."

"But aren't you flying then?" I was getting nervous. He was close to his mother. Maybe her grief had made him change his mind?

"Yes, on Friday. The funeral is on Thursday, thank God. I couldn't leave Mum alone now—well, I mean, for the funeral," he added, and his words extinguished my shred of hope. There was no way we could meet before then. His parents probably did not even know of my existence. My head spun, but this was not the moment to complain.

"I have to go. We have so many things to organise. Please don't be angry."

"Of course not," I said. I wasn't angry, but disappointed. And immensely sad for both of us.

Germany 1990

37

"Karl, drop Pippa's bag by the washing machine."

Karl lunged towards the canvas holdall. Pippa firmly held onto the handles.

"Mum, I'll do it later."

"What's the matter, young lady? Is your mother not allowed to see your silky underwear?"

Karl chuckled as his face flushed. A sensation he hadn't known for many years surged up from his groin. Savouring it, he let out an indiscernible moan.

"It's just that I don't want to cause anyone extra work," Pippa said.

"Since when did you consider us?" Karl grumbled and pinched Pippa's hand as he grabbed the bag. "Now, give it here. Or is there something in there you're keeping from us?"

Pippa flinched as he ripped it from her hands.

Her mum gave a resounding sigh. "Tell me the truth. Are you hiding something?"

Pippa's mouth twisted with frustration.

"What are you talking about, Mum?"

Before Waltraud could answer, Karl clutched the blue bag tightly. He pushed his face close to Pippa's.

"Let me tell you this, young lady. Just because you're a student does not mean you have the green light to behave however you like."

He felt his daughter's body heat as tears gathered in her eyes.

Without a chance to escape his intense stare, Pippa's voice quivered. "Mum, please, what's he talking about?"

"If we find out you're on the pill, that there is a boyfriend back in Cologne—not only can you do your laundry but also find another sponsor for your studies!" He air-quoted the last words.

Pippa kicked her shoes off and launched them into the hallway corner. She slipped her coat off her back and bundled it over the bannister before following her parents through the kitchen into the utility room.

The unmistakable smell of washing powder burned her nostrils. She wiped her nose with the back of her hand.

"Mum, let me …"

She bent to the bag, but her mum was quicker. With one hand, Waltraud restrained Pippa from reaching into her laundry whilst tipping the contents on the floor.

"You have no idea how the machine works," she said, pulling the washing from the bag.

Whilst Waltraud sorted shirts, trousers, and socks into piles on the floor, Karl squeezed his eyelids and focused on his wife's movement until he spotted what he'd been looking for. One arm lying on his back, he leaned in, stretched out the other hand, and took hold of a pair of black knickers.

Pippa blushed as she watched her dad dangle the flimsy piece of cotton in the air, studying it with amplified interest.

"Dad, please put that down, please." She took a step forward to grab her clothes, but her dad stretched his arm further into the air, out of her reach.

"Look at this, Waltraud," her father said, unruffled by Pippa's presence. "Do you think our daughter is spending time studying English when she's not with us? I wonder if she's up to very different activities."

He hoped his wife and daughter hadn't noticed the excitement in his loins.

38

Karl closed his car's boot, moved onto the pavement, and inspected the distance between the parked cars behind and in front. *Let's hope we get this done before any of these Turkish Kanakes smashes into my car.*

"Dad, are you coming?" Pippa stood halfway inside the four-storey building, holding open the door made from weighty safety glass with one hand whilst dragging a large suitcase with the other.

"Careful with that case. I promised Mum to bring this back in one piece." Karl shook his head at the sight of his daughter, narrowed his eyes, and tilted his head back. *The state of those windows.* Why did she have to move in with a hoard of uncivilised hubble-bubble suckers?

He followed Pippa and lifted the heavy luggage.

"Don't touch anything here," he muttered, and as Pippa hoisted herself up, holding onto the bannister, he repeated his warning in a stern tone. "You've no idea what you might catch."

"Dad, please. Yvonne said there was a cleaning rota. Will you please stop being so paranoid?"

"Watch your smart mouth, young lady. Just because you're a student doesn't entitle you to speak to your father like that." He pulled a handkerchief out of his coat pocket to protect his hand whilst holding on to the wooden railing.

Pippa stopped before a plain white door when they reached the third landing. Karl bent to read the label above the doorbell.

"Oh, there seems to be a lot of comings and goings in this establishment," he said, without trying to hide his sarcasm.

"Dad, please. Yvonne and I will replace it now that we are the permanent tenants."

"Let's hope it's not unduly permanent, Phillippa. This is scarcely the surroundings for…"

The door opened. "I thought I heard voices. Why didn't you ring? I would've helped. Is there more stuff downstairs?" The girl standing at the entrance spoke in a flurry whilst jostling to take the heavy bag off Pippa.

"Dad, this is Yvonne."

Yvonne blushed and bit her lip. "Oops, excuse me. You must be Mr. Olbig. Very pleased to meet you."

"Yes, I must be." Karl couldn't resist giving the young woman a mocking, fake smile. He glanced at her baggy T-shirt, which caressed her naked thighs. *Is she not wearing a bra?*

Mesmerised by the sight of the carefree student, Karl continued to squeeze past, holding in his belly. Yvonne smiled and pointed her arm toward a door at the far end of the long corridor. *She smells delicious.*

"Pippa's room is right over there."

Karl tightened his eyes and turned, his gaze resting for a moment on the girl's petite waist.

"I see," he said and swallowed, his Adam's apple jumping like a cat held in a sack.

Germany 1992

39

The sky's reflection in the language department's windowpanes irritated Yvonne's eyes. She fluttered her eyelids and glanced up into the heavens. It was odd weather today—not a hint of sunshine, yet bright enough for sunglasses.

I wonder how Pippa is doing. Yvonne hoped for her friend to succeed in her last exams. *God knows she deserves it.* In the last year, they'd had a lot of fun, and out of the group of students Yvonne had lived with, Pippa had become a close friend. Her stomach crunched at the thought of her departure, despite the selfishness of it. *She hasn't even met Tom yet. They'd hit it off immediately.*

The whiff of warm coffee and paper hit Yvonne as she pushed the entrance door open.

When she let the heavy door close behind her, she heard a bang, followed by a loud groan. "Ouch."

Yvonne turned. "Sorry, let me help you." She held the door ajar for the young mother, who balanced her toddler under one arm like a sleeping bag. The boy giggled and swung his arms like a swimmer doing lengths.

"Hi. Is this little man joining you for lectures?"

Susanne nodded and cradled the boy in her arms.

"Yes, Vincent is joining me whenever I can arrange it."

Yvonne reached out. Vincent leaned into her, and the mother let him sail into Yvonne's arms. "He's at this beautiful age where he has faith in everyone."

Yvonne held Vincent up, and they beamed at each other with joy. The child's pink lips glistened. A thin trail of saliva emerged from his mouth, shining in the light like a spider's web.

"Mind you, today it's just for bringing back a few books." Susanne let a bag thump to the ground and reached for her son.

"Thank you," she said, positioning the toddler to sit upright on her hip. "And first, young man, we're having a scrumptious piece of cake." She tickled his nose with her finger. Vincent chuckled.

Susanne turned to Yvonne with a sunny smile. "Fancy a coffee?"

"No, I can't this morning," Yvonne replied. "I'm meeting Pippa. She's about to finish her final exam." Yvonne breathed out a sigh. "Professor Werther."

Susanne laughed. "The pipe-smoking feminist, right? I hope Pippa passes okay. I guess you'll have to advertise her room for next semester?"

"I'd love for her to stay on, but if I'm honest, she needs to escape."

Susanne opened her eyes. "Escape?"

Yvonne pressed her lips and blew out through her nostrils. "I shouldn't be telling you this, but her parents are hard work. She gets the blame for everything and no credit when she does well. In their eyes, she can't do anything right. They expect her to move right back in with them so that they can keep her under their thumb."

Susanne quivered. "Brrrr ... that sounds depressing. I hope she'll break away."

"So do I. But independence doesn't appear to be something that her folks value. They are extremely oppressive. Including her sister."

The boy on Susanne's arm wiggled.

"Sounds like a proper crab bucket," the mother said. "Remind me never to do that to you, Vinny." She nuzzled her nose against her son's.

"What do you mean, crab bucket?" Yvonne looked at Vince and next Susanne, puzzled.

"If one crab tries to break free and climb the sides, another will yank it back into the bucket."

"I get it. If I can't be happy, neither can you." Yvonne's eyes glazed as she recalled the afternoons she had spent comforting Pippa after another depressing visit from her parents.

"Absolutely. A shared demise is easier to endure, kind of thing." Susanne twitched her nose. "Now, speaking about demise, I'd better check this fellow's nappy before we queue for lunch."

Yvonne laughed. "You do that. It was nice talking to you. Take care." She stroked Vincent's cheek and turned to skip to the library.

40

"Karl, did you wipe the table?" Waltraud stuck her head out the kitchen window, watching her husband set up the plastic garden furniture.

He shot her a firm look. "Waltraud, let's keep it down. The neighbours."

His wife turned to check the neighbouring garden. The conifer hedge they had planted as a boundary remained less substantial than the garden centre had said.

She leaned out further and spoke softly. "I'm just saying, Karl. It's been stored in the cellar for a year. You need to wipe it." She tossed a wet cloth onto Karl's shoulder, and he yanked it from his shirt.

Heat flared in Karl's neck. "Bloody woman," he muttered. "The house is clean enough to eat off the floor."

The ringing of the telephone broke Waltraud's train of thought. "Hang on, the phone."

"You'd better get it. It'll be your sister with something new to moan about, without a doubt."

He exhaled with relief when he turned and saw the window empty. *Now, how do I put together this monstrous contraption?*

He was about to tie the flowery cushion to the sunbed frame when Waltraud hurried through the door. Karl widened his eyes. His wife stopped on the pebble wash tiles, as she wasn't wearing any slippers.

"What on earth…?" He halted mid-sentence when Waltraud put her finger to her lips and pointed her head towards the house.

Maintaining eye contact, he placed the cushion on the table. It slid off and fell to the ground, covering his toes. Waltraud gestured for him to enter the kitchen after her.

Karl followed the instructions. Waltraud lingered by the telephone. Her husband furrowed his brows and mimed, "What?"

"Phil-lip-pa," Waltraud gestured back.

Karl coughed to clear his throat. He grabbed the receiver out of her hand.

"Phillippa?"

The line was quiet for a second.

"Phillippa, it's your father. What did you just say?" Karl breathed into the receiver. He threw a disapproving look at Waltraud, who leaned back when he searched for eye contact again. "You said you wanted to join my company." Karl listened intensely. "Aha. And when will that start? You haven't finished your exams yet."

Waltraud observed a thick artery pulse in his neck. Karl's eyes closed.

"Pippa, listen carefully—" he said, but his daughter interrupted him. Karl looked perplexed, then gathered himself. "If you do that, young lady. If you go off to England, you're no longer a daughter of mine."

Waltraud flinched. Her eyes shimmered with tears. Karl wiped his eyes and forehead.

"You heard me: if you go off to England, Phillippa, you cease to be our daughter. Your mother and I will disown you, and you'll be on your own. What you do next is your decision. Goodbye."

Waltraud shielded her mouth with both hands and stared at Karl. How she admired his forcefulness. It would bring their youngest daughter to heel.

He slammed the receiver onto the telephone. "A teacher training course in England. Over my dead body." An image of Pippa strolling across Tower Bridge in London came to his mind. As a young man, he had perused travel books and the pictures of the British capital with its historic buildings and elegant inhabitants had been one of his favourites. Pippa would not stay solo for long. His groin ached.

Waltraud let out a brief shriek.

"What did she say, Karl?"

"What do you think she said? She stuttered and stammered and switched on the waterworks."

Waltraud bit her lip. "Shall we ring her back? I mean …" She struggled to speak.

"Waltraud, I don't give a damn about your opinion. I meant what I said, and I hope we stand together on this."

Waltraud responded, "Of course we do, Karl. Of course." She watched her husband walk back and forth in the hallway. They had presented Pippa with endless opportunities for happiness. God knows, they'd cut corners so their daughter could go to university. *Infuriating how she prioritizes her own happiness over the family. How ungrateful.*

"She's had all her fun in Cologne. I mean, it's obvious what she's been up to." Karl paced around the room.

Waltraud nodded.

"There's a complete apartment up there for her to move into." He tilted his head up to the ceiling. Waltraud followed his movement with her eyes. "There are schools over here, teaching jobs over here, and plenty of young men over here. But no, Madam fancies an Englishman." White traces of saliva formed in the corner of his mouth.

With every step closer to the telephone, Karl stared at the receiver.

Eventually, he stopped before the compact leather-bound directory and flipped the cardboard pages to "S".

He took hold of the receiver and dialled. "Sandra, it's your father. We just had a call from your sister. She wants to relocate to England."

There was silence on the far end of the line. Waltraud listened but could not hear.

Karl nodded, pressing the receiver to his ear. "Yes, absolutely. Yes, that's what I said. Yes, you do that."

He ended the call. "Sandra will go over there and talk some sense into her sister."

England 1993

41

I spent the next few days in numbness until a letter from Archbishop Thomas School reminded me that I, too, was embarking on a new chapter in life. It was an invitation to get to know my colleagues and prepare for the coming school year—a welcome distraction, as the funeral arrangements completely absorbed Chris.

Alex, the Head of the Department, and Erica, a teacher I had met at the interview, greeted me and led me into a classroom. They had joined several desks to form a large square.

"This is Anne," Alex said, pointing to a youthful-looking woman making moves to stand up.

"Good afternoon and welcome. I haven't been here that long either. I teach French." Anne introduced herself with an elegant accent. She held out her tanned arm, her hand resting in mine. Her brown eyes glowed, and dark curls framed her face.

"Hello, nice to meet you," I replied, struck by her radiant beauty.

"And this is Pat ..." Alex began, but she interrupted him.

"We've met before," Pat announced, "at your interview." She laughed and waved across the table. I shrugged with an apologetic smile.

Muttering sounded from the corridor. Someone kicked the door. We looked around and saw a stack of books appear in the opening, carried by a tall, young man with short, black hair that matched his dark eyes.

"Here they are, just delivered. There are still boxes in the hall downstairs."

With a dull thud, he placed the books on a table. Gasping for breath, he looked at me.

"Hi, so you're Pippa. I'm Jim; I teach German, too."

"Hello, nice to meet you," I lifted my hand for a brief wave. "I hope I can remember everyone's name." I smiled and shrugged.

"We've all been there." Jim held his arm out and tilted his head back. "You felt the same way, didn't you, Anne?"

His colleague nodded and snorted. "Ah oui," she said, widening her eyes, "in the beginning it was a nightmare. And the names of the children … mon dieu …"

She waved mid-air and laughed.

Jim walked around the seats and stopped behind me. He tapped my shoulder.

"It'll be alright. I have the classroom next to you. If you want to, I'll take you under my wing for a bit."

"Thanks, that's a kind offer," I replied and looked at Alex, who gave Jim an approving nod. "I think …" I added.

I turned around to look at Jim and noticed tiny scars and dimples on his neck and face. He must have had bad acne in the past.

"Coffee or tea?" Pat had stood up and placed a mug in front of everyone.

"You'll have to excuse our mismatch of cups, Pippa. There are no coasters either," she said.

"Coffee for me, please." Anne offered me a biscuit. As I took a bite, I leaned back and looked at my new colleagues. I could not wait for the term to start.

Pat gave me a tour of the building before Jim explained the layout of his classroom and helped me position the tables into a giant horseshoe, with my desk at the front. We shared out the textbooks and stationery and cleared the walls of tattered posters—witnesses to the past school year. By the end of the afternoon, names and anecdotes of parents, teachers, and students were bouncing off the inside of my skull.

"Can I do anything else?" I flicked through the top of the pile of dictionaries in Alex's room.

"No, Pippa, I don't think so. You must be exhausted."

"Yes, you'd better go home and digest everything. There will be enough time to finish things just before term starts." Pat said and walked into the room with a bloated bin bag, scraps of paper sticking out.

"Bye, everyone, and thank you so much for making me feel welcome," I shouted and turned to walk down the corridor, clutching a set of books to my chest.

Shouts of "You too," "Bye, Pippa," and "Auf Wiedersehen" echoed from various rooms.

I had not seen John since I'd moved, and I was excited to tell him about my day. Just before I reached the stairs to the main entrance, I heard a voice behind me.

"You're Pippa, aren't you? Glad I caught you."

I turned around.

"Hello." The tall young man smiled and stretched his arm out in my direction.

"That's right, Pippa Olbig. Hello," I replied. The books tumbled to the floor as I aimed to accept his hand.

"Shit," I swore and apologised at once.

"Not to worry, it's my fault for jumping on you like that." He crouched and helped me pick up the volumes from the floor. He wore a washed-out denim shirt. I noticed his long, dark hair tied in a ponytail.

"Sorry. I was going to drop by your classroom at lunchtime. I'm Martin." He handed me the books. He wore two small, golden loops in his left earlobe. I tried not to stare as I heard my father's tutting about men and jewellery.

"You're not a language teacher too, are you?"

"No, I'm the counsellor. I work with students as well as colleagues."

I blinked in astonishment.

He gave me a mischievous smile, "… and for the kitchen staff, the gardeners, the caretakers. The list is endless."

"Do they need a *counsellor* in this school?" I shook my head in disbelief. "It's idyllic."

"Well, fortunately, I have not had a request from the gardener yet. If *he* needs counselling, things have gone bad indeed." He laughed. "I was going to introduce myself sooner, but there are quite a few new members of staff to see. So far, I've met Matthew, a maths teacher. Before then, Alicia from the science department. I'm pleased I've bumped into you."

"Indeed. It's just … I need to …"

Martin raised both hands in the air. "No, no, I don't want to keep you. It's been a long day. We can meet another day this week. Unless you want to join me at the local animal shelter."

He studied my puzzled face, then explained. "I do voluntary work with the RSPCA on the other side of town."

"Oh, have you got time for that?"

"I make time. Voluntary work is more rewarding than it's time-consuming. They welcome new volunteers." He smiled at me.

"Anyway, it would be nice to have a proper chat. How about tomorrow?"

"Yes, I could come back in the morning. I've got nothing better to do, anyway."

Martin grinned. His blue eyes matched the colour of his shirt.

"Oh, no, I didn't mean it like that." I felt heat rising up my neck. "I mean, I'll be back tomorrow."

"Fine. Shall we say ten o'clock?"

"Yeah, great."

"See you tomorrow then," he chirped, turned towards a door and disappeared.

After walking along the country road, I reached the university campus and saw John from afar. He stood in front of the college, leaning on a broomstick with his eyes closed, facing the sun.

I cheered from afar. When he spotted me, he stretched his arms out wide, the broom swinging back and forth.

"Pippa, all alone?" He raised his brows and sharpened his focus on the path behind me.

"I was at school all day, John. It was great," I replied.

"Ah, that makes sense. I wondered where you'd left your other half." John lifted his chin.

"Chris is with his parents."

John's puzzled reaction reminded me he had no clue about recent events. When I told him what had been going on, he let out a deep sigh.

"I'm doubly sorry, Pippa. About his grandmother's death, of course, and the fact that your last days together were cut short so abruptly."

"You can say that again. It's dragged me down the last few days. But being at school has lifted my spirits."

"That's good to hear, very good, and you'll see each other …"

The front door opened from the inside, and a girl with long black hair stepped out. "Are you the caretaker?" She spoke with a Spanish accent.

John looked at her and smiled.

"Yes, I'm John. You can call me by my first name. We all do here. Carmen, isn't it?"

"Si, eh, I mean yes. Where do I find the letterbox?"

John pointed inside the building. "You passed them on the way out right next to the caretaker's booth."

The young woman turned her head towards the door, thanked John, and disappeared inside.

"She arrived this morning. It's the same course as you were on. I should have introduced you. I think she could do with meeting a friend."

"Maybe another time. Looks like I'll meet plenty of new people soon enough." I made a circular movement through the air with both arms. "I'd better go, John. See you soon."

"I'll look forward to it, Pippa. When you speak to Chris, please give him my condolences," he said.

I nodded. "Will do."

Then I walked home.

That evening, I did not hear from Chris. I imagined him and his parents writing funeral announcements, speaking to the vicar and undertaker, and selecting flower arrangements. Meanwhile, I busied myself with textbooks and wrote a list of stationery I needed to buy.

My heart swelled with happiness as I arrived at school early the next day and encountered Alex in his classroom.

"Have you already made the acquaintance of our counsellor?" he asked.

"Yes. Martin. We briefly ran into each other yesterday and arranged to meet this morning."

"That's all right then," Alex said. "Once school starts, things can get hectic. There's often not enough time to talk about stuff. But Martin has an open door. He's the best we've had for the job so far."

At ten o'clock, I stood at the door of Martin's office. *Dr. Munro, School Counsellor.* I paused as I read the nameplate before I knocked. I had not touched the handle as it opened from the inside.

"There you are, quick, come in." He turned, and I saw his eyes scan the room before he closed the door behind me. "I need to keep it shut. We're not alone. Do sit down." With an inviting gesture, his outstretched hand glided through the air above a sofa and armchair.

"Not alone?" I repeated as I lowered myself onto the small blue sofa, gave him a quizzical smile and shrugged.

Martin relaxed in a dark blue armchair opposite me and tilted his head towards the windowsill decorated with various flowerpots differing in colour, shape, and content. Plants we used to keep as students: easy-to-care-for evergreens, parlour palms and a solid stem with thick, rubbery leaves that shone pink as the sunlight reflected on them.

"Yes, you hardly notice him," Martin said, and in that instant, I spotted the oval brown wicker basket in the far corner, next to a spider plant with long air roots dangling in front of the radiator. I stretched my neck and detected an animal's grey, long fur move up and down.

"Oh, may I?" I exclaimed. I stood up and stepped towards the window without waiting for an answer.

"That's Jeb, he's a Ragdoll."

"A what?" I held the back of my hand above the animal, just high enough for its back to touch me with its next inhalation.

"The cat seems to have made himself at home on that spot. Well, if you can still call a feline that size a cat."

I lowered my hand and felt the warm body move undisturbed. His head was hidden between one white, fluffy paw, and only the tip of an ear was visible.

"He seems so relaxed. I'd better leave him to soak up the sunshine," I said and sat back in my seat, eyes focused on the windowsill.

"Yes, Jeb is very quiet. I keep checking whether he's still breathing. He's not mine, you see," Martin explained. "The former owners dropped him off at the shelter."

"Yes, you mentioned you did voluntary work there." I sat upright as a sensation of familiarity resonated. "My friend adopted her dog from a shelter." When I heard the childish enthusiasm in my voice, I cringed, but Martin leaned forward, eyes wide.

"A fellow animal lover, great. Loving an animal adds a completely different and beautiful dimension to one's life." He gave a muted huff toward the cat's sleeping place. "This fella here had a tough time. His twin brother died, and the owner claimed that he could not handle being alone. So, they had the 'brilliant idea' of bringing him to the shelter to be with other cats."

He sighed, tutted, and shook his head. "You can't mix a Ragdoll with other cats easily. They're far too soft. Our Jeb here got bullied by the other inmates at the shelter. Instead, I took him in to give him peace and quiet." Martin exhaled and looked at the wicker basket. "I can't keep him long term, but I won't let him go anywhere he isn't loved."

The corners of my mouth moved up. I could not hide my joy and admiration for Martin's passionate intentions. Our eyes locked, and all I could say was, "How good of you. And how lucky for Jed."

"It's Jeb. His real name is Jebediah. A biblical name meaning 'beloved friend.' Although, one might suggest, being dumped for showing one's grief is not exactly how to treat a *beloved friend,* is it?"

"Yes, it's cruel," I said. "Anyway, he found a good—"

Before I could finish, Martin held his hands up in protest. "This can't be his forever home, but I will look after him as long as it takes to find him one."

I heard a thud, and we both turned. The cat had left its sunny spot and, with a "meow", stared at me with ice-blue eyes.

"Hello, Mr. Jeb," I said with a high-pitched voice, "forgive me for getting your name wrong." The cat opened its mouth wide, yawned, and then shifted its large body to stroll in our direction.

I turned to Martin. "I wonder why they called him Jebediah?"

"I guess they named him after someone to remember a loved one. We hear this a lot in the shelter," Martin mused.

"He's gorgeous," I said, "I've never seen a cat with blue eyes."

"That's typical Ragdoll. He's a real pedigree." Martin leaned over and tipped the floor with his fingertips. "Psst, psst, come here, boy." Its bushy, grey tail dancing like a column of smoke from a chimney, the cat approached us, rubbing its ears against Martin's hand, then moving over for me to stroke it. As soon as I buried my fingers in the soft, warm coat, his body vibrated as he purred.

"He likes you," Martin said, then grabbed the armrests of his chair and straightened his back. "Forgive me, please. I have not even offered you anything to drink." He got up and turned to a small cupboard with a kettle, tray of cups and tins. "I filled the kettle before you came. What's your poison?" He held a jar of instant coffee and a box of teabags in the air.

"Coffee for me, please," I said, still leaning over in my seat, with my fingers deep in the silky coat of the purring cat.

Alex was right; the atmosphere of peace and calm was palpable, and something was soothing in Martin's presence. He had decorated the walls with wildlife photos and pictures that students must have painted. Letters, written in children's handwriting, expressed thanks in large, ornate letters.

When he passed me a hot drink and offered me a chocolate digestive, I leaned back in my seat, watched the cat sniff at the furniture and listened to Martin speaking in a subdued voice about trust in the workplace, stress, lack of time, and the importance of having a dependable sounding board when things were overwhelming.

"So, what made you move over here? You must miss home?" he asked, his eyes following Jeb as he jumped onto the sofa beside me without a sound.

"I've wanted to live in England ever since I learned my first nursery rhyme at school," I said and soon expanded on my studies, navigating around the topic of my family.

"Will you return home to Germany for the holidays?" Martin asked, and I caught myself before speaking aloud: *Home is here now.*

"No," I said, focusing on a photo of an iceberg in shades of white and blue behind him. "I've just moved and need time to sort out the house."

I tried hard to avoid eye contact. To my great relief, he asked no further questions. Instead, he told me more about his studies, his PhD in social care and how he'd had different jobs around the country but felt that York was where he wanted to remain.

Later that evening, I spoke with Chris on the phone. I was burning to share my new impressions with him but held back. His voice sounded tired, and the pauses between our sentences confirmed we were worlds apart already.

On the day of his grandmother's funeral, we did not speak. The night before, I had wished him strength for the following day. Our words sounded half-hearted. All that connected us was a sense of our separation to embark on different paths.

It was still dark when the phone rang. I grabbed Chris's heavy bathrobe, which was hanging over an armchair, and hurried down the stairs. The street light outside shone a grey light through the window.

"Hello," I gasped into the receiver. There was silence. "Chris?"

My heart pounded in my chest. I squinted at the calendar beside the telephone. It was his departure date.

"Hi, Pippa," he whispered. "I woke you up, sorry."

My eyes adjusted to the dim light. It was 3.20.

"Don't apologise. I hoped to hear from you before you left."

Then we were quiet for a moment before Chris asked, "Did you find the record player?"

"No, crap. I forgot. There was so much to do. I was at school the last few days. How did it go yesterday?"

"Listen to that record, please. What I feel for you … I can't express it better than the words in that song."

"Chris, my darling," I was surprised I had voiced this term and cringed at myself. "I'll do it today, I promise. Now, tell me about yesterday."

"It was exhausting. We buried my grandma, and I said goodbye to all my family who were there. It was so depressing. Can you understand?"

"Yes, I can imagine." I sensed how bad he felt.

"And the worst thing, Pips: I couldn't say goodbye to the one person who means so much to me. I miss you terribly."

Was he crying? I pulled the dressing gown tighter around my middle. Chris sounded so vulnerable. What could I say?

"Are you still there?" I asked.

"Mmm, mmm."

"When is your flight?"

"Quarter to seven. I need to be at the airport in two hours." His voice sounded flat. I could not detect any emotion for the new challenge he faced in his voice. Had he come to regret his decision?

"Are you excited?"

"No. Everything just feels numb. I'd rather get on a train to York and snuggle into bed with you."

"Oh, don't say that. It'll make me even sadder. But I'm counting the days until you are back."

"Heartless as it sounds, the positive about all this is that I'll return in December. Mum's grieving so much."

She's not the only one.

"I've talked to my parents. They want to meet you and have invited you for Christmas." His voice gained energy.

"Oh wow, that's great."

Less than half a year and we would meet again. A wave of relief rippled through my body.

"I have to go."

A weight pressed on my stomach. My throat tightened. "Call me when …"

Yes, when would he be able to call again? Countries, place names and times buzzed through my head like bees.

"When I'm in Taiwan tomorrow evening. I have a few hours' stay there and will try. It'll be night-time for you."

"Never mind, call me. The main thing is that I hear your voice. But if not, then from Na—"

"Nagoya. Sure, I'll get in touch right away."

We were silent for a moment.

"I have to hang up." Chris's voice sounded tender. "I love you, Pips."

My mouth widened into a wide smile; tears welled up in my eyes at the same time.

"I love you too, Chris," I replied, and added a quick, "Take care of yourself."

"You too." Then he hung up.

Handset in hand, I stared out the window. The glass bird hung motionlessly; the street looked deserted. I exhaled. We'd ended our last call in the same country. The next one would be shorter, with a poor connection.

Had I said everything I needed to? Yes, it was fine. He loved me. I'd see him again at Christmas.

42

He should be on the plane now.

I was kneeling in the black space under the stairs, pulling out one dusty box after another. In the far corner, protected by a plastic bag whose contents felt soft, I discovered the record player. Someone had wrapped the cables around the speakers. There was a crack in the lid of the turntable. It had come off one of its hinges. This device looked frayed, an entangled mess.

As I disentangled the twisted wires, parties in my flat in Cologne appeared in my mind. Urs falling asleep with her head on the windowsill, Yvonne blaring her heart out to Alanis Morissette, me bobbing around the kitchen. Underneath another carton of abandoned regalia, I pulled out a crate of records. I bolstered it with both arms, fearing the tired cardboard would give way before it saw daylight. Shoving everything back and closing the door, I manoeuvred the items into the hallway with my foot.

The records undoubtedly belonged to Chris. Randy Crawford, Sister Sledge, Gloria Gaynor. I reflected on our evening at the nightclub. A huge desire to experience that magnetic atmosphere once more overcame me.

After clearing a space on the shelf in the bedroom, I assembled the stereo. As I was fixing the hood back in its place, the doorbell sounded. Through the window I saw Eleanor standing on the pavement, peering at the front door. I dashed to open it, and she embraced me before I could say "Hi."

"It's so great to see you. I was up at uni and I had to pick up a couple of papers. I thought I'd come and check how you are settling in."

Delighted with this impromptu visit, I hugged her tight. "That's excellent, Eleanor. Chris has left, you know," I said.

She nodded. "Is he terribly upset?"

"His grandma? Yes. It's such a rotten thing, now of all times."

"There's never a convenient time for death, Pippa."

"Come on in. Fancy a coffee?"

"I'd love one." Eleanor sounded relieved and followed me into the kitchen.

I put the kettle on and grabbed a pack of biscuits. We chatted like she had never left. Eleanor still belonged in this house. I loved the ease with which she poured another coffee, got the milk from the fridge, and ran up the stairs to the bathroom.

"I found bags of clothes under the stairs. Are they yours?" I said.

"Oh, dear. They can go to charity." She peered in the door's direction. "I wanted to go into town next. Fancy joining me? We could drop off a few bags."

"Yeah, why not? I don't need to wait for a call from Chris today. He's up in the air by now." I pointed to the ceiling.

"Great. Let's get rid of that ancient clobber." Eleanor jumped up and went to the cupboard. I listened to her mutter, a giggle, followed by a thud. "Bloody hell, I had forgotten how cramped it is in there." She appeared with two bags in one hand, rubbing her head with the other.

On the way into town, we handed the bags in at the RSPCA charity shop and wandered into the town centre, past my favourite café opposite the cathedral. I hadn't been there for weeks and hadn't visited many souvenir shops, but the city was in the mood for the summer holidays.

I hooked arms with Eleanor. "I'm so pleased you came," I said, laughing, and she clutched onto me.

We had dinner in an Indian restaurant, and I told her of my initial encounter with this kind of cuisine in Whitby. Eleanor reacted with "aww" and "bless" and called Chris and me the perfect couple who "certainly will be married sooner rather than later."

My hand shot up in protest, and we both laughed.

"With at least three children," she added. My mouth uncoiled, and I turned to look out the window.

"What, not enough?" Eleanor leaned in to catch my eyes.

I forced a smile and confessed that envy had consumed me when our friendship began. This was sufficient to divert her from the topic. She assured me that Chris was like a brother to her. "He's a good mate, that's all."

"I believe you." I recalled his words, "I love you", and my body and mind softened and mellowed.

"Another glass of wine?" asked Eleanor, waving to the waiter.

"I'd love one. What time is your train?" I looked at my watch.

"Oh, shit, no idea. I still feel so at home here." It was after nine.

"Stay. There's still a bed in Don's room."

"Seriously?" She looked at me with her eyes wide.

"Yes, seriously," I reiterated, "Stay for the weekend. You still have a few clothes under the stairs."

"I'd love to, Pippa. Honestly, I'd be up for it. We could have a beautiful couple of days. Have you done a boat trip on the river?"

"No, but it'll be a lovely distraction from waiting for a call from China or Japan or God knows where."

We both snickered and toasted each other.

On the way home, we bought another bottle of wine. Eleanor assembled the record player back at the house while we flipped through Chris's record collection. We closed the curtains and danced to his music.

Eleanor collapsed into a chair by the shelf and grabbed her glass of wine. She removed a strand of hair from her forehead. As she returned the glass, she spotted the single.

"Oh, wow, where did you get that?" she yelled, holding up the sleeve.

"Chris left that for me under my pillow," I said, embarrassed. "I haven't listened to it yet."

"You don't know *this* song?" Eleanor straightened her back to sit upright and held the record up like a red card. "May I?" she asked, lifting the single higher.

"Yes, why not," I replied, and Eleanor set about putting the record on.

After fiddling with the settings of the record player, she took my hand and guided me to a chair. "Sit and listen to this."

"Yes, Miss," I muttered as the sound of harp and guitar permeated the room. Tiptoeing over to the bed, Eleanor sat on the edge.

A warm female voice whispered the first words. Soft guitar guided the lines in which she remembered the night she met her love for the first time. I turned to Eleanor. She raised her index finger to her mouth, signalling for me to follow the lyrics.

I dared not speak. Instead, we listened to Roberta Flack describing how she first saw, kissed, and slept with her lover. She half sang, half spoke the text, and all the while, Eleanor glowed and nodded with expanded eyes.

A cocktail of romantic happiness and intense melancholy overflowed my soul. *This is what Chris wanted to tell me.*

I reflected on the evening we met. When had I looked at his face in the glow of a street light after the cinema. How he had come back weeks afterwards, and our first kiss.

I grinned at Eleanor. This woman was singing about Chris and me, and he knew it. This most intimate of gifts, would he approve of me listening to it with our friend?

As if she could read my mind, Eleanor interrupted my thoughts. "Here comes the most beautiful bit."

Her eyes glittered as she mimed the lines, singing them to me, muted, and I looked back to how I had listened to Chris's heartbeat the night before his sudden departure. She raised her index finger again, like a teacher.

I thought our love would last until the end of time, too.

"See what I mean?" Eleanor said. "You two are meant for each other."

I understood what Chris had tried to say to me. He was on his way to the end of the world and had no idea that I'd understood his message at that moment.

"Well, what do you think?" asked Eleanor, looking at me quizzically as the needle slid over the final grooves.

"That Chris is an incredible romantic. That's what I think," I replied, returning the record to its sleeve.

"I never had him down as a true Romeo, Pippa. If a man ever quotes Roberta Flack to me, let alone gets me the record …" Eleanor said.

She looked at the candles flickering on the table. She yawned.

"I'm tired too," I said. "Chris's call woke me in the middle of the night. I need to catch up on some sleep."

We gathered blankets and pillows and wished each other goodnight. With the lyrics and sound of the song in my head, I settled into bed and was glad that Chris was nearing his destination. Soon, I could thank him for his parting gift.

He did not ring the following day, and we explained the silence as due to time changes, crowded airports, and a lack of options.

"Who knows if there are any phone boxes close. Plus, he will need local change." Eleanor consoled me. I didn't leave the house for the whole day.

"I'll cook us something luscious. Do you like lasagne? I make a superb one, my speciality."

I sat at the kitchen window, the phone within easy reach. "Yes, that's fine," I replied, longing for Chris to make his special tortellini for us instead.

Eleanor clutched the keys and picked up her bag. "I'll go to the shops for a pint of milk," she said.

After the front door had fallen into the lock, I took the piece of paper from the noticeboard on which Chris had written his parents' number. I searched my mind for the proper words.

Good evening. I'm Pippa, Chris's girlfriend.

No, I didn't want to introduce myself in that way.

Good evening. My name is Pippa. Have you heard from Chris?

That seemed overly formal.

When Eleanor returned to the kitchen, I pinned the note back onto the board and put her shopping on the table.

"Right, I hope everything is still in its place," she said, opening the cupboard next to the fridge. I heard the cluttering of pans and drawers being opened and shut while I gazed at the glass bird in the window.

After scraping the last of the lasagne stuck to the sides of the oven dish, we leaned back in our chairs, the empty plates in front of us.

"Well, that was delicious, if I say so myself. I could finish another helping," Eleanor said, licking the last of the sauce from the serving spoon. "Have you had enough?"

"For God's sake, if I eat one more bite, I'll burst." Laughing, I rubbed my hand over my bloated belly.

As Eleanor watched, she laughed out loud. "Are you sure that's the food? Looks like twins to me." She giggled.

I gave her a stern look.

"Oh, sorry, I didn't mean … You're not fat at all. Did I offend you?" Her words rushed out, jumbled.

"No," I replied.

"You're perfect. And I am sure Chris would agree if he was here."

I bit my lip.

"I did it again, didn't I? Put my foot in it. Sorry."

"I miss him so much. How am I supposed to endure this for two years?"

"It's serious with you guys, isn't it? And I am here, making silly jokes. I'm sorry. Sincerely though, can you imagine having children with him one day?"

Eleanor's question caught me off guard. Like a bomb, her words struck every cell in my body. Heat rose inside me. I leaned forward and clutched my water glass.

"Jeez, Pippa, what's the matter? You're shaking." Eleanor frowned as she spoke.

"No, it's not you. It's just … oh, you know …"

My head was on a merry-go-round. Thoughts raced by before I could grasp them. How would she react if I told her? She might condemn me for the abortion itself and not telling her earlier. Or she might pity me for the same reasons.

"I'm going crazy waiting. I wish he'd arrive and ring. I wish it was tomorrow."

"I understand." Eleanor squinted at me, her eyes sharp. "But don't wish your life away. Not one single shitty day." After a brief pause, she added, "Let's go dancing tonight. What do you think?"

I turned to the window and glanced at the phone and the clock. It was still early in the evening.

Eleanor read my thoughts. "Right," she said, "we'll give him a few more hours. In that time, we'll clear the place, get ready and …" She looked at the clock and counted the hours in a whisper. "… nine, ten, eleven…" Then she said with vigour, "If he hasn't called by eleven, we'll hit the road."

"Hit the road," I repeated, laughing. "You make me laugh. But yes, it's a great idea. You cooked; I'll do the dishes."

We finished half a bottle of wine as we got changed and foraged through my makeup bag. Eleanor and I were the same size, and within an hour, we had dressed and were ready to go. My friend was right: Chris would call me at the latest when he reached his destination. Until then, distraction was the best medicine.

The dance floor was crowded by the time we arrived. I leaned over the bar, handing our jackets to the bartender. Eleanor stood at the edge of the pulsating crowd and beckoned me to join in. Stretching my arms wide, I danced towards her. She grabbed my hands and pulled me into the middle. We jumped to the rhythm of the music and spun around until the DJ announced the last song.

Eleanor's face was gleaming, and her hair stuck to her sweaty skin. She mimed "Four o'clock" and imitated ticking a wristwatch. I replied by putting a glass to my mouth and returning to the bar.

The music was playing a slow song, "On My Own." How apt, I thought, when a man squeezed beside me and leaned over to say something.

"What did you say?" I shouted, and inside my head, my voice was a dull drum. He tilted his head towards the dance floor. His lips moved, but the music drowned out his voice.

He brushed my hair back from my ear and leaned in closer. Before I had time to react, Eleanor turned up and dragged him aside, her eyes flashing She pulled the stranger towards her by the shoulders and pushed her face close to his with both hands.

He looked at me and mimed "sorry" before disappearing into the crowd.

By the time we got home, my ears had recovered. Exhausted, we dragged ourselves up the stairs, giggling.

"That guy. What did you tell him?" I laughed.

"That you're already spoken for," Eleanor replied.

I am already spoken for… I kept repeating her words in bed until they fused into the song we had played earlier that evening.

43

A sharp ringing hauled me from my sleep. Eyes shut, I struggled to identify the sound. The phone ... I hurled back the duvet, dragged the bathrobe off the hook, dashed down to the kitchen and squinted at the clock. It was gone half past noon. Like a swarm of bees, my insides tingled with trepidation. I had one arm tucked through the sleeve of the gown when I reached for the receiver.

"About time, Mister," I said with a laugh. My voice was throaty. I coughed.

There was silence on the line.

"Chris, can you hear me?" I imagined my words being carried to the other side of the world.

"Erm, hello, this is Graham Jones, Chris's father. Am I speaking to Phillippa?" The man's stale voice resonated down the phone. This was no international call.

"Yes." My hand sought a grip on the back of a chair.

"Phillippa." His tone wobbled. "There's been an accident, a plane crash."

Squeezing the receiver to my ear, I sagged onto the seat behind me. My stomach plunged in free fall.

"Our son Chris was on ..."

I choked, my head spinning. "What has ..." I went ahead.

"There are no survivors."

"What happened? How's Chris?"

"He ... Phillippa, he didn't make it."

"Is he ...?" My throat tightened and produced a squealing noise.

"Yes, he's among the fatalities. He was in that machine."

The man had recaptured his composure. I crunched my eyelids, my lips together, my whole face together.

"Are you still there, Phillippa? Can you hear me?"

"Mm, mm," I muttered. "I don't understand," I whispered. "Is Chris alright? Has he called?"

Mr. Jones rehashed the information he'd been given. The plane Chris was on had crashed, and there were no known survivors. He spoke of Taiwan ... a follow-up call from the airline ... and wait and see.

The receiver became heavier with each word he spoke. "This cannot be ..." I whimpered.

"I'm afraid it is."

"We'll call you when we have more information. You must have been waiting for a sign from ..." He corrected himself. "Waiting for a call." His speech broke, and only a heavy sob prevailed. "Excuse me," he said, and the line went dead.

I glared out the window and imagined plane parts, water, jungle, and pieces of wreckage. Then the pain struck. Like a harpoon, it pierced my heart, and sharp agony spread through every cell of my body. Hot tears burned their way through the cavities in my face to my eyes. I turned in my chair and scanned the kitchen with a blurred gaze. I recognised Eleanor in the doorway. She came towards me, and her outline became sharper.

"What happened?" she asked, startled, and put her hand on my shoulder.

I opened my mouth, but instead of words, a shrieking scream escaped, followed by convulsed sobs.

I forced my hands to my face to block the pain. Eleanor knelt before me, her voice telling me her head was close. Her hands rested on my knees.

"Pippa, my poor dear Pippa …"

She placed a tea towel in my hand. I pressed my face into it.

"Pippa, what is it?" Eleanor's voice trembled with fragility. "Did I just hear that right? Is Chris … has there been an accident?" she asked.

I nodded and felt hot tears on my face.

"Plane … crash …" I stammered, gasping for breath.

Eleanor slapped her hands over her mouth. As if she were in a shipwreck, she snorted for air.

I clutched her wrists. "That was his father. The plane crashed. Chris is dead, he said."

"No." Eleanor cried out, ruffling her hair. "When? Where did it happen? Where's your radio?" she yelled and checked the time.

"I don't know. He didn't say …"

I tried to recall his words. Had all the passengers died? Had they found Chris's body?

Eleanor shot upstairs. Her footsteps stomped in the bedroom above me, next on the stairs. With the radio in her hands, she knelt by a socket and plugged it in.

The last bars of Oasis' "Wonderwall" faded, and I heard the newsreader's voice.

"A China Airline Airbus … on route from Taiwan to Nagoya … after take-off … in the late evening hours local time … of unknown cause … no survivors …"

Eleanor and I stared at each other in disbelief. It was true. I bit my lips. She shook her head in resignation and unplugged the radio.

"What did Chris's father say?"

"The airline told him everyone is dead." My voice was still hoarse. I tried to remember the exact words. Had I missed something? Perhaps it wasn't certain that Chris was among the victims.

"Maybe it's a mistake," I stammered, turning to the glass bird. "What am I going to do?" I burst into tears.

Eleanor wrapped her arms around my body. Trembling, I clung to her.

"Shhh… shhh…" she repeated, rocking us back and forth like a mother consoling a baby. She held me until I calmed down.

"If you like, I'll call his parents in a bit and see if they know any more," she offered as she put the kettle on. She trembled, but her voice sounded firm.

"Yes, please. I can't face speaking to them."

With shaky hands, I took the cup that Eleanor had poured. The tea scorched the inside of my mouth. I winced, put the mug on the table, and stared into the air.

"Shall I run you a bath? Is that their number?" She pointed at the paper on the notice board. I bowed my head.

From the bathroom, I heard disjointed sentences from the kitchen. No, she couldn't go back home, Eleanor said. She had to stay with a friend. A bereavement, yes, a dear member of the family, a partner. Another call and she sobbed as she spoke about the plane crash.

The comforting warmth of the bathwater calmed me. I loved its pressure cradling my body. I waited in vain for it to dull my pain as I stared at the wall tiles. I closed my eyes and thought of how Chris had joined me, sitting on the side of the tub. Could he hear my thoughts? As a child, I had believed the souls of the deceased continued to exist around us. I placed my hand on the edge of the bath. The air felt chilly.

Are you here?

In my mind, I implored him to come back.

Let it all be a dream, please.

A shiver ran across my spine. This was how I had communicated with our unborn child. I had apologised and tried to justify my decision. Was this my punishment?

My guts tightened. I straightened and sat bolt upright.

This was retribution. I had to repent. I remembered my mother kneeling in the pew with her eyes looking at her hands. She had clasped her fingers until her knuckles turned white. *Hail Mary, full of grace, the Lord is with you ...* As I knelt beside her, I tried to figure out what the reason for her suffering was. *Mea culpa. My fault.*

I bent my legs in the bathtub, enveloping my knees with my arms.

Stop, stop these thoughts.

"Hey, can I come in?" Eleanor knocked on the door.

"Yeah," I said, gliding back into the water.

"How are you feeling?" she asked, looking washed out and pale.

"I don't understand. I keep thinking that Chris is about to walk in the door."

I sobbed the last words rather than speaking them. "But he's not coming, is he?" I continued.

Eleanor shook her head. "No," she said, "I just got through to his parents. It was his mother's turn. They're heartbroken. They're waiting for news from China about the transfer of Chris's body. That's all they know."

Eleanor stayed with me for two further days. During that time, she was my link to the outside world. She did the shopping, cooked, and held me when I hunched on the floor and cried. At the pharmacy, she got me a valerian product to help me sleep. Holding me in her arms, she watched me breathe. However, the most significant help was that she updated our friends. After she had told Don, Naomi, and a few others, I asked her to tell John and David at the university.

My face was pasty and blotchy, my eyes red-rimmed, my cheeks hollow. I had not washed my hair since his father's call. Greasy, it framed my pale face.

Eleanor took on this task, too, and told me about the reactions of the others. Naomi herself was in Japan with her family. David offered his sincere condolences. The news had especially struck John.

"The colour drained from his face, Pippa. He had to sit for a while."

"He likes Chris …" I said and welled up.

"Yes, I could tell. He cried. And I couldn't control myself either."

"Thank you, Eleanor, for taking this on yourself. I couldn't face John."

"He really took to you, Pippa. I know it's his job to look after us all, especially the freshers. But you are quite special to him."

"He's a good judge of character. Had it figured out pretty quickly that things are difficult with my family. Maybe that's why he supported Chris and me."

"He's become a bit of a second dad to you, right?"

"Perhaps that's why I couldn't tell him."

"John asked for you to come by when you're ready. He'd like to see you."

"Yes, I will," I vowed, feeling supported by her tender voice. "At the moment, I can't face anyone who I care about, who cared for Chris and knew what we meant to each other." I wept.

When Eleanor had to return to London, anxiety overwhelmed me.

"I don't know how I can bear being alone in this house."

"What about your friends back home? Have you called them?"

I lifted my head and exhaled towards the ceiling. "No, not yet."

"That girl who visited, Urs, do you have her number? I'll ring her."

"No, I will do it soon. Promise."

"Good. Don't keep this bottled up. Take each day hour by hour. Sometimes, you will have to take it second by second. One breath at a time. They say it will hurt less." Eleanor stood before me in the hallway. She pulled me towards her and held me.

"I'm still in shock. I need to process all of this. Thanks for your help."

She kissed me on the cheek and pulled the door shut behind her.

As I turned, I noticed the sleeve of Chris's winter coat peeking out from underneath the jackets on the coat rack.

"Far too heavy to take on the plane," he had said, adding with a laugh, "You wear it, and I'll be with you."

I lifted the tight fabric from the hook and held it against my face. Inhaling, I remembered him in front of me at the cinema. I recalled how he strode across campus whilst I watched from up in the library. With swift steps, his coat fluttered in the autumn wind. I slid my right, then my left arm through the sleeves and jerked the garment over my shoulders.

"My dear, beloved Chris." I pulled the giant coat around me. "Where on earth are you? What am I going to do without you?" Weeping, I stroked the sleeves. Outside, I heard children's voices. Laughing, they ran past the house and down the streets. How could life continue as if nothing had happened?

Still draped in the coat, I made myself a valerian tea. Cup in hand, I climbed the stairs to the bedroom. I relived the evening when I had sat on the bed after the disco, and Chris served me a cup of tea. I turned on the record player, put on his farewell gift and switched the little button to "repeat".

When I woke up ten hours later, I was still hugging the coat.

44

The curtains remained closed the following days. The only voices I tolerated were Don McLean, Roberta Flack, or any other of Chris's favourites. I sipped tea and tap water and scraped by on toast and jam. When the cheese ran out and the last slice of bread slipped into the toaster, I picked up the phone and dialled Ursula's number.

"Pippa, what a lovely surprise. It's wonderful to hear from you. Is everything ..." Ursula stopped halfway.

"Urs, something awful ..." I gasped for air.

"Pippa," her anxious voice shook with emotions. "The flight ... the crash ... oh my God ... was Chris...?"

Before she could finish her sentence, I interrupted. "Yes, Urs, he was on it ..." I burst into tears.

Ursula said nothing. I heard the sharp intake of her breath. Then, "Oh no ... oh my dear Lord, you poor thing ...no, no, no ..." Meanwhile, I was sobbing into the phone.

We cried on the phone together for a few moments. Just as I gathered myself, she took a deep breath and, with a strong voice, said, "Right, I am coming over. I will be on one of the next flights available."

"Okay," I said, and as if on autopilot, I hung up and turned to Chris's coat draped across his favourite kitchen chair.

"I have to go out, Chris," I whispered.

It was time to visit John. When I reached Alcuin College, I was relieved to find it deserted. I drew in a sharp breath and opened the glass door. John hastened towards me.

"Pippa, my dear." As he hugged me, I welled up. Mindful not to smudge his jacket, I pulled my head back and dipped in my pocket for a tissue.

"I am so sorry, so sorry." He struggled to suppress his tears, the rims of his eyes glinting red.

"John …" I sputtered, "I … I… am …" I gasped. My chin quivered. I pressed my lips tight.

"Come, sit down. I'll make some tea, or do you want coffee?"

"Tea is fine, thank you."

We sat in the room where I had spilt my heart out to him many times before. John looked aged as he listened in silence. The skin underneath his chin was saggy and shadowy circles surrounded his eyes.

"You know what I keep thinking, John? That it's retribution."

He lifted his eyebrows. "Pippa, what are you talking about?"

My voice became firmer as if to persuade him of my suspicion.

"It's punishment. You know, for my sins. The death penalty follows murder."

"Pippa, you mustn't talk like that."

"But why else did it happen? Why am I being punished like this?"

"Pippa, more than two hundred people died in that crash."

"Why does it feel that I am the only one affected by it?"

"How do you mean? Anyone close to someone on that flight is feeling the same pain you are."

"The cashier at the corner shop just grinned and moved my groceries over the counter. He grinned, John, while my heart is slashed in two."

"Pippa, we all suffer. The whole world knows about this disaster."

"It's my punishment …" Tears kept flowing. I wiped my face with my flat hand.

"If life worked like that, I wouldn't still be sitting here, believe me."

John spoke fast with a raised voice. He was determined to talk me out of the notion I couldn't expel from my head.

"But John ..." Now I couldn't hold back the tears. "I can't stop thinking about it. And I can't shake off the thought that Chris might still be alive if I hadn't ... if I'd kept the baby. Our baby."

"Pippa, please calm down."

I buried my face in my hands. I felt John touch my head.

"Come on, Pippa. Look at me. You've got to get rid of this thought that you're sinful. Get rid of this guilt."

"But if I'd kept the baby, maybe he would never have left and got on that plane."

"Maybe, Pippa, maybe. But you do not know that. Nobody knows that. You ... you chose what was the right thing to do at the time."

"The money, John. I guarantee I will repay you as soon as I get salary."

"Look, what you're doing: it's guilt-tripping. We agreed there was no hurry for that."

I shook as tears ran down my face.

"Oh, Pippa, you're all mixed up inside. Stop telling yourself this nonsense about punishment and retribution."

I accepted the tissue he held out and nodded. Meanwhile, a quiet voice in my head muttered that I had brought on this insufferable pain myself.

"In time, Pippa, your wounds will heal. First, there will be a scab, reminding you each time you look at or touch it. It will heal into a scar. We will never forget what happened. But this gruelling pain you feel will subside. With time."

I looked at John with a furrowed brow. I could not imagine the pain receding or my grief easing. But John was not one to proclaim platitudes.

"I know grief, trust me. And look, I'm sitting here and can still enjoy life. Someday, Pippa, you will be happy."

He lifted his hand when he saw I was about to oppose him. "And Chris will be with you, Pippa. You'll carry him in your heart and your memories. Always."

I choked. If only I still carried his child under my heart.

"Have you been to the philosophy department? Everyone knows of your tragedy."

"Not yet. I needed to see you first."

"If you go over, Pippa, there's a memorial desk for Chris there. You'll need to be prepared."

I wept.

"There is a condolence register, and some students and lecturers have left small mementoes. The idea is to hand it all over to Chris's parents."

I bowed. "Thank you. It's good you told me."

"You can come here anytime, you know that. When does school start? Do they know …?"

"Nobody knows. We begin September."

"Do you know if there will be a funeral and when?"

"No, it's horrible. They haven't recovered any …"

I wavered and had to clean my throat.

John's eyes revealed a despair of helplessness. There were no magic words, no incantation to transform my cruel reality.

"All right, Pippa. Please let me know when you hear anything."

"Mm, mm, I will. And thank you," I said, placing the teacup on a shelf.

"Come here." John stood up and held his arms out to embrace me. I sank my face into his shoulder and smelled a refreshing scent of soapy cologne.

The meeting with David was less emotional. When I arrived, Gill sat behind her desk, taking her reading glasses off her nose.

"Pippa, I'm so sorry for your loss. My deepest condolences. How are you?"

I heaved, but David walked into the room before I could answer her. He expressed his sympathy and looked at me, waiting for me to answer Gill's question about how I was.

"I'm okay. About how you'd expect, given the circumstances," I said and was relieved they did not poke the wound. They smiled. David sighed and put a hand on my shoulder. His steely blue eyes looked watery and bloodshot.

The memory of my first day in York flashed by. Was it fate that Gill discovered my application just moments before I entered this building? With hindsight, how right was the title they played on the radio, "I'm gonna be (500 Miles)"? And David's words when I told him that nobody was waiting for me back in Germany: *I am sure you will soon make friends here.*

I could not help but attach a profound meaning to everything that had occurred in the last year. "Stop it, Pippa," I heard John say, and I told David and Gill that I would pop in when the term had started.

The closer I got to the building where I used to meet Chris for coffee or lunch, the heavier the pressure grew in my heart. On a bench by the lake, I paused until my pulse normalised. It was peaceful. A few students walked alone around the campus, just like that day when I went to the cinema. If I had stayed in my room back then, the pain I felt today might belong to someone else.

When I forced open the entrance door to the philosophy department, it appeared heftier than ever. It was like someone was pushing against it from the inside, delaying me from coming in. Breathless, I stepped into the hall. A student stopped in front of a vending machine. He turned around and said "Hi" before he returned to the display and lifted his hand to insert change into the slot.

I walked along a corridor that served different seminar rooms. One door had a white paper with a black written sign pinned to it. "Condolences: Chris Jones." My breath floundered. I couldn't feel my knees as I depressed the handle.

An intense scent of incense urged me to come in. Someone had closed the curtains to keep out the radiant daylight. Broad, silvery candles filled the room with a tranquil glow. I closed the door, not wishing to upset the serenity. As my eyes became accustomed to the light, I spotted Chris's photo mounted on a table by the wall. An abrupt cry emerged from deep inside of me.

"Oh, Chris, Chris," I moaned.

His picture was in a simple black frame. He was wearing his academic robe and smiling at the camera. The heavy candles on either side quivered as I sat before it. A white orchid stood in a narrow glass vase.

I stared at the photo. The silence stifled me.

"Why, why? We were just at the beginning …"

With a dark sigh, I pulled the deep green leather-bound book towards me and opened the gilt-edged pages. Words and signatures were scribbled on the page: professors, lecturers, fellow students.

"Far too young", "deeply shocked", "incomprehensible".

I turned the thick leaves until I found an empty page. What was I going to write? I studied Chris' face. His eyes flashed, an expression I knew so well.

"You'll think of something," he seemed to say.

I leaned back in my chair. "I listened to your record." I started crying.

"I would have liked … to listen to it with you … Chris," I stammered in a broken voice.

"I want to tell you … so much."

I kept my eyes on his face.

"You know, I never told you. But I was … in love with you from the first day we met."

In my mind, I heard Chris laughing, "Ha, I knew it—and I felt the same way."

I clutched the picture frame, held it in front of me, and wailed.

"Chris … Chris …?" I begged, but the room remained hushed, apart from my sobbing.

I lay the photo on the table with my arms around it and rested my head on my hands. Huddled over the picture, I wept with closed eyes. My body twitched as I gasped for air. After a while, the rivulets of my tears became thinner. I heard Roberta Flack's voice in my head, the sound of the harp, the dark bass underplaying the rhythm. Our love song now sounded like a funeral march.

"Thank you for everything." I straightened my upper body, grabbed the pen and wrote, *As close as I got to you, it was never enough …*

I signed, *Always, your Pippa xxx*, took the photo frame and kissed the cold glass.

Epilogue
Six months later

"Hi, I am here to meet Martin." I breathed in the smell of muddy paws and faded animal urine mixed with an edge of a bleaching agent. Dog barks boomed in the distance.

"Martin, someone's here for ya," the lady hollered over her shoulder into a corridor behind the reception. "Have you come to volunteer?" She looked at my shoes, nodded, and sank her hand into a jar of dog treats. "There you go, love."

I stashed the biscuits in the pocket of my fleece. "Thank you."

The howling and yapping increased. Doors slammed. Martin approached at the end of the passageway, wearing washed-out dungarees. Unruly strands of hair had broken free from his ponytail. His rubber wellingtons squelched on the wet floor.

"Hi, Pippa, so you made it." We hugged, our bodies not touching. "Excuse me, I'm filthy."

I squeezed in a short "Hello", but Martin kept talking. "Shall we go?"

"Yes, let's," I shrugged and wriggled my arms, hands in my jacket pocket. "Can't wait."

Together, we retraced his steps as he led me through the cattery. "Have your magic treats ready," Martin rambled on. "Brace yourself for commotion." How different he was here, outside the tranquillity of his school office. I had often sat with him after school hours, peeling off the layers of my grief. He knew about the loss of Chris, and I had recently lifted the edge of the veil covering the estrangement from my family.

He halted. I raised my hands to bolster the impact of our collision.

Martin turned and steadied me by my shoulders. "Sorry, Pippa, are you all right?"

"Yes, yes," I laughed, "no harm done."

"I'm pleased you came. You'll see, the love of a dog has natural healing powers. Are you ready?"

I could not contain a smile and nodded.

Martin opened a metal door into the yard of the RSPCA. As we stepped out onto the grass, an orchestra of barking bellowed through the quadrangle. I crunched my face and protected my ears with my palms.

"I warned you," he shouted, waving for me to follow. The kennels were built on all four sides of the courtyard. The four-legged residents jumped and flung themselves against the fencing, creating deafening blasts.

"How do we choose?" I laughed, still covering my ears.

"You'll find they do the choosing. But if you offer them a treat, there'll be a second respite."

I did as I was told, and a small Jack Russell mix seized the biscuit through the wire. A large dog of indiscernible breed drove it back into my hand, unable to grasp it with its teeth. Balancing on my toes, I reached across the top and let the crumbs rain down. He hoovered them up in one go, chomping.

A scruffy mongrel with a wiry black coat caught my attention in the following enclosure. Unlike other dogs, he sat silently by the gate, tail brushing the floor.

I knelt and met his striking amber eyes. "Who are you, handsome fellow?"

"This is Jake." When Martin moved into sight, Jake launched himself in the air, landing on all fours. Martin wiggled his fingers through the webbing. The dog turned, leaning into the fence for maximum contact. "He's a lurcher."

"Can we take him out?"

Without reply, Martin opened the latch, coaxing Jake to step back, his voice tender. "Good boy, where's that leash of yours?" The dog tiptoed on its paws, dancing with joy.

Once Martin had handed me the leash, Jake dragged me through the entrance of the building, his body weight straining forward. Only when we reached the riverbank, he slowed, and I could slacken the strap, which I had twisted around my wrist.

"Wow, he's got enough energy for two. How old is he?" I asked as we rested on a bench overlooking the Ouse.

"We guess he was one when he turned up. He was a stray. So that makes him two years old."

"Are you telling me he's been in kennels for a year?" I drew Jake closer and placed his head in my hands. He lifted his eyebrows. "You poor thing." I kissed his forehead. Jake placed one paw on my knee.

"Yes, luckily, he is such an easy dog. Otherwise, he might have been put down."

My heart throbbed. Impossible to think that nobody wanted to adopt this majestic animal and that he might have been killed. My gut twisted.

Jake put his second paw onto my knee and nudged me with his snout.

"Oh, he likes you," Martin laughed. "And who can blame him?"

"He's gorgeous," I said, still holding on to the dog who started climbing onto my lab. "What's he doing?" I tried to cover the quiver in my voice with laughter. "Hey Jake, you're too big." I had not completed the sentence before he had installed himself onto my thighs, his body pressing against me, propping his head on my shoulder.

Fervour scorched from my stomach into my heart while every cell in my body reverberated with excitement. My eyes burned. I blinked.

Martin smiled. "See what I mean? The love of an animal. A unique dimension." He patted Jake's side. "Excellent choice, boy. Excellent choice."

On the way back, Martin tried to persuade me to adopt Jake. "He's the softest dog we've had in a while. You saw how gentle he is."

My heart pounded, and blood rushed through my veins. *What would my father say?* I shuddered as I realised I had not thought of my parents for months.

"I'm not sure I have the time or space for a dog."

"Your house is certainly large enough. And as far as time is concerned, I can be your standby," Martin said and nudged me with his arm as we entered the building.

Jake placed his paws on the counter, stretching his slender body, coat gleaming, tail wagging.

"I don't know, Martin. I need to think this through." I sighed. "This was meant to be a social visit. I hadn't planned on leaving with a dog."

"Quite right. You must know you can care for him for the next twelve years." Martin sounded apologetic, unaware that his excitement had rubbed off on me.

"It's not just that," I said. "I worry that he might feel lonely when I'm at work."

"Jake lonely? All he wants is a mum. Isn't that right, Jake?" Martin's words pierced right through my heart. *A mummy. Could Jake be my redemption?*

"I'll have to get on. It's feeding time. Think about it. Jake will still be here," Martin said.

I waved goodbye. "See you at school on Monday."

On my way home, thoughts spun whilst my stomach twisted. Could I fulfil my childhood dream? There was one person I had to talk this through with—someone who would not burst my bubble but would give me genuine and balanced advice. I lifted the receiver and dialled Ursula's number.

"I might adopt a dog. Do you think that's nuts?"

"No, Pippa. It's a wonderful idea. Does your counsellor friend have anything to do with it?"

I recounted my visit to the RSPCA.

"Aw, he sounds so sweet. I wish I could have been there."

"Guess what happened when I asked them to reserve Jake for next week? The woman behind the counter shouted across her shoulder, 'Someone wants to reserve Jake.' And all the volunteers laughed. 'Reserve our Jake?' they said. 'Not a single soul has paid any attention to him for over a year, love.' Honestly, Urs, I felt quite foolish. Thank goodness Martin had left by then."

Ursula chuckled. "Sounds like you two are meant for each other." I pulled the receiver from my ear for a second.

"What? Martin and I? He's just a colleague," I insisted with a smile. Then added, "and has become a bit of a confidant."

"No, you and Jake, silly," Ursula clarified. "Honestly, if you adopt him, that dog will think he's died and gone to heaven."

I gulped and smiled at my little bird dangling in the kitchen window.

"And as far as the rest is concerned, you'll know when you're ready. In the meantime, get back to that kennel and get Jake out of there."

I let her words sink in before I replied. "I will, Urs. Thank you. I will go back tomorrow and bring Jake home."

Printed in Great Britain
by Amazon